DEATH
RATTLE

An Arizona Borderlands Mystery

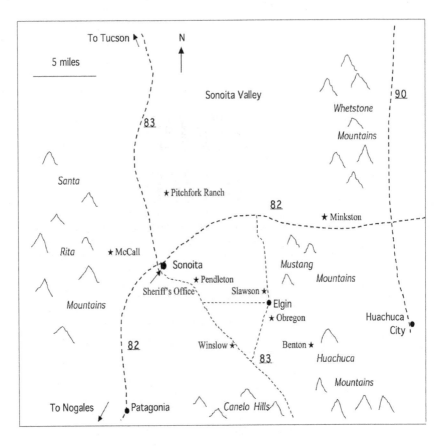

Map of the Sonoita Valley and Vicinity,
Santa Cruz County, Arizona

DEATH RATTLE

An Arizona Borderlands Mystery

Carl and Jane Bock

ABSOLUTELY AMAZING eBOOKS

ABSOLUTELY AMAZING eBOOKS

Published by Whiz Bang LLC, 926 Truman Avenue, Key West, Florida 33040, USA.

Photo credits: cover – Linda Kennedy, Movjave Rattelsnake – Rogern Cogan, author photo – David Norris

For information contact:
Publisher@AbsolutelyAmazingEbooks.com

ISBN-13: 978-1945772511 (Absolutely Amazing Ebooks)
ISBN-10: 1945772514

DEATH RATTLE

An Arizona Borderlands Mystery

Prelude

The man had taken the snake from the others at high noon and placed her in the box. She had been in a damp dark place for over two weeks, and it had left her deeply lethargic. It was late October on the high plains of southern Arizona, a time of cool nights but warm days. At first she had been too cold to move, but by late afternoon the sun had been beating down on the box for more than three hours and now she was becoming dangerously over-heated. She had explored all corners of the small confining space, testing its walls and the air with her tongue. Her lidless eyes found a faint rim of light at one end of the box. She had coiled then, with her head facing the light.

The snake was nearly dead from the heat when the sensitive scales on her belly picked up ground vibrations. Their magnitude and rhythm told her that the approaching object was far too large to be food. She raised her head and neck, pulling them back into the taut arc that would enable her to strike in self-defense. For the moment her rattle held still, her fangs and their deadly content folded back against the roof of her mouth. But she was ready.

~ ~ ~

Andy Slawson tightened one last piece of barbed wire around the old juniper fence post, twisted it into place, and slowly straightened his tired frame. Andy was nearly six feet tall, but he looked shorter because of a perpetual teenage slouch. For perhaps the tenth time that day he cursed the heat, the dust, old man Winslow's half-baked ranch, and work in general. He pulled a dirty blue bandana from his hip pocket and used it to wipe sweat from a sunburned and freckled *face. Then he pawed at his mop of ragged red hair and ambled back toward the ranch house. On the way he walked past Moss Winslow's little vineyard. Each row of grapes was pruned and weed-free. The Mexicans had been there from dawn to dusk the day before. They had worked their butts off as usual, so Moss had given them a break while Andy had to keep working. It pissed him off all over again. Didn't those guys know when to quit? He was pretty sure they did it on purpose, just to make an ordinary American like him look bad.*

Andy Slawson did odd jobs for Moss Winslow and for anybody else willing to hire him. He probably was the only white yard boy in the whole damned valley, but he knew his Aunt Grace might send him away if he quit working. He would have left this godforsaken place a long time ago, except nobody back up in Tucson would have anything to do with him. What Aunt Grace didn't know was that one of his jobs might be turning into something bigger. It definitely could be more profitable, and it might just allow him to get the hell out of this desert land once and for all.

Andy reached the house and collapsed in the shade of the porch. He needed a break before starting the long walk home. Aunt Grace lived over three miles away, but she wouldn't let him drive even though she had that old pickup that hardly ever went anywhere. It was bad enough that she made him work for the old man, but then to make him walk – well, it was an injustice for sure.

Moss Winslow came out on the porch carrying a stack of mail. As usual he was dressed in a baggy Hawaiian shirt, Bermuda shorts (even in winter), and white tennis shoes. Didn't the old man know how ridiculous he looked? Whoever heard of a rancher that always dressed like he was headed for some sort of perpetual luau?

Andy Slawson knew that ranching wasn't Winslow's real passion. *Instead it was those damned grapes, and, even worse, his thing about flying saucers. He just wouldn't stop talking about them, about all the landings he'd seen, the weird lights at night. Just blah, blah, and more blah. One time Andy made some lame joke about little green men. Moss had flown into a rage, turned purple right in front of him, and threatened to throw him off the place. So he never did that again. Not that he actually liked working for Moss, or anybody else for that matter, but he knew what might happen with Aunt Grace if he got himself fired.*

He stood up to leave, when Moss Winslow caught him short. "Say Andy, would you put these envelopes in my box at the end of the drive on your way home? Maria Obregon does her mail route in the morning before I like to get up, and there's a coupla things need to go out."

The boy sighed, scratched at a piece of skin that was flaking off the top of his right ear, and reluctantly took the stack of letters. Then he walked down the lane toward the battered old mailbox, oblivious to his surroundings. Grasslands of the Sonoita Valley held absolutely no interest for him, nor did anything else outdoors. In decreasing order of importance, the things that mattered most to Andy were sleep, television, beer, cars, and getting laid. The latter made the list only if it involved minimal expenditures of either time or money. But at least Aunt Grace would be off his back when he got home, because he had put in a full, if lethargic, day's work.

Andy reached the box, pulled down the door, and leaned over to peer inside. In an instant the Mojave rattlesnake struck, buried her fangs into his cheek, and pumped out a lethal dose of poison. Andy reeled backwards and grabbed at the pain. Then he started to run. For one of the few times in his short life, and certainly for the last, he was totally alert.

Nobody ever figured out why Andy Slawson had not simply returned to the Winslow ranch house that afternoon instead of trying to find his way back home, but it had been a fatal mistake.

Chapter 1

"Well, those Border Posse boys are at it again. This time they've set up outside the fairgrounds." Larry Hernandez had just come in off patrol and was helping himself to a late cup of coffee. It was burned and stale by this late in the day, but that was his business.

Larry and I are Santa Cruz County deputy sheriffs, and we work together in the Sonoita station. We're pretty much all there is to law enforcement in this part of Arizona, if you don't count the Border Patrol or the occasional state patrol officer who drives through. Luis Mendoza is the sheriff. He prefers to stay down at headquarters in Nogales most of the time. He usually lets us run things by ourselves in a part of the county he considers remote and, most of the time, not very interesting.

"Did you check to see if they have a permit this time?"

Larry shrugged. "Uh, no, guess I should have."

I didn't blame him. The handful of locals who called themselves the Border Posse had two main activities. First, they made so-called 'security patrols' along the Mexican line, looking for people they considered suspicious or undesirable. Second, they liked to stand around in public places holding up signs that left no doubt as to just who those suspicious and undesirable folks happened to be. Their signs said things like:

"Illegals go home."

"Take back America."

You get the drift. Of course Larry Hernandez and

his family have been in this part of Arizona longer than most of the Anglos, but still it must have been hard.

I got up from my side of our shared desk. "Guess I'll leave you to it. I'll drop by the little gathering on my way home. Maybe they screwed up this time."

Harlo Henshaw was the self-appointed leader of the Border Posse. He and I had been high school classmates down the road in Patagonia, but afterwards we'd definitely gone our separate ways. He owned and operated a little pawnshop on the northern edge of Nogales, except when he was busy making America safe from undesirables.

I pulled the county Blazer up in front of the little demonstration and got out. At the moment it was poorly attended. In fact, I was the only one present besides the six members of the posse themselves. They stood around holding their signs, and they all stared right at me. They had attached two flags to the fence on opposite sides of the main gate leading into the fairgrounds. One was the stars and stripes. The other one was a vertical tricolor of green, white, and red. At first I thought it was the flag of Mexico, but when I got closer I could see that there was a coiled rattlesnake in place of the regular coat of arms in the center. Underneath the snake, in big gold letters, it said "*No Más.*" At least they'd gotten the accent right.

Harlo ambled over in my direction. He was tall and gangly, with a big beaky nose and a prominent Adam's apple that waggled up and down when he talked. The other kids had made fun of his looks back when we were in school. Maybe that had something to do with his charming personality.

Harlo knew who I was. "Hey Cal, good to see you. And before you ask, yes we do have a permit." He showed me a piece of paper and then turned to the other five posse members. "Boys, I'd like you to meet

Calvin Creede, our local deputy sheriff."

They were all wearing red, white, and blue vests adorned with little pins and badges. Two were carrying sidearms, but public display of weapons was legal in Arizona under most circumstances, so I couldn't touch them on that. I didn't bother getting close enough to read what it said on their little badges.

So far as I was aware these guys hadn't caused any real trouble other than making the job of the actual Border Patrol harder than it needed to be. Unfortunately there was no county ordinance against being a xenophobic bigot, and I could see no point in attempting to engage any of the little group in conversation. Instead, I got back in the Blazer and drove east out of town on route 83, on the way to see my long-time, smart, beautiful, and (did I mention?) sixth generation Hispanic lady friend, Maria Obregon.

Maria and I had been all set to get married in the summer that had just ended, until a flash flood tore up her house and the little goat dairy she ran. Now we were busy putting her place back together, and the wedding was on hold. Between her day job delivering the mail and my obligations to the county, there were only so many hours left for the work we'd both rather have been doing. But things were progressing, and I was optimistic about our future together.

The monsoon rains that brought the flood also had worked their magic on the grasses. Lush green hills rolled away in all directions, tinged with reds and golds that signaled the start of fall. Mountains that surrounded the Sonoita Valley rose clear and crisp against a bright sky that matched my mood. One small group of local vigilantes notwithstanding, life felt pretty good. Two months previously, Larry and I had solved a major cold case involving murder and ancient artifacts. It had made the sheriff so happy that he'd promoted me to the rank of detective, which meant I could handle a lot of cases by myself. Things seemed to have settled back into a normal routine.

I should have known it wouldn't last.

Chapter 2

Moss Winslow owned and operated a two-section ranch that lay up against the Canelo Hills at the southern edge of the Sonoita Valley. It had been in his family for three generations. Sometimes I drove past his place on my way to and from work. Following a local trend he recently had added a small vineyard to his property. While the rows of grapes looked tidy and well tended, from my perspective some of the plants didn't look so hot, and I wondered if a cattleman like Moss really had any business starting a vineyard. Of course the Winslow family never had been strictly ranchers. Those 1,280 acres might sound like a lot, until you factored in that it took at least thirty of them to grow just one cow and her calf sustainably in the arid grasslands of southeastern Arizona. The only thing that made it work at all was that the property included one strong artesian spring. This not only kept the cattle watered but also made it possible to adequately irrigate the vineyard.

So what else did Moss Winslow do to keep the wolf from the door? I wasn't sure of all the details, but apparently he was into science fiction, especially about flying saucers and such, and he actually made some sort of a living at it. I didn't know it yet, but some of his ideas about visitors from outer space were way beyond spooky.

The Winslow ranch headquarters included a barn, some corrals, and a windmill, in addition to a large frame house painted white. A gravel lane led from the county road back to the house, and there was an oversized mailbox attached to a post at the end of the drive. I'd noticed the box before, and asked Maria why the old man needed one that big. It was just a casual question at the time. Funny how things like that can turn out to be important later on. She'd grumbled that a person's mail was supposed to be confidential, but then she must have decided it was okay to tell me what she knew, at least in general terms. She explained that Moss subscribed to a bunch of magazines about UFOs, space aliens, and the like, and he also rented a lot of movies that came on discs in the mail. Some days the box was nearly full.

On the drive past the Winslow place, I was surprised to see that his mailbox was open and there were letters lying around on the ground beneath it. Technically this wasn't sheriff's department business, but retrieving errant mail seemed like a neighborly thing to do, so I pulled off onto the lane and got out of the Blazer. The letters consisted of three legal-sized envelopes, stamped but not cancelled, and addressed to somebody other than Winslow. I took this to mean they had been intended for Maria to pick up for delivery when she drove her route the next day. Moss must have forgotten to close the box, and somehow the letters had fallen out.

It was when I bent over to pick things up that I heard an unmistakable hiss and buzz. At first I couldn't figure out where the sounds were coming from, but then I realized there was a rattlesnake inside the box.

What the hell?

I don't really like snakes, even in places where they belong. On the other hand Maria is sort of crazy about them. She took a class in herpetology when she was a student at The University of Arizona. Over the years of our acquaintance she had recited a number of snake factoids, most of which I did not find interesting. However, one useful piece of information she did share is that rattlesnakes cannot climb. This meant that a relatively low but solid wall was a good way to keep them out of your backyard. So how did a normally earthbound rattlesnake end up in Moss Winslow's mailbox? The only reasonable answer was that somebody must have put it there. But who and why?

I walked closer to the mailbox and looked inside. The snake had gone silent and appeared lifeless, but I knew better. I took a shovel from the back of the Blazer and worked the wooden handle around in the box until the snake fell out. It hit the ground with a heavy slap. Then it coiled and struck toward but well shy of my right leg. I un-holstered my sidearm, took careful aim, and shot the snake through the top of its head. Despite the resulting cerebral damage, which was massive, the body continued to writhe and thrash about on its own. Taking no chances, I picked the snake up using the shovel and placed it in a box that happened to be in the back of my vehicle. Then I secured the area around the mailbox with yellow crime scene tape, and drove down the lane to Moss Winslow's ranch house.

The man came out on his porch as I pulled up. He was small and wizened, mid-sixties or so, with a burr haircut and wire-frame bifocals. He had on short pants and a Hawaiian shirt that was mostly yellow but with lots of flowers and birds of different colors. Ranchers around Sonoita came in various shapes, sizes, and political persuasions, but nobody looked or acted less like one than this little man. In my experience, which was substantial, his phenotype just didn't fit the cowboy model.

Winslow held up both hands to shade his eyes against a fiery orange sun that was about to drop below the Santa Rita Mountains. "Is that you, Cal? I can't hardly see."

I got out of the Blazer, stopped at the bottom of the

short staircase leading up to his porch, and related what I had just seen out by the highway. "Do you have any idea how that snake might have gotten into your box, or how your mail ended up on the ground?"

The old man shook his head. "But I know what was supposed to happen, and this doesn't look good."

"What do you mean?"

"It's about Aunt Grace Slawson's nephew Andy. He does odd jobs for me? And today when he was heading home I asked him to put some letters in my box. So he must have, you know, well either he put that snake in the box, or else . . ."

There were several possibilities, some more ominous than others. "Did you see anybody around here this afternoon besides Andy?"

Moss Winslow shook his head again. "Nope. But I've been inside most of time, so I probably wouldn't have noticed even if there had been."

"Anybody else working on your place?"

"Not today. Normally my field hands would be here tending the vineyard, but they had the day off."

"Do you have a local phonebook, Moss? The first thing I need to do is talk to Andy. I know he lives with his Aunt Grace over near Elgin, but I don't have her number."

"Sure, come on in and I'll get it for you."

I had never been inside Moss Winslow's place before. The outside looked like a typical ranch house. The inside did not. We walked into the living room and it looked like a planetarium. The ceiling was painted entirely in flat black, except for a profusion of golden spheres of various sizes that I took to be images of stars and planets. The walls were adorned with pictures of flying saucers and humanoid creatures of the extra-terrestrial variety. There were even some movie posters featuring fifties sci-fi classics with titles like "It Came from Outer Space" and "Zombies from Pluto."

The heavy wood furniture, most of it upholstered in cowhide, didn't come close to matching the space alien motif. I assumed it must have been left over from earlier days. The whole place smelled like old leather mixed with another scent I couldn't place – sort of musty, but with an edge. Winslow had followed my eyes. "I fixed up this room to look just like the night sky around Sonoita. Did you know there have been more UFO sightings around here than almost anywhere else? Except maybe around Roswell, New Mexico. I've seen plenty of 'em myself. Even had one close encounter."

"Encounter with what?"

Moss squinted up through the top half of his bifocals and gave me a look that I guess was the one he reserved for nonbelievers. "A saucer, of course. It was right out there, off toward the Mustang Mountains. It was on a moonless night, just before dawn, five years ago April. I'd gotten up to go to the bathroom, and I saw this glow hovering just above the hills. So I went out there, you know? And then I think maybe they took me on board, but I can't remember."

"Why not?"

Again he gave me a look like I was some sort of ignoramus. "Because that's what they always do. They clear your mind, so you won't be able to give away their secrets. The only thing I remember was the sky serpents."

"Sky serpents?"

"Sure, Cal, some of their ships are not like saucers at all. Instead they're great long twisted things. I learned during my abduction that's where the real interstellar forces reside. The saucers are just their scouts."

I'd always known that Moss Winslow was an eccentric, but this was getting way too creepy. We also

9

had drifted off the subject at hand – that being a mailbox and a snake and Andy Slawson. But the old man was not to be deterred, and he started up again before I had a chance to interrupt.

"So anyway, after that night, that's when I knew for sure. And that's when I started the magazine."

"Magazine?" Why did I keep asking these questions?

"Yep, and it's doing real good too. It's called 'We Are Not Alone.' Now I even have a website. Like to take a look?" Winslow pointed off toward a side room where I could see an aged desktop computer dwarfed on all sides by stacks of books and papers.

Even if I had been interested in learning more about Moss Winslow's hobbies, this clearly was not the time. "I really do need to see that phonebook, Moss."

"Oh sure, sorry. Have a seat and I'll be right with you."

~ ~ ~

Grace Slawson lived near the village of Elgin, at the east end of the Sonoita Valley. It was not far from Maria's place. About seven years ago she had retired from a lifelong career teaching generations of local kids at the Elgin School. Somewhere along the way she became 'Aunt Grace,' though nobody could remember exactly why. It puzzled and sometimes annoyed newcomers to the valley, but that was her name to the rest of us. Though no longer in the classroom, Aunt Grace remained active in local affairs, particularly if they had anything to do with the environment. Andy Slawson had come to live with her two years ago, apparently as a refugee from some bad things to do with his parents and their home up in Tucson.

She answered my call on the third ring. "Why hello, Cal. How are you?"

"I'm fine Aunt Grace, but I need to speak with Andy

if he's around. It's kind of urgent."

There was just a moment's hesitation. "I'm sorry, but he's not here. He's been working over at Moss Winslow's place. Can I have him give you a call when he gets in? And what's this all about? I hope he's not in some kind of trouble."

It was way too early to get into details. "Not that I know of. Please just have him call the office in the morning. And thanks."

I disconnected and turned my attention back to Moss, who by now was looking both anxious and angry. Apparently his thoughts had begun to converge on mine. "What are you going to do, Deputy? You don't suppose that kid put the snake in my box, do you? I know he pretty much hates my guts because I make him earn an honest day's pay. But I just can't imagine he's organized or ambitious enough to do something like this." Winslow stopped and shook his head. "But still, I could have been killed!"

Likely Moss was wrong about that. My friend Maria Obregon would have been the next person to open the box when she delivered the mail early the next morning. Had she been the target?

It all seemed a little crazy, especially because there were two things that didn't fit. First, as far as I knew Maria and Andy Slawson didn't even know each other. Second, and more to the point, if Andy's plan had been to harm or at least scare somebody with that snake, why did he drop Winslow's mail on the ground and leave the box standing open? It didn't make sense. There was another possibility that did.

I handed the phone back to Moss, and stood up to leave. "Let me check down the road toward Elgin to see if I can find the boy. In the meantime, don't go near your mailbox."

"Why not? You took the snake, didn't you?"

"Sure, but that's not the point. Until we figure out what happened out there, we need to treat the whole area as a possible crime scene."

Chapter 3

I drove back and forth between Winslow's place and the village of Elgin three times before I found him. Andy had fallen into a roadside ditch full of tall vegetation that had obscured everything except the lower part of his left leg, which stuck up out of the grass at an awkward angle. His foot was still wearing a battered old red tennis shoe, or I might not have seen him at all.

I braked to a stop, put on the flashers, then jumped out and ran to where Andy lay face down in the remains of a rain puddle. He wasn't moving and at first I thought he was dead, maybe even drowned. But the boy moaned as I knelt down and carefully rolled him over. It was hideous. The whole left side of his face was red with bluish purple blotches, and it had grown to twice its normal size, giving him a grotesque lopsided appearance. His left eye was swollen shut, and I could see fang marks on his cheek.

Andy's breathing was shallow and ragged, but at least it was still there. I bent down close and said his name, but there was no response. Clearly he wasn't going to be able to tell me what had happened, at least not any time soon. Still, it seemed pretty obvious. I went back to the Blazer, got an old horse blanket that I have been using to cover up a tear in the back seat, and wrapped it around Andy's body.

No one had died from snakebite around Sonoita in all the years I'd been on the job. The fact is that rattlesnakes rarely strike humans, and even then only a small fraction of the bites result in death. Although he looked pretty bad, I thought Andy might be okay if

13

we could get him to the hospital for anti-venom shots within the next hour or so. But two things about the present circumstance were worrisome. First, a bite on the face was unusual and extremely serious because the venom could reach the heart or brain much more quickly than from the usual strike on a hand or lower leg. Second, the most common viper on the treeless grassland around the Winslow ranch was the Mojave rattlesnake, and I knew it was an exceptionally venomous form. Most rattlesnakes carry a poison affecting blood and tissues. However, Mojaves also produced a second kind that attacked the nervous system, a neurotoxin, which can lead to paralysis and death. Andy Slawson probably had been bitten in the face by the most dangerous serpent in North America.

A bunch of things needed to happen fast, the most important of which was to get Andy to a hospital. I called emergency services and gave the operator directions to the spot where he lay. Once I had described Andy's condition, there was no problem convincing him to dispatch both an ambulance and a helicopter. An ambulance crew happened to be in Sonoita at the time, and the dispatcher told me I could expect them in about twenty minutes, tops.

I took the snake out of the box and laid it on the road in what was left of the evening light. Then I called Maria. Proper identification was essential, so that personnel at the hospital would know which specific anti-venom to administer. I had my suspicions, but I was anxious to get Maria's confirmation before making the call. She didn't live all that far from where I was parked, but I was unwilling to leave before the ambulance arrived and so I hoped a description of the snake would be sufficient.

Her cell rang four times before she picked up, and she sounded out of breath. "Sorry, Cal, I was out in the barn milking the goats. What's up? When will you be home for dinner?"

I explained the circumstances, and my reason for calling.

"Good grief Cal, that's awful. And you're right, there's no way that snake could have gotten up there by itself. I'm familiar with Mossy Winslow's mailbox, and it's just too high off the ground. So tell me about the snake. Do you have it in front of you?"

"I'm looking at it now."

"Is it intact?"

"Well, sort of. I mean I shot it through the head, so that part's kind of a mess. But everything else is here."

There was a pause. "That's not so good because the one sure way to tell the local rattlers apart is from the scale patterns on their heads."

Oops.

"But anyway, let's work with what we've got. I have three questions. How long is it, does it have black-and-white rings around the tail, and what about the colors on the body?"

I stretched the snake out on the road and made an estimate. "It's about three feet long, maybe a little more. It does have black-and-white rings around its tail. Otherwise the color is sort of mixed, but I guess you could say the overall appearance is a sort of greenish-yellow. Does that help?"

"Definitely. For sure we can eliminate the black-tailed rattlesnake, because its tail is all black like the name suggests. There are only two other kinds of rattlers that are at all likely to be found around here. From the color, I'd say it most likely is a Mojave and not a western diamondback. Diamondbacks tend to be larger, and they usually have a speckled grayish-brown, almost a salt-and-pepper sort of look. You know that's not good if it's a Mojave. They're really dangerous."

"Yeah, you told me that before."

" You should notify the hospital, tell them it almost certainly is a Mojave, and remind them about the neurotoxin. I assume he'll be flown to Sierra Vista, and I know they keep the right sorts of anti-venom on hand."

"I'll call the hospital right now. And then I'll be bringing the snake over so you can make sure, once I've taken care of things out here. But it may be a while."

I'd heard the siren as Maria and I were finishing up our conversation, and the ambulance pulled up just as we were disconnecting. Two EMT's got out, a woman named Ginny Ballentine and a man I'd never seen before. They got right down to business, and I let them do their job while I called the hospital over in Sierra Vista and told the people in the emergency room to be ready to treat a Mojave snakebite.

Next I called Larry Hernandez, who was still finishing up in the office. My instructions to him were simple once I'd brought him up to speed on what was happening. "Get out to Moss Winslow's place, let him know you're there, and then stick by that mailbox until I get back in touch."

"Got it."

One of the things I liked best about Larry was he knew how to get down to business when the occasion demanded.

Next I got on the radio to headquarters in Nogales, explained the circumstances, and requested a crime scene unit. Bill Cummings was on the desk that evening, and he was a lot more skeptical than Larry had been. "You sure about this? I mean, what sort of a crime are we talking about here?"

I thought about going around him straight to the sheriff, but Luis Mendoza probably had gone home for the day, and I knew he didn't like to be disturbed unless it was an emergency. "I know it sounds strange, Bill, but there's just no way that snake could have gotten into the mailbox by itself. Somebody had to put it there. As far as I'm concerned that somebody committed a crime, and there could be evidence at the scene, like fingerprints and footprints. So I really do want some help."

"Couldn't it wait until tomorrow?"

"Well, I've got Deputy Hernandez out there watching the place, but I'm reluctant to ask him to stay all night since he's been on duty since eight this morning. And, there's other things I've got to do related to the case."

That seemed to satisfy Cummings. "Okay, let me check on who's available. I'll get back to you."

At this point I heard an all-too-familiar 'whump-whump-whump' and looked up to see a helicopter approaching. The sound brought back memories from Afghanistan that were neither welcome nor pleasant, but I pushed them aside and got to the business at hand. By now Ginny and her partner had Andy secured on a stretcher, and they were signaling the pilot where to land in the fading light. He touched down on the road and kept the rotors turning while I kept an eye out for any oncoming traffic. In less than five minutes they had him loaded up, and I watched as the helicopter rose and headed off to the east with Andy Slawson and Ginny on board.

Right about then Cummings radioed back. "Got some good news and some bad news. The good news is that Julie Benevides from crime scenes is available, and she's a first-class investigator. The bad news is that she won't be able to get out there until about ten tonight."

"Tell her I appreciate it, Bill."

I called Larry with the bad news. He was already at

the scene, and he must have anticipated something like this. "Good thing I brought a thermos of coffee, isn't it? Old stale stuff from the office, but it should do the trick. I'm sure you've got other things to take care of."

Like I said, Larry is a good man, and I'm happy to have him as a partner. And for sure there was something else to take care of, something I had been dreading most about this whole mess. As soon as I dropped the snake off at Maria's place, it was time to go see Aunt Grace.

Chapter 4

Aunt Grace Slawson lived in a tidy two-bedroom adobe on about fifteen acres she'd inherited from her father. It was just north of Elgin, backed up against the Mustang Mountains. Their cave-pocked limestone slopes rose directly behind her house, but by the time I pulled into her driveway it was too late to make out anything but a dark silhouette. She was on her porch because I'd called ahead, and she looked ready to travel. I'd already told her where we were going and why, but I'd skipped over the details until it was possible to deliver them in person.

This was going to be tough.

Aunt Grace rose from a straight-backed rocker as I walked up onto her porch. She was in her mid-sixties, about five-five, with a trim figure that testified to the amount of time she spent in various outdoor activities. Her short wavy gray hair framed a tan face that showed strong even under the pale light of a single energy-efficient bulb. She looked up at me expectantly. Her blue eyes were partially hidden by reflections off a pair of gold-rimmed glasses, but still I could see the worry.

"How is my Andy?"

"Not so good, Aunt Grace. It was a serious bite."

"How did it happen?"

I told her what we knew, or at least what we guessed. She was a good naturalist and so she understood what it all meant. Her look of disbelief quickly changed to something much worse. "In the face? By a Mojave?" She bowed her head. "Dear Lord, please help my boy. Oh Cal, I hope he is strong enough to make it. Dear Lord, dear Lord."

Grace Slawson was an exceptionally gifted teacher. She had taught at Elgin School for forty-one years, first in an old wooden building near the village of Elgin itself, later in a much more expansive facility built closer to Sonoita. Both Maria and I had been her pupils. We attributed our mutual interest in the natural world directly to her, but that was far from all that we had learned.

Although I was too young at the time, in hindsight I had come to appreciate two things about Grace Slawson as a teacher. Both were much in evidence that night as she and I drove to the hospital. First, she was an instinctively kind person who understood that positive reinforcement worked better than threats and intimidation. Not every teacher understands that, believe me. But second, she could be tough as nails when circumstances called for it. I was pretty sure tonight was going to be one of those times.

We drove north along the west flank of the Mustangs, then east on state route 82 into Cochise County and on toward the town of Sierra Vista. It surprised me some, but apparently Aunt Grace wanted to talk. I was happy to oblige because I was anxious to learn more about Andy. "I know everybody around here calls me Aunt Grace, but here's the funny part. Andy actually is my nephew. His father is my brother-in-law."

It was news to me that she even had a brother-in-law. "How did Andy come to live with you?"

"He just showed up one night and knocked on my door. Turns out his father had kicked him out of the house."

"Do you know why?"

"You mean other than the fact that my brother-in-law is a big jerk, just like my late husband?"

I glanced over at Aunt Grace sitting next to me.

Even in the darkened interior of the Blazer, I could see that she was getting uncomfortable. Never before had I heard her utter a sarcastic word about anything or anybody. "Sorry. It's none of my business, unless maybe what happened today is related in some way to his past troubles."

"Well, apparently there were problems with drugs up in Tucson, and maybe some petty theft. I never learned all the details. Didn't want to really. But how could that tie in to anything down here?"

"Probably doesn't. It's just my job to consider all the possibilities."

"Such as?"

"Such as, do you know if he has an interest in snakes?"

As I may have already said, Aunt Grace is a sharp lady, and right away she figured out where I was headed. "You don't think somebody put that snake in Moss Winslow's mailbox to get Andy, do you?"

She answered the question herself before I had a chance. "Of course you don't. How would they know it would be him that opened it? No, you think Andy was the one with the snake to begin with, and somehow he got bit trying to get it into that box so it would hurt somebody else. But why? Why would he do that?"

"I have no idea."

At that point we went back to a time when she was the teacher and I was the pupil. "Now you wait just a minute, Cal, and listen here. My Andy is a good boy. He's had his share of troubles, for sure, but mostly it wasn't his fault. I know what people think of him around here, that he's lazy and good for nothing. Well, maybe he is and maybe he isn't, but that doesn't mean he would try to hurt anybody. So you can just put any such idea right out of your head."

We drove in silence the rest of the way.

21

~ ~ ~

I've been in lots of hospital emergency waiting rooms over the years, and they're all pretty much alike. The atmosphere of dread and fear is inescapable, no matter how perky the receptionist might be, or how many high-end plastic plants they scatter around, or how often they replace the used magazines or the stale coffee. There's no one to blame. It's just what these places are.

We waited for five hours, far into the pre-dawn morning, until we were the only ones left besides hospital staff. The same doctor came out to talk to us three times, a young woman named Morganstern. The first two times we got pretty much the same story. Andy was in intensive care, and unconscious. They were doing their best, but he'd had a strong allergic reaction to the anti-venom, which limited what anybody could do. His heart had stopped once, but they'd managed to get it going again. They would let us know if there was any change. It could be a long night.

The third time was different. Dr. Morganstern came through the door and motioned us to accompany her into a side room. She closed the door behind her, and invited us to sit.

Aunt Grace declined the invitation. "Please just tell us, doctor."

"I'm sorry. We did everything possible, but there was just too much poison."

Grace sat down in the nearest of three brown leather armchairs, took off her glasses, and laid them on a low table next to the chair. Then she bent forward and buried her face in her hands. But it wasn't long before she looked back up and I could see that her eyes were clear.

"I want to see him."

The doctor hesitated. "I'm not sure that's a good idea."

I decided to get involved. "Aunt Grace, maybe we

should wait." I started to say we should wait until the funeral, but caught myself just in time. "Or at least let me go in with you."

That seemed to galvanize her into action. "No. You wait here. The doctor is going to take me in. It won't be long, and then you can drive me home."

And that's just the way it happened.

Chapter 5

Maria and I were at the breakfast table the next morning, sharing a plate of chorizo and scrambled eggs. She had a Labrador Retriever named Boomer who liked her Mexican food. This was no particular recommendation because he'd eat almost anything with calories, even dead things that had been lying around out of doors for way too long. So he was sitting nearby, patient but drooling. He knew he'd get to lick the plate when we were finished.

The sun was just coming up over the Huachucas. I was on my third cup of coffee, and we were both preparing for a busy day. I had cop business as usual, except that 'usual' didn't often include snakes, and they were not my favorite subject. Maria needed to get out to the barn and tend to her goats, and then start on her mail run. She was a contract worker, not an official post office employee, so her exact hours were up to her as long as the job got done. She drove her own vehicle, a little Honda that was both fuel-efficient and all-wheel drive. She often timed her route so that we could have lunch together in my office in Sonoita.

I looked around the interior of the old Obregon adobe that Maria had inherited from her late husband Tony. We were fortunate that the flood had left the basic structure intact, no doubt testimony to the brick-making skills of Tony's great-great-grandfather all those years ago. We still had some plastering and painting to do on the interior walls, and the kitchen cabinets needed refinishing. But we were making progress.

Before we went our separate ways, I wanted to ask Maria a couple of questions. Turned out she had some for me as well. Given the late hour, we'd barely spoken when I had gotten back from Sierra Vista the night before.

"Aunt Grace must be devastated, Cal. I can't imagine. Do you know what happens next with Andy? Will there be a funeral?"

"She and I talked about that on the way home. She wants a service for sure, but it may take a while. The doctor over in Sierra Vista told me she would certify cause of death as heart failure due to snakebite. But because of the unusual circumstance, I'm sure the sheriff is going to want an autopsy."

Maria nodded. "You may not know this, but Luis was one of Aunt Grace's pupils way back when. So I'm sure he'll move things along fast as he can."

I remembered from somewhere that the sheriff also was Maria's godfather. "That's good. I don't imagine a medical examiner is going to find out anything we don't already know. The question isn't how Andy died, but why."

Maria swallowed a last bite of chorizo. "It sure is an odd case. I suppose anybody could have put that snake in Mr. Winslow's box. But even if somebody wanted to kill him, why attempt to do it that particular way?"

I'd been having exactly those same thoughts, but with a twist. "I think you may be jumping to at least one premature conclusion."

"How so?"

"When you make your deliveries today, be careful when you're opening up all those mailboxes, at least the big ones."

She got a look, but it didn't last long. "Oh that's ridiculous, Cal, why would anybody..."

I cut her off. "Just be careful, okay? But you're probably right. Another possibility I need to consider is that Andy might somehow be involved in all of this."

"You mean besides just being in the wrong place at the wrong time?"

I nodded. "Aunt Grace told me last night that Andy

had been in some trouble up in Tucson."

We sat in silence for a while, sipping the remains of our coffee. Then some of the goats started to get noisy out in the corrals, and Maria rose to leave. She paused at the door and turned back. Her long dark hair glowed, backlit by the morning sun. "You know, it might help if we knew where that snake came from."

"Is that possible?"

"It might be. You remember I took a class in herpetology from a lady professor at the university? Her name is Hazel Smith, and she happens to be an expert on rattlesnakes. If she's still around, maybe we could take her the snake that killed Andy, and she could tell us more about it. You want me to give her a call? Would you like to go along if I drive up there?"

"Yes to both, of course. But why do you think this could help the case?"

"It might not help at all. But snakes vary a lot from place to place. For example, some of the Mojave rattlesnakes I've seen down in the Sonoran Desert are a lot greener than the ones around here."

"What about the one I showed you yesterday?"

"Well, it didn't look all that unusual, but there may be subtler differences that Dr. Smith would know about. Wouldn't it be useful to learn that your snake came from the Tucson area instead of from the grasslands down here? Or maybe from a mountain range over near Tombstone instead of someplace down on the Mexican line?"

It seemed like a long shot, but I couldn't see any downsides. "Sure, then, let's check it out. And thanks."

I kissed Maria goodbye, got in the Blazer, and headed off for work. I took the upper Elgin road, which is the shortest distance from Nanny Boss's Dairy to my office.

Fall days in southeastern Arizona are among the

best in the year, usually crisp and clear, with deep azure skies and relatively little wind. This was going to be one of those days. As I was driving west toward Sonoita, I spotted a pair of coal-black Chihuahuan ravens on the road ahead. They reluctantly rose up off the county blacktop as I approached. I had disturbed them at breakfast, which in this case was the bloody remains of a jackrabbit somebody had hit the night before. Ravens are smart birds, quick to adapt to human-created opportunities. They have learned to follow roads across the Sonoita Valley, always keeping an eye out. I guess they're sort of like deputy sheriffs that way.

I came to the end of the county road, at the point where it merged with state route 83. On my immediate left the students were arriving for another day of classes at Elgin School. Unless things had changed since my grade school days, most of the girls were happier to be there than the most of boys, except maybe for recess. I wished all of them well.

Chapter 6

L arry Hernandez was brewing coffee as I walked into the little office that we shared in Sonoita. We were situated at the intersection point of two state roads. Highway 82 ran from Nogales northeast into Cochise County, while route 83 originated at the interstate east of Tucson and ended down near the Mexican line. The only place they met was right here in town.

There was space for only one desk in our office, but the sheriff had found an old partners version that had places for chairs on opposite sides. The scarred oak surface was big enough for two computers, one landline phone, and a cradle for the county radio. The rest of the room was crowded with file cabinets, two straight-back chairs for visitors, and a small refrigerator. Our coffee maker sat on top of the refrigerator, next to a little sink. There was a pegboard on the wall above the sink that held the usual assortment of cups of uncertain origin that tend to accumulate in shared spaces. A tiny half bath was appended to the north side of the office. The plumbing was problematic because the roots of a willow tree in the vacant lot next door kept growing into the septic line.

We had only a single window. At one time it had consisted of four good-sized panels, but now there were only three. The fourth spot now held one of those little swamp cooler inserts. It may have done some good in the hottest and driest times of the year, but otherwise it just raised the humidity and made the place smell damp and musty.

The sheriff had been after us to move to a bigger

and better space. There was one available in a new mall just down the road. We'd almost ended up there the previous summer, until the builder got in trouble with the law, which was us. The little mall had a new owner, but still I was dragging my feet. The fact is I liked it where we were. For one thing, our little window opened to the east with a fine view of the Huachuca and Mustang Mountains in the distance. Closer in, we could see the rear entrance to the Santa Rita Saloon, my favorite local watering hole. Another bonus was an enormous old cottonwood that grew along the south wall. It provided great shade in summer, and there was something sweet, almost nostalgic, about the sound cottonwood leaves made when they slapped against each other. It was like a thousand little hands clapping whenever the wind blew, which was most of the time.

I poured myself a cup of coffee and sat down opposite Larry. "How did it go last night out at Moss Winslow's?"

He stretched, yawned, and tilted back in his chair. Larry was in his mid-twenties, about two inches shorter than my even six feet, but broader across the shoulders. He had black hair and eyes, and a deep tan. "It went fine, I suppose. How did it go at the hospital?"

"Not good. Andy died early this morning."

He shook his head. "Geeze, that's terrible. Poor Aunt Grace. Guess I'm not surprised though 'cause of what you told me about the bite."

We discussed the case a little bit, mostly agreeing that none of it made any sense.

"So anyway, it looks like we could have a homicide on our hands. Tell me what the crime scene crew found."

"The woman came alone. Said she couldn't find anybody else who was able to go that late." Larry took a small spiral-bound notebook out of his shirt pocket and consulted his notes. "Her name is Julie Benevides. Cute little red-haired gal. I liked her style, but there really wasn't all that much to do. She dusted the mailbox for prints, and then took a set from Moss for comparison. She looked around for footprints, but there weren't any worth casting. Then she took lots of photos of the whole area, and left."

I liked Larry a lot, but he was prone to occasional lapses in the PC area. I decided to niggle him. "So, did you happen to tell that cute little red-haired gal about Andy Slawson?"

Larry took his medicine without comment. "What I knew at the time, sure. She said she needed to get his prints. I guess now maybe somebody can do that in the morgue."

"Yeah, I'll check with the sheriff about that. And speaking of our leader, I'm sure he's expecting my call by now."

Larry got up and took his empty cup over to the sink. He rinsed it out and hung it back up on the pegboard. "Guess I'll head out on patrol. Let me know if you need anything."

"Will do. Oh, and while you're at it take a drive past the Winslow place. Let me know if you see anything."

"Like what?"

"No idea. Just anything that looks new or unusual."

Larry paused at the door and turned back. "Now that you mention it, I did see something out there a couple of weeks ago. I don't know if you'd call it unusual exactly. In fact, I'd forgotten all about it. But now, in light of what's happened..."

"What?"

"There were two people standing out in the middle of Winslow's vineyard, all by themselves. One was Moss, and I'm pretty sure the other was Andy Slawson."

I didn't see what was so unusual about that, and said so.

Larry nodded. "Yeah, but it looked to me like they were having some sort of argument."

"How could you tell?"

"I couldn't tell for sure, because it was just a momentary look and then I was on down the road. But Moss was right in his face, and the kid was backing up."

~ ~ ~

I may have mentioned that the sheriff and I had a working relationship that was different from most in the department. Luis Mendoza liked it that I usually took care of business alone in my end of the county, and the only thing that had changed recently was the addition of Larry Hernandez. On the other hand, he didn't like surprises, and I'd learned the hard way that the jungle drums never stopped beating in Santa Cruz County.

Luis picked up on the first ring when I punched in the number that went straight to his personal cell. Sure enough, he'd already heard the news. "Morning Cal. I'd been expecting your call. Too bad about the Slawson boy. I didn't know him of course, but *Tía* Grace and I go way back. Please give her my condolences."

That certainly took care of the preliminaries. "What about Andy's body? I know Aunt Grace wants to have a service as soon as possible."

"I've arranged to have it sent up to Tucson. As you know, we use the Pima County medical examiner for most of our autopsies. I'll do my best to expedite. Anything else?"

It seemed like the sheriff was in a hurry, but I didn't know why. "Just that it's a weird case. I'll keep you posted if we can figure out who put the snake in that mailbox."

I almost disconnected, but then I remembered

something else. "While I have you, what can you tell me about a group calling themselves the Border Posse?"

The sheriff grunted. "Those *pendejos*? Not much I suppose. A couple of my deputies have seen them driving around down along the border. They claimed they were looking for crossers. We warned them not to do anything except call the Patrol. I hate this sort of vigilante stuff, but I don't think anything has come of it so far. Why? Does it have something to do with the Slawson case? Are those Posse boys working around your area?"

"They had one of their little demonstrations yesterday outside the fairgrounds. Turns out I know their leader, a guy named Harlo Henshaw. We went to school together. But no, I can't see any connection."

That was about to change, because about five minutes later I got a call from Moss Winslow. The Border Posse had showed up.

"What are they doing, Moss?"

"Well, I'm looking out there right now. They're out on the highway. They've got these signs and some flags, and they're yelling things at my vineyard crew. And no, wait, now there's two of 'em walking out into my field. They haven't got that right, do they?"

"Not without your permission they don't. I'll be right there."

~ ~ ~

I pulled my Blazer up behind an old Chevy Suburban that had carried the half-dozen members of the Border Posse to this day's event. Harlo Henshaw must have seen me coming because he'd called everybody back out onto the road. This time I wasn't planning on a quiet exit.

I put on my flashers and parked the Blazer on a diagonal blocking the county road. Then I got out, went up to the man, and put my face directly into his. "What's going on here, Harlo?"

33

He pointed toward the vineyard, where about a half-dozen workers were milling around. Some of them looked like they were about ready to run. "Just doing your job, that's all. Them's illegals out there, everybody knows it. And that Moss Winslow knows it too. He just don't care. All he cares about is cheap labor."

"Now first of all, Harlo, even if you're right, that's a job for the Border Patrol and not for you or me. I think you know that. And second, you've got no right to go out into those fields. That's private property. I could arrest you for trespassing."

"But..."

I didn't let the man finish. "And third of all, you're blocking a public road. So I have a suggestion."

"What suggestion?"

"That you get the hell out of here before I change my mind and start issuing citations."

There was a lot of muttering, but I guess Harlo figured I wasn't bluffing because he quickly did a Posse roundup. "Okay, boys. We've made our point. Let's put everything back in the truck." Then he turned back to me. "But we're not done with this."

They were rolling up the fake Mexican flag when something occurred to me. I addressed the whole group. "Any of you guys interested in snakes?"

A bald guy with an oversized gut took one step closer and asked why.

"No particular reason I suppose, except you've put a picture of a big rattler on your flag there, and I wondered what that was all about. Seems sort of intimidating."

"Maybe that's the idea."

After the Border Posse rode off into the sunset, I drove on down the lane to Winslow's house. He'd been watching from his porch the whole time. He was dressed in his standard garb, except today the

Hawaiian shirt was mostly blue instead of yellow. We sat on his porch together in matching wicker rocking chairs. I noticed his field workers were still eyeing me warily, standing between the rows of grapes.

"Tell them it's all right, Moss. Nothing's going to happen, at least not today."

He walked across his drive to the fence bordering the vineyard, and yelled something in Spanish. It was too fast for me to catch, but it must have worked because pretty soon everybody went back to work.

A brief gust of wind swirled some dust up into the air above Moss Winslow's corrals as we returned to the shade of his porch. Looking west I could see the top of Mount Wrightson, the high point of the Santa Rita Range, shimmering in the late morning heat.

Evidently Moss had followed my eyes. "Just about the best view in the valley, isn't it? Not like it used to be, though. Too many damned houses, and all those lights cluttering things up at night. I think it intimidates them."

"Who?"

The old man apparently thought it was a foolish question. "The aliens, of course. They just don't come around as much as they used to." Winslow pivoted in his chair and pointed north, toward a range of mountains beyond the Mustangs. "When I was a kid my dad sent me up into the Whetstones every summer to tend the cattle we put out on a grazing lease. From up there the air was so clear it felt like you could see all the way to California. And the night sky was spectacular. That's where I had my first sighting."

I had to ask. "Sighting?"

"Of a UFO. That's when I got hooked. Lots of evidence up there in terms of landing spots. Whoever's flying those things in, they must like the Whetstones as much as I do. You ever been up there?"

"Never have."

"Beautiful, except for the snakes."

"Snakes?"

"Yeah, the place is full of them. Lost more than one horse to bites over the years. Still, I loved those summers. And speaking of snakes, how's the Slawson kid?"

Apparently our conversation about space aliens had ended, and I was just as glad. "That's one of the reasons I came out here, Moss. He didn't make it. He died early this morning over at the hospital in Sierra Vista."

The old man looked pensive. "That's too damn bad, Cal. The kid was pretty worthless, but nobody deserves to die like that."

"Now that we have a killing on our hands, and maybe even a murder, there's something I need to ask you about."

"What's that?"

"It's something Larry Hernandez saw out here. He was driving by your place on his way home, maybe a couple of weeks ago, and he thought he spotted you and Andy out in the vineyard together. Apparently it did not look like a happy occasion. Can you tell me what that was all about?"

Moss waved his hand dismissively. "Oh, that was nothing. We had a little disagreement about his wages. He's lazy and maybe a little greedy. Sometimes I feel sorry for Aunt Grace having to put up with him."

"So why do you hire him?"

"Good question. Guess maybe I'm just a softy. So anyway, Cal, not that Andy wasn't important, but hasn't it occurred to you that the snake could just as easily have gotten me? After all, it's my mail box."

I didn't mention Maria, but he had a good point. "Have you had any troubles lately? Anything new going on I should know about?"

"Well, you know about those posse guys that were out there today. And then there's J.L. Minkston and our development deal. That's not going so good, and I think he's kind of pissed off at me. But still..."

The old man stopped and shrugged.

J.L. Minkston was a new land developer in the valley. I'd seen him around town, but we had yet to meet. In fact he was the one who'd bought the half-finished mall where my new office was supposed to be, and I'd heard he was looking for land and water. I didn't know he had anything to do with Moss Winslow. "You think he could have done something like this? Are your troubles that serious?"

Moss shook his head. "Don't see how. I expect we're gonna work things out. Just thought I'd mention it is all."

I made a mental note to look into the affairs of J.L. Minkston. "Well, I suppose that's it for now. I've got just one more question."

"What's that?"

"It's about your workers. Technically this is none of my business, but nevertheless I'd like to know if they're legal."

The old man did not hesitate. "Absolutely. Most of them's got driver's licenses and social security cards, and the rest have green cards. Believe me, I checked. 'Course I suppose they could be fakes, but how am I supposed to figure that out? And anyway, it may not matter much anymore."

"Why?"

"Because my little grape business probably won't be around too much longer."

Again, I asked why.

"Too much competition. You must have seen it yourself. All those new vineyards popping up around here. Seems like there's a new one every week. Mostly it's those big boys from California, with their tasting rooms and other fancy shit. Hell, it's gotten to the point where I can't hardly sell my crops anymore. And just the other day I heard that French fellow that runs the Santa Rita Saloon, that maybe he's gonna start growing grapes too. So much for the little guy, huh?"

"So you're having a hard time, Moss?"

It was like he hadn't heard me. "You know when I was a kid you could make a pretty good living just raising beef. I mean my Dad had to lease public land because our place wasn't big enough, but we did all right. Not anymore, though. Now even with grapes and the magazine, plus the cattle, I'm barely hanging on."

"So is that why you're going into business with J.L. Minkston?"

"Sure, but he's a real sonofabitch, you know? I just wish I could go back."

"Back where?"

"Back to where all these people would just leave me the hell alone." Moss Winslow paused and pointed to the sky. "Sometimes I think the only friends I've got left are the ones up there."

I'm pretty sure he wasn't referring to dead relatives.

Chapter 7

Andy Slawson's funeral was on Sunday afternoon, which was an unusual day for a burial service. The reason was that Aunt Grace wanted to have it on the weekend to convenience working people, and there hadn't been time to get things ready by Saturday. The service was at the Valley Christian Church, with burial scheduled immediately afterward in the Black Oak Cemetery. The church was packed, certainly more in tribute to Aunt Grace than to Andy. Pastor Bob Atwood was tall and blond with a narrow-lipped eagerness, but he was almost totally lacking in spirit or imagination. It quickly became obvious that he had not known the deceased. He spoke only platitudes over the remains of Andrew J. Slawson, and I thought he spent an unnecessarily long-winded time doing it.

Maria's parents, Cecelia and Ernesto Contreras, lived nearby in Patagonia. They had joined us for breakfast at the Obregon homestead, but we had driven separately to the funeral. Maria and I hung back on the church steps after the service ended, and I took the opportunity to survey the parking lot. Sometimes there were useful things to be learned at such events, in terms of who was mixing with whom. Two groups caught my eye. First, I was surprised to see Aunt Grace and Frenchy Vullmers together, deep in conversation. Frenchy, all two hundred plus pounds of him, owned and ran a place in town formally known as the Santa Rita Café and Lounge. That sounded a little snooty to most of the locals, so they just called it the Santa Rita Saloon. By either name the Santa Rita didn't seem like Grace Slawson's kind of place, and I couldn't remember ever having seen her there. So how and why did she and Frenchy even know each other? I made a mental note to ask about it the next time I saw him.

A second interesting group included Moss Winslow, J.L. Minkston, and Sally Benton. Sally owned and operated the V-9 ranch over in Lyle Canyon. I knew her mostly as one of the regulars at the Santa Rita, but I'd also helped her track down a Hereford bull that had been rustled off her property the previous summer. She was a classy lady, obviously well off, but serious about running her ranch the right way. It was hard to imagine what business she could have with Minkston and Winslow. Watching the three of them, I got the distinct impression that the developer was doing most of the talking, and that Sally was less than comfortable. Finally, she shook her head a couple of times, and then turned and walked away toward the green Jaguar sedan she always drove.

Just as everybody was getting ready to leave, a young man I had not seen before emerged from somewhere and joined Aunt Grace and Frenchy Vullmers. He was tall and thin, with shoulder-length curly brown hair and a goatee that was way too sparse and scraggly to have any chance of improving his appearance. Grace caught my eye and waved me over, at the same time that Frenchy and the young man were shaking hands.

We jointed the group, and Maria gave Aunt Grace a big hug as we both expressed our condolences. Grace looked sad but resolute. She made the introductions. "Cal, Maria, I'd like you to meet a new neighbor, Ambrose Pendleton." We shook hands all around, he without enthusiasm. "Mr. Pendleton is a member of the Elgin Nature Club, and quite an amateur herpetologist."

I belonged to the club because Maria had signed

me up, but I usually didn't go to their meetings. As far as I could determine Aunt Grace was its president for life, or at least nobody else ever seemed to be running things. It was an active group, with interests ranging from geology to botany and zoology.

Ambrose Pendleton, who apparently went by 'Brose,' seemed anxious to talk. "I heard about the snake, of course, the one that bit Ms. Slawson's nephew. Terrible thing. What can you tell me about it?"

Clearly this was neither the time nor the place, and I said something to that effect. Frenchy Vullmers must have agreed, because he conspicuously rolled his eyes, took Aunt Grace by the arm, and led her quickly away toward his vehicle.

Pendleton persisted. "You didn't kill it, did you? What is the species? I'd like to have a look at it, if you don't mind. I have a collection at home. Rattlesnakes are a particular interest of mine."

I needed to get rid of this guy, at least for now. "No, sorry, we're keeping the snake as evidence in a possible crime."

Apparently the man was not easily deterred. "But what about the species? That could be really important."

"That has already been taken care of, thanks. And now if you'll excuse me, it looks like everybody is about to leave for the cemetery."

Ambrose Pendleton III (I learned about that part later) looked hurt and maybe a little bit angry as we walked away. There was something about the young man that struck me wrong, but perhaps it was just my usual suspicions about anybody who professed a fondness for snakes. Except Maria, of course. At least she didn't keep a bunch of them around the house.

Maria and I were nearly to the personal Jeep I drive when off duty, when a familiar voice called out from across the parking lot. I turned and spotted Dan McCall, our local game warden, along with his wife Vicky. Dan had begun his career with Arizona Game and Fish working out of their Kingman office in the northern part of the state, but they had transferred him to the Sonoita area two years ago. Both he and Vicky were active in the nature club, so Maria knew them better than I did. However, I'd had occasional dealings with Dan in his capacity as a wildlife law enforcement officer.

Maria waved as Dan and Vicky walked over in our direction. They were a handsome young couple. She was a petite blue-eyed blond. He was a good head taller, with green eyes and curly red hair. We exchanged the usual polite things one says at a funeral, including our mutual admiration for Grace Slawson. However, it quickly became apparent that Dan had something else on his mind. With apologies to the women, he motioned me aside.

"I couldn't help noticing you talking with Ambrose Pendleton over there. How well do you know him?"

"Not at all, Dan. Aunt Grace just introduced us. Why?"

"Oh, he's sort of up on my radar screen."

I made an informed guess. "Does it have something to do with snakes?"

"Yep. The department is aware of some recent activity in the illegal possession and sale of rattlers."

I couldn't imagine why anybody would want to buy one, and said so.

"You'd be surprised, Cal. Now the common ones, like the diamondback and Mojave, or even the black-tailed, not so much. But we have three varieties around here that are rare and highly valuable. Mostly they live up in the mountains. It's illegal even to possess one without a scientific permit, but there are collectors out there willing to pay up to a thousand dollars for a single live specimen."

"Which snakes are we talking about?"

"The twin-spotted, the ridge-nosed, and the banded rock rattlesnake. All three, but especially the first two, are unusually small compared to the species down here in the valley. Just tiny little things, really, but they still pack a wallop just like all the rest."

"And you think Pendleton might have some of those, or he might even be selling them?"

Dan McCall shrugged and shook his head. "Well, he has a pretty big snake collection in his house, but so far we haven't been able to catch him with any of the protected species. Once, after a meeting of the nature club, I asked if I could see what he had. He invited me over like it was no big deal and gave me a tour."

"And let me guess. You didn't see any of those rare types, right?"

"Right. Of course I made my feelings known that I thought excessive hoarding of any Arizona wildlife was a bad idea. But everything he had – or at least what he let me see – was legal."

"So you're stuck. Is there anything I can do to help? I doubt if we can get a search warrant without some kind of evidence."

"Just keep an eye out, Cal. Pendleton drives a green Toyota 4Runner. Let me know if you or any of the other deputies spot it, especially if it's anywhere up high."

"Will do."

~ ~ ~

The hearse carrying the body of Andy Slawson pulled out of the church parking lot and headed for the Black Oak Cemetery, which was in the foothills of the Canelo Hills about fourteen miles south of the Sonoita Crossroads. Aunt Grace followed immediately behind, riding with Frenchy Vullmers in a big old Peugeot. We all got in line behind them. Custom held that only long-term residents of the area could be interred in the Black Oak burial grounds, but apparently Aunt Grace had pulled some strings. She wanted Andy to be buried in the Whitfield family plot next to her parents and other relatives.

Grass in the little cemetery was green but largely untended, and the oak trees were alive but stunted, just like they were everywhere along this part of the hills. The sky was an uninterrupted pale blue, and a fitful breeze swirled around the mourners as the coffin was lowered into the freshly dug grave. The late afternoon heat was palpable, and the procession of cars had left a fog of dust over the proceedings. Once again Pastor Atwood made up in longevity for what he lacked in profundity. I could sense that the mourners were relieved when the graveside service finally ended, and they departed as soon as was tactfully possible. Most in the group were headed for Aunt Grace's house, where neighbors and other friends would supply a potluck meal. I had learned at breakfast that Maria's mother would be a major contributor.

~ ~ ~

I was anxious to talk to Maria alone, but the first opportunity did not arise until that evening after we had gotten back home from the wake. She'd finished the afternoon milking. My offer of help had been rebuffed, as usual. Apparently I made some of the animals nervous, and we had developed a mutually wary relationship. I thought her LaMancha goats were sort of funny looking because of their stubby little ears, and I actually didn't think their milk tasted all that good. But Maria was intensely proud of her little herd, and I appreciated her dedication toward making the business a success. Exactly how the goats might fit into our long-term relationship was an issue still under negotiation, but Maria had made it clear the animals weren't going anywhere.

A wooden bench made out of mesquite planks sat up against the north wall of the old Obregon adobe. It was our favorite place to sit and watch the evening light change on the Mustangs. They started out limestone gray, then faded to yellow and pink. Finally they glowed burnt orange just before the sun dipped below the western horizon.

I'd grown up with a view of the Mustang Mountains out my bedroom window. They always seemed a magical place, almost like they were haunted. I hiked up there once to explore the caves, and found one that went all the way through from north to south at a narrow point along the ridge. Standing in one spot inside that cave I could see all the way to Mexico in one direction, then turn around and see Rincon Peak east of Tucson in the other.

The Mustangs are relatively barren compared to the other ranges that surround the Sonoita Valley – an arid, scraggly, almost archetypical western landscape. You might recognize them even if you've never been to southeastern Arizona, because of all the old movies that have featured them as a backdrop. My favorite of these was the original black-and-white version of *Red River*, with John Wayne and Montgomery Clift. The story was about a cattle drive supposedly going from Texas to Kansas. But during the actual filming they just kept driving the herd around and around the Mustangs until they finally got to Abilene, except that it actually was Elgin. That was back when a railroad still ran through the valley.

Maria and I were sharing a bottle of *Pacifico*, which was her favorite. I took a sip and handed her the bottle. "I thought Aunt Grace looked okay, under the circumstances."

Maria nodded. "You know her life has not been

easy, so I guess maybe she wasn't surprised by one more disappointment."

This was news to me. "I know about Andy, but what else?"

"Her life up in Tucson. My parents told me about it a long time ago. Apparently she got married while she was a university student. She got pregnant right away, but then she lost the baby. To top it all off her husband turned out to be a real bum. I think he's dead now, and I guess Andy was her last hope for any sort of real family."

"And now he's gone, killed by a snake of all things."

"Speaking of that snake, I finally got through to Dr. Smith on Friday. She said she'd be glad to take a look at it any day this week. You know I have Wednesdays off, so that would be best for me. Wanna go up there?"

"Good idea. Maybe we could combine it with a visit with my parents, if you're up for that. I haven't seen them in over a month, and I know they're anxious to talk about how we're doing after the flood. Oh, and to nag us about getting married of course."

My parents, Harold and Doris Creede, had owned and operated the Pitchfork Ranch just north of Sonoita the whole time I was growing up. They were retired now and living in Green Valley, a senior community south of Tucson. It was the right decision, given their ages. We still owned the Pitchfork, but we had leased it out to a couple from west Texas. They were doing a good job, but I knew my parents, and especially Dad, were disappointed their only child had been unwilling to take over. I'd thought about it of course, but not hard and not for long.

My time in Afghanistan had been rough, and I still had not fully recovered from the trauma. But I'd volunteered for the MPs over there, and it wasn't all bad. There was something clean and satisfying about police work, even in a war zone and even in that godforsaken desert. Ranching's different – just an endless string of worries about things like rain and grass and disease and the price of beef. I was back home from the army only two weeks when a job with the sheriff's department opened up. I jumped at the chance, and so far it seemed like the right decision. Maria and I had talked about someday maybe going back to the Pitchfork, she with her goats and me with a bunch of cattle. But that was part of such a distant planning horizon as to be virtually invisible.

Apparently Maria was comfortable with a trip to Green Valley. "Sure. Let's go see your parents. I'll take your mom some goat cheese." Then she changed the subject. "I'm really anxious to find out what Dr. Smith can tell us about Mojave rattlers in general, and especially about the one that bit Andy. By the way, my boss told me the Postmaster General's office might be sending somebody out from D.C. to look into the crime. It could be a federal offense because it involved a mailbox."

I felt sure we didn't need a big city fed from back east under foot, but decided not to share my opinion with Maria. "Speaking of that mailbox, the Nogales crime scene people found no usable prints on it except those belonging to you, Andy, and Moss Winslow. And nothing else useful turned up, no foot or tire prints, no more snakes, no personal effects. Just nothing."

Maria rose from the bench. It was nearly dark now, and dead quiet except for the hollow boom of a nighthawk swooping around someplace out over the San Carlos wash. Maria was a very good naturalist, and she knew what that booming sound was all about. The bird was demonstrating his aerobatic prowess to a potential mate. "You know, after I've tucked in the goats and we've had something to eat, I think it's time for a little courtship of our own."

Later that night I lay awake thinking about the case. I was virtually certain that Andy Slawson had been murdered. But why, and by whom? I had dealt with only a handful of violent crimes in my years with the county. With one or two exceptions they were straightforward events involving things like alcohol or jealous lovers, and easily solved.

The main problem was that using a snake as a weapon was a very strange way to go about killing or even just hurting somebody. Put simply, there was nothing to guarantee results. Whoever the intended victim might have been, the odds were at least fifty-fifty they would have seen the snake in plenty of time to get out of the way. And who were those possible victims besides Andy? Perhaps Moss was right that the snake had been meant for him, or maybe even Maria. After all, she opened the mailbox and put her hands into it almost daily.

Possible motives were an even greater puzzle. Was there some connection with Andy's problems up in Tucson, like revenge for a drug deal gone bad? I'd have to check that out with local law enforcement in Tucson and Pima County. Maybe Aunt Grace knew something, although she'd claimed ignorance the other night. And what about Harlo Henshaw and the Border Posse? Clearly there was no love lost between them and Moss Winslow, to say nothing of his field crew. But murder? The snake on their battle flag was an interesting coincidence, but I couldn't imagine it was anything more than that.

I finally drifted off a little after two in the morning, but what little sleep I got that night was punctuated by a strange dream. I was in the barn with Maria's goats, and there were rattlers in every corner. My job (why was it my job?) was to keep the snakes away from the goats. They hissed and coiled and struck, not so much at the goats but at me. There were other men who kept coming into the barn and then leaving. They were dressed in camouflage and their faces were painted black, like they were dressed for night action. Some of the men carried big cages with more snakes inside. I thought they'd come to help catch the snakes, but instead they were letting them out. I called out for Maria, but she would not come.

None of the dream made any sense, but then mine never do.

Chapter 8

It was Monday morning after Andy Slawson's funeral, and I was in the office tidying up some boring paperwork. Larry had gone off to a campground east of the Canelos over in Lyle Canyon. Apparently there had been vandalism down there over the weekend. It was a recurring trouble spot.

About nine o'clock a man I did not recognize walked in the door. He identified himself as Percy Butterfield, a reporter for the *Tucson Gazette*, and he wanted to talk.

Butterfield looked to be in his mid-thirties, short and round, with a moon face to match. I learned later that his colleagues at the paper sometimes called him 'Butterball,' but he had their respect for his uncanny ability to sniff out a good story. In retrospect, it was not surprising that the man's nose had taken him directly to the Sonoita substation of the Santa Cruz County Sheriff's Department, which was me and Larry.

The local paper in Nogales had already run a story about the Andy Slawson death, of course. But the sheriff had connections there, and so it had been little more than a bare bones re-write of the departmental press release. It turned out Percy Butterfield had juicier things in mind.

I knew Luis didn't like it when his deputies dealt directly with the media. Instead, we were under orders to refer all such inquiries to his press officer. I tried that with Butterfield, but it didn't work. Instead, and without invitation, he plunked himself down in Larry's chair. Then he placed a little cassette recorder on the desktop between us, fired it up, and started asking questions.

I told him to turn the recorder off, or otherwise my answers to everything would be 'no comment.' He sighed conspicuously, but eventually he did as I asked and replaced the recorder with a notebook. At that point I decided to humor the man and answer a few questions, just as long as we stuck to facts about the Slawson case already available in the public record. In hindsight, probably even that was a mistake.

Butterfield flipped open his notebook, clicked on a ballpoint pen, and began the interview. "Is it true that somebody must have put the snake in Mr. Winslow's mailbox? That it couldn't have gotten there by itself?"

"Yes."

"Yes, what?"

"Yes, it is my understanding that rattlesnakes cannot climb. So a logical conclusion is that somebody must have put it there."

"Do you have any suspects?"

"We are pursuing several possible leads, but we are not prepared to name any suspects at this point in our investigation." I knew that sounded like public relations jargon, and apparently so did he.

"Yeah, right."

Butterfield paused and asked if he could smoke. I nodded in reluctant agreement, and reached in my desk drawer for an old glass ashtray that rarely saw daylight anymore. He tugged a pack of Camels out of one shirt pocket and an old Zippo lighter out of the other. I noticed yellow-stained fingers as he lit up.

He took a big draw and exhaled a blue cloud in my direction. "So if you can't or won't name any suspects, what about victims?"

"I don't understand. The victim was a young man named Andy Slawson." I knew that was far from the whole truth of the matter, and not surprisingly it didn't fool Butterfield.

"No, Deputy Creede, what I mean is, how could the perpetrator have known in advance who was going to open that mailbox?"

"I suppose he couldn't."

"He?"

"Sorry. He or she."

"Sure. Now let's assume for the moment that it was Mr. Winslow and not the Slawson boy who was the intended victim. Then would you have any ideas as to a suspect or a motive?"

"That's too hypothetical for me to answer."

"I see. Well then, what can you tell me about a group that calls itself the Border Posse?"

Percy Butterfield obviously had done his homework, and I was beginning to doubt the wisdom of having let the man into my office in the first place. I described what I knew about the posse in general terms, expressed some reservations about their activities, but pointed out that as far as we knew they had not yet done anything illegal. I didn't realize it at the time, but that last part eventually was going to get me into trouble.

This didn't seem to satisfy him in any event. "What do you know about Border Posse activities around Mr. Winslow's vineyard?"

Where had he heard that? My respect for Butterfield was growing, but it sure wasn't making me any more comfortable. Still, it seemed at this point there was little to do except tell the truth. I described the circumstances of the posse's protest, and then emphasized its peaceful resolution.

"So you don't think there's any chance this posse or whatever it is might have put the snake in Mr. Winslow's mailbox?"

Clearly it was time for Mr. Butterfield to leave. "I

really have no idea, and I will not comment on unfounded accusations. Now if you'll excuse me, I have some work to do outside the office that cannot wait. If you have any more questions, please get in touch with our press officer down in Nogales."

"I've already done that, Deputy, and I cannot imagine a reason for doing it again. But I thank you for your time."

I gave Butterfield five minutes to clear the parking lot because I didn't want him to ambush me with "just one more question." Then I locked up the office, got in the Blazer, and headed off once more to see Moss Winslow. He'd said something puzzling the other day about that new developer in the valley, J.L. Minkston, and I wanted to follow up.

The familiar drive through the Sonoita Valley took me past the full spectrum of current land uses. Thousands of acres remained as undeveloped rangeland, mostly the remnants of a land grant that had passed from Spanish-American to Scottish-American hands during a big drought at the turn of the 20th Century. It was picture-postcard beautiful, with a spring-fed marsh called a *cienega*, and open rolling grasslands dotted with appropriately scattered cattle and horses.

Elsewhere, formerly large cattle operations had been divided up into 'ranchette' parcels ranging from five to perhaps forty acres. I hated to see unspoiled parts of the valley slipping away, but I understood the pressures that old-time ranchers were facing to sell out. Economics of the cattle business went up and down, while the value of their property as real estate never stopped climbing.

Three horses, one steer, and a couple of sheep were grazing one of the first ranchettes I passed on my way out to the Winslow place. A newly constructed Santa Fe style house sat in the middle of the property, plastered in stucco and painted tan so that it looked like real adobe. Behind the house were two metal mini-barns and a matrix of small corrals. The remaining portion of the property not taken up with structures looked like a moonscape. It was so overgrazed that whatever homegrown nutrition the animals received came only from a few scattered weeds. Local ranchers knew it took at least thirty acres of grass to feed just one horse in a sustainable manner in this part of Arizona. These new landowners had no clue about the carrying capacity of their land, or maybe they just didn't care.

Not everybody was treating the land that badly. Some owners, most in fact, took pride in leaving their parcels in as natural a state as possible. It was surprising how well native plants and animals could do if you just left things alone. Maria did that with her quarter section, except for the goats of course, but at least they were confined to her corrals.

Moss Winslow's place included another new land use in the valley – namely, the growing of wine grapes. Some vineyards were much bigger than his and included their own cellars. I did not know where Moss sold his grapes, but one or more of these local operations seemed the most likely.

Something strange caught my eye as I was approaching Elgin from the west. It was a medium-sized house trailer, festooned with a bunch of flags and colored pennants attached on wires or ropes extending out in all directions from one corner of the trailer, like spokes on a wheel. The flags and pennants flapped insipidly in a fitful breeze. The place looked like a low-rent used car lot, except there was only one vehicle in sight – a big pearl-white Cadillac Escalade. Either the whole setup was new, or I had been asleep on the way to work that morning.

I slowed for a closer look and then stopped, still on the county blacktop. The trailer had only one door, which was standing open. A sign on the wall next to the door informed me this was the sales office for something called 'Mustang Estates.' While I was reading the sign a man came out of the trailer. He was carrying a hammer in one hand and a roll of duct tape in the other. It was J.L. Minkston. I had been meaning to have a conversation with the man, and this looked like a good time, so I pulled off onto the short dirt track leading back to his little office.

Minkston was a big man gone soft, with broad shoulders but an even broader waistline. He had a big jowly face under a full head of curly black hair tinged with gray at the edges. The corners of his undersized mouth were turned up in what passed for a smile, but his dark deep-set eyes remained cautious. It was one of those 'jackass-eating-thistles' sort of grins, where the lips moved but the eyes didn't follow. It made me suspicious. I guess the feeling was mutual.

I wanted to put the man at ease so I got out of the Blazer and extended my hand. "Morning. I'm Cal Creede, from the sheriff's office over in Sonoita."

His grip was firm enough, but decidedly damp. "Morning. I'm J.L. Minkston. Is there some sort of a problem?"

"No, not at all. I just wanted to introduce myself. I like to get to know everybody in the valley, make sure they know we're here and on the job. My partner's Larry Hernandez. I expect you'll see him around because he's the one that's usually out on patrol."

Minkston scruffed around in the dirt with his left boot, then fumbled in his shirt pocket like he was reaching for a smoke, but changed his mind. "Well thanks, Deputy. Appreciate it. Believe I've met your boss down in Nogales."

I wondered when and how that happened. "I understand you recently bought the mall that's partially finished outside Sonoita. So it looks like you've got some more property right here in Elgin?"

"Yep, just closed on the fifty acres behind us here." His hand swept the horizon, indicating a broad rolling grassland well populated with flowering yuccas. As far as I could determine, the property approached but did not quite reach the foothills of the Mustang Mountains off to the northeast.

I handed Minkston one of my cards, which he accepted and put in the shirt pocket without the cigarettes. It was pushy for sure, but I decided to take a chance. "If you don't mind my asking, what are your plans for this area?"

It was like somebody threw a switch. Minkston's face lit up. "Well, why don't you come in the office and I'll show you."

It was hot and stuffy inside the trailer, as if it had been closed up until just recently. There were only a few items of furniture, a desk with a couple of chairs and a filing cabinet. The thing that struck me was the profusion of maps and drawings that took up nearly every wall space. They were all in color, and from what I could see at first glance, it was scary as hell.

Minkston followed my eyes. "I know what you're thinking, Cal. Is it all right if I call you Cal?" I scarcely had time to nod before he went on. "Everybody around here thinks of Elgin as just a sleepy little village, out of the way, hardly a town at all. But they're missing the bigger picture. This place has incredible potential, and I hope to realize it. This whole valley is a secret paradise, and Elgin is the jewel in the crown."

"But there already is quite a bit of development, especially around Sonoita, and what with the economic downturn and all..."

J.L. Minkston held up a hand to stop me. His dark eyes flashed with a self-assured light. "No, no, you're wrong. The housing market is looking up. Everybody knows it. People are hungry for something new, something not already built-out. You gotta have vision, Cal. This place is gonna be the next Green Valley!"

He likely noticed my skeptical look, but it didn't slow him down. Instead he insisted on giving me a tour of the maps and drawings, pointing out the highlights as we circled the interior of his little trailer. "We'll have lots of individual housing units, of course, including both stand-alone and patio homes. But there's also gonna be a top-rated hotel with pools and a golf course, riding stables, maybe even a dude ranch. There's so much open space here, the sky's the limit."

I had a pretty good idea what the limit actually was around Elgin, and it definitely wasn't the sky. "So your development is called Mustang Estates?"

"Well, this is only a start, just the first fifty acres right behind us here. I've got my eye on some other properties, and they're going to be essential." Minkston paused. "Speaking of which, I understand your friend – Maria's her name, right? – she might have some land available? She could get in right on the ground floor, be almost like a partner if we could work out the right arrangements. It could make her rich, Cal."

I had to give J.L. Minkston credit. He certainly knew how to cut to the chase. How in the hell had he found out about me and Maria, and what else did he know? At first I'd just been skeptical about the man's plans. Now it was personal.

Chapter 9

I was half expecting to see Moss Winslow already outside as I drove into his yard, because we had set up our meeting in advance. But there was no sign of anybody around, not even his field hands. The rows of grape vines across the fence were clean of grass and weeds, and at least some hung heavy with ripe purple fruit. A half-dozen steers were bawling and milling around inside a corral out behind the house as if they were expecting either food or water. Otherwise it was dead quiet.

I went up on the porch and knocked. There was no response so I knocked again and identified myself. Still nobody came to the door, but I thought I heard voices coming from somewhere deep inside the house. Officially I had no business going any further with this, except a suspicion that something might be wrong. After all, the rancher was not a young man and we did have an appointment. I tried the front door and found it unlocked. I took one step inside. Nothing looked out of the ordinary, but neither was there any sign of Winslow. Then voices started up again, from somewhere off to my right. This time they were accompanied by music and what sounded like a muffled explosion. What the hell?

I un-holstered my weapon and walked farther into the living room. Something was wrong about the whole scene. The voices and the sounds continued, clear but faint, as if they might have been coming from someplace outdoors. But I'd just been outside, and there had been no such voices or sounds.

Suddenly a door opened, and Moss Winslow walked in. At the same time the voices and sounds got much louder. He was carrying a glass of amber liquid in one hand, and a lighted cigar in the other. I found myself enveloped in a cloud of pungent cigar smoke, mixed with the unmistakable odor of bourbon.

Eerie sounds were coming from the dark room behind Winslow. He quickly turned back to shut the door, and I took the opportunity to re-holster my sidearm. Whatever was going on, the man seemed to be okay.

I was expecting an explanation, but it sure wasn't the one he gave me.

"*It Came from Outer Space.*"

"What?"

"You know, it's a fifties classic. Sort of dated now, but I kind of like those old ones." He lifted his glass and took a swallow. A half-inch of ash dislodged from the end of his cigar and fell to the floor, unnoticed. "So anyway, Cal, why are you here?"

I reminded him we'd had an appointment.

"Oh shit, that's right. Sorry. Must be the booze. That other fella really upset me, so I kinda started early."

"What other fella?"

"Some little fat guy. Said he was a reporter. Asked a lot of rude questions."

It looked like Percy Butterfield had gotten here ahead of me. "What did you talk about?"

"He wanted to know all about the snake in my mailbox, of course. And about Andy Slawson and the Border Posse. All that. But then he sort of got distracted, I guess, with my stuff about UFOs. So that's what we ended up talking about. And it really pissed me off."

"Why is that?"

"Because he just laughed, that's why."

Moss Winslow and I took seats on opposite sides of a heavy low table, in matching chairs upholstered in Hereford cowhide. Moss put down his cigar in a copper ashtray shaped like a flying saucer. Then he took off his glasses, pulled out a red bandana, and gave the lenses a quick wipe.

I pointed toward the room from which Moss Winslow had just emerged. "So, you have some sort of home theater in there?"

"Yep. It's got one of those high-definition big screen TVs, a couple of luxury recliners, and a whole wall of shelves for my tapes and CDs. And I subscribe to the sci-fi channel on satellite, even though it costs me extra. You should come over some time on your day off. We can watch a flick together. I can make popcorn, just like the real deal. But I hope you like sci-fi, 'cause that's all I've got. You have any favorites?"

Funny he should have asked. "Yeah, I do as a matter of fact. The first *Star Wars*."

Moss Winslow frowned. "Good film, I suppose, and it sure grossed a helluva lot of money. But it was fluff. No substance at all. I don't even own a copy. Nope, it's the ones about close encounters that I like the best. If I put on the right old film it's easy to imagine that saucer is coming down right here in my back yard."

He paused and took another sip of bourbon. "Or maybe it lands up there in Whetstones like when I was a boy. Takes me back to when things were just so clean and simple. Then, at least for a little while, I can forget about all the mess that's *really* going on out there."

Now we were getting somewhere. "What mess is that, Moss?"

The old man gave me a look that said he knew I was smarter than that. "You damn well know what mess. Okay, sure, it doesn't necessarily have anything to do with the sheriff's department, but don't tell me you haven't noticed or don't care about the way our valley is getting carved-up by these damned developers."

He had me there. "You mean like J.L. Minkston?"

Moss Winslow was staring out one of his front

windows. For a while it was like he hadn't heard me, didn't even know I was there. Then he snapped out of it. "You know I grew up around here, don't you?"

I wasn't sure what any of this had to do with flying saucers, but it seemed like a good idea to humor the man. "We both grew up here, Moss."

"Well, then you can imagine what I'm missing. So you're damned right, like J.L. Minkston. Him and some others. Greedy bastards."

"But aren't you in business with Minkston? I thought you said something like that the other day, when I was out here about the Slawson boy."

Winslow's cigar had gone cold, but he made no effort to light it back up. He shook his head, but not in a way that told me I was off the mark. "J.L. and I got a deal, you're right. But I only did it for the money. Listen, Cal, do you have any idea how hard it is to stay ahead in the cattle business anymore? I'm not a wealthy man. I mean the magazine does all right, but it's not enough to live off. And that little vineyard of mine? I thought at first it might help, but now I'm not so sure."

"How so? I thought your grape crop looked pretty good out there when I was driving in."

"It's okay, I guess. But you gotta factor in the costs. First there's the watering system, and then the fertilizer and the pesticides, to say nothing of labor. Even those wet – uh, those field hands – they cost me a bundle. I did make some money the last couple of years. But now, I don't know if you noticed, but some of my vines don't look so good. That's new this fall. It's like they're dying or something. One damned thing after another. Now I'll probably have to fatten out a couple of my steers and sell 'em, just to break even."

Chapter 10

Two great air masses compete for space over my part of Arizona. The monsoon comes up from the south, mostly in July and August, building into thunderheads that can drench the ground and make the summer grasses grow. The Navajo call these male rains. I have a theory about that. Lots of times those same monsoon clouds just show up empty, promising life-giving rain but delivering only noise and wind.

Female rains usually come in winter, off the Pacific. Only rarely are they violent, but they can last for days, sometimes covering the whole region in a gray, gentle, mist. In between there is fall, normally a dry time of year when the grasses have time to cure and the animals get busy doing whatever they must in order to make it through the winter.

It was mid-October in the Sonoita Valley, normally too late for the monsoon but a bit early for the winter rains. Yet as I was driving to town that evening low, dark, clouds began to fill the western sky. Tucson radio and television stations were reporting that it had rained the day before in San Diego, which is where our female weather fronts usually made landfall. Scattered drops were beginning to wet the parking lot at the Santa Rita Saloon as I arrived for my regularly scheduled Monday night appearance.

Three years ago Frenchy Vullmers, owner of the Santa Rita, started what he called 'Two-fers Monday,' where the beer was half-price from five until nine. His goal was to increase business. It had worked, but with an unintended side effect. Namely, the crowd sometimes got a little rowdy, which is where I came in.

It had become my habit to enjoy one of Frenchy's ribeyes and a bottle of *Bohemia* on Monday nights, just in case. It didn't hurt that he cooked a mean steak on his mesquite-fired grill. Plus, I liked the man.

Frenchy was retired military, but far from the usual sort. Born in France, his real name was Patrice Vieumilliers and he'd been a long-time member of the French Foreign Legion. He got himself attached to nearby Fort Huachuca in some capacity I'd never fully understood. Then he'd quit the military and gone into the bar and restaurant business while I was overseas. The Regulars at the Santa Rita Saloon had come up with the name Frenchy Vullmers. They had no idea that Patrice was the French equivalent of Patrick, and they thought it sounded sort of girly. So 'Frenchy' replaced 'Patrice.' And he *was* French, after all. They had no problems like that with Vieumilliers. But nobody was sure how to pronounce it, so they converted it to Vullmers.

The place was quiet as I slid into my usual booth, a spot up near the front where it was possible to intercept anyone as they were coming or going, depending on the occasion. I sat with my back to the wall, where I had a clear view of a long bar to my left and a line of six booths opposite. The booths and the barstools were upholstered in red. Individual tables took up the center of the room. The grill was next to the bar, along with a swinging door that led to the kitchen. Two pool tables and the restrooms were at the far end.

A short, middle-aged Hispanic woman was behind the bar, wiping glasses with a blue-and-white towel. I had not seen her before. She was chatting with Al Treutline. Al owned the Quick Stop gas and grocery place in Sonoita. He was one of the most regular of the Regulars, and he rarely missed a Two-fers Monday. Al was the only customer at the bar. This was unusual for a Monday, but three parties already were in booths having dinner.

Two middle-aged couples were seated in the booth closest to mine. They were over-dressed by Santa Rita standards, the men in tailored western wear with southwestern design, the women in heels and formal black dresses. They spoke in rapid, animated Spanish. Based on their attire I guessed they had come up for the evening from Nogales, Sonora.

Two men were seated in the second booth. The one facing me looked out of place in a shiny black suit and a white shirt with no tie. The other man was dressed more like a local, and when he turned toward the bar I recognized Ambrose Pendleton. He caught my eye for an instant and then looked quickly away. Shortly after that the man in the black suit called for the bill, which Frenchy delivered in person. The man handed Frenchy some cash, then he and Pendleton got up and left their table without waiting for change. The young snake collector gave me a nod on the way out, but he hurried past my booth without any pretext of introducing me to his companion. I thought about my recent conversation with Dan McCall, and what the game warden had said about recent traffic in illegal snakes. Just a coincidence?

Sally Benton was in the third booth along with two younger people who might have been family, although as far as I knew Sally lived alone on her V-9 Ranch. Sally was her usual immaculate self, in jeans, boots, and a turquoise blouse with lots of matching jewelry. She and her party were having margaritas, but unlike the Hispanic couple they were not yet eating. Sally caught my eye and waved, then looked back expectantly toward the grill.

As if on cue, French Vullmers emerged from the kitchen with three plates already loaded with potatoes and salad. He had a large white towel wrapped around his midsection, and he was wearing a cook's hat. His face was red, and he was perspiring heavily. He stopped at the grill, deftly forked two steaks and one large hamburger onto the plates, and carried them over to Sally's table. They chatted briefly, and it looked like Sally was introducing her guests.

Frenchy went back to the bar and said something to Al Treutline. Then he asked the lady bartender for a chilled glass and a bottle of *Bohemia,* and headed my way. He set the beer on my table, and then he actually bowed before joining me in the booth. "Good evening my friend, and thank you once again for gracing my establishment." He had a distinct accent, which made things seem especially formal. Frenchy was like that, but I knew he meant it.

"So you're working the kitchen tonight?"

He rolled his eyes. "Ah the joys of owning a place such as this, in the middle of nowhere. The help is always coming and going. Right now it is mostly going. I am fortunate Lucinda was able to come in and do the bar. She lives over in Sierra Vista, married to an army sergeant named Alturas. I knew her from my previous life."

Then I said something really stupid. "Well, at least you're not all that busy. I mean, given the lack of help and all, maybe it's just..."

I trailed off, no doubt looking as sheepish as I felt.

Frenchy, in his usual impeccable style, let me off the hook. "I'm sure things will pick up later in the evening. In the meantime, however, I am just as glad, because there is something we need to discuss."

I poured some beer and took a swallow. "What's that?"

"It is about the funeral the other day. I am sure you noticed that Grace Slawson and I were together, and that I gave her a ride to the cemetery. I wanted to explain."

I shook my head and shrugged. "No explanation required. I hope you two are friends. Aunt Grace could use one right about now. And certainly it has nothing to do with the sheriff's department."

"I hope that you are right, but I am not so sure."

This was news. "I guess maybe you'd better tell me what's going on, Frenchy."

"As you say, it may be nothing at all. But there is a man - from what I can tell not always such a nice man - who is making life unpleasant for Grace."

That stopped me in mid-swallow. "Who's that?"

"His name is Minkston. J.L. Minkston. Do you know him?"

"We've met."

"Do you know about his plans for Elgin?"

"Yep. Or at least some of them. Why do you ask?" I wondered how much Frenchy knew.

It turned out he knew a lot. Vullmers took off his cook's hat and ran a beefy hand through his thick head of close-cropped gray hair. "Well, he's after Grace's little piece of land, and he also wants her water. She has a wonderful spring on her place, and I guess that's unusual because the groundwater situation around Elgin is - how do you Americans say it – somewhat iffy? So maybe he wants the water even more than the land."

This was interesting information, especially in light of what I knew about Minkston having designs on Maria's place. But I still didn't see how any of it was connected with Frenchy, or why the man thought it might be a matter for the sheriff's department.

He must have read my mind. "You are wondering why this is any of my concern, no?" He didn't wait for a response. "Well, here is why. Grace Slawson and I may be about to embark on a joint venture, to start a little vineyard on her place. I know something about grapes, because of where I grew up. The soils and slope on her property are ideal for certain varietals, to say nothing of her water."

"But even if Minkston wants her land, there's no way he can make her sell."

Frenchy Vullmers shook his head. "Perhaps he cannot make her sell, but he can try to change her mind, no?"

"But how? And I still don't see what any of this has to do with me, in an official capacity that is."

"Perhaps that is because you do not know Grace Slawson was well as I? Perhaps you do not know just how important Andy was to her?"

"I think I have some idea about that, yes. And I have known Aunt Grace for nearly my whole life. But what does that have to do...?"

Frenchy Vullmers held up his hand. "That vineyard was to be for him, Cal. It was to be Andy's future. And now he has no future, and so perhaps Grace has no future out there either. And would that not fit right in with Minkston's plans?"

He let that settle in. It was a stretch, but I got the connection.

"Of course it may be nothing, but I thought you should know these things."

"I think you have a suspicious mind, Frenchy."

"You are perhaps correct. The business I was in before coming to Sonoita? Well, let us just say that I learned to be suspicious."

There was one other aspect to this whole thing that troubled me. It was personal and not professional, so I decided to put it straight out to the man. "I know that Aunt Grace has her retirement from the school district, but I am not sure she's in a position to set up a vineyard. Aren't there a lot of front-end expenses? And then what about the costs of tending and harvesting the grapes?"

Frenchy Vullmers shook his head. "No, no, my friend. Perhaps I did not make myself sufficiently clear. Ours will be a true partnership. She will provide the land and the water, while I cover all the rest. If she does decide to go ahead with our project, there will be no costs to her. I have some savings that will be more than sufficient to get us started, and I have every confidence that our venture will soon be profitable."

Frenchy slid out of his side of my booth and stood. "But now I must return to the kitchen. Are you ready for that steak? And do I remember correctly that your favorite cut is the ribeye, cooked to medium-rare?"

The next half-hour passed quietly. A few more of the Regulars drifted in, while the parties in the booths, minus Ambrose Pendleton and his mysterious companion, lingered over coffee and after-dinner drinks. It looked like this Two-fers Monday would end without incident, as had been the case recently.

Then in walked Harlo Henshaw and two of his buddies from the Border Posse. Each was dressed in camouflage from their baseball caps clear down to their boots, and they looked tired and dirty. I suppose they had been down along the border, helping to make America safe again.

The trio walked up and took stools at the bar. Harlo did the ordering. "Three beers for my friends and me, nice and cold."

Lucinda gave them a look. "Any particular brand?"

"Whatever you got on tap, as long as it's American. We aren't buying any of those Mex brews. Don't believe in it."

It got real quiet in the Santa Rita Saloon. Al Treutline picked up his beer and moved farther down the bar. Lucinda seemed to be having trouble finding three mugs that were clean enough. Off to my right, the two couples from Nogales had fallen silent and were just sitting there, staring down at the cups and glasses in front of them.

Sally Benton apparently had a different plan. She rose to her feet and walked over to where the three men were anxiously awaiting their drinks.

"Evening boys! You guys sure do look hot and thirsty." She turned her attention to the bartender. "Lucinda, would you pour these fellas a big ice-cold pitcher? And it's on me."

Harlo Henshaw was quick to respond. "Well thank you, ma'am, that's mighty nice of you."

Sally Benton reached for the pitcher. "Least I can do, under the circumstances." Then she dumped the whole thing in Harlo Henshaw's lap, said 'oops,' and walked back to her table.

It fell to me to return calm to the place. If it had been up to me personally, Sally Benton would have gotten some sort of a reward. But as a sworn deputy my duties lay elsewhere. Peace was restored only after I persuaded Sally to apologize, which she did with some reluctance. Frenchy Vullmers supplied towels for cleanup and free beer on the house for the rest of the night. Even Al Treutline got in on it, although I noticed he never said a word or made eye contact with Henshaw or his buddies. Frenchy wouldn't let the foursome from Nogales pay for their meal. He thanked them for coming and hoped they would come back soon. He said these things in pretty good Spanish, but I don't suppose it made much difference.

Chapter 11

It had rained on and off for most of the night, and the roads were still wet when I headed to the office on Tuesday morning. There was no sign of life as I passed J.L. Minkston's little office trailer, and I saw no fresh tire tracks in the mud puddles surrounding it. Two of the poles supporting his ropes with little flags and pennants had sagged, giving the whole place a forlorn look. Apparently the newest development in the valley was off to a slow start.

The sun broke through the clouds as I pulled into my usual space beside headquarters. Larry's Jeep was out in back, and he was typing something into the office computer as I walked in. He pointed over his shoulder, but didn't look up. "Coffee's ready. Be with you in a second."

I helped myself to a cup and sat down on the opposite side of our shared desk. I had time for three good swallows before the printer came to life and Larry pushed back in his chair.

"Morning boss. What's new?"

I summarized events at the Santa Rita from the night before.

Larry laughed. "Glad it was you and not me."

I pointed to the printer, which had just fallen silent. "What's up with you?"

"Had a little incident yesterday over in Lyle Canyon, at Gus Barlow's place. Just finished writing up the report."

I knew Gus ran a decent-sized cattle operation over in the mesquite hills at the base of the Huachucas. "What happened?"

"You know that windmill and stock tank of his out next to the road?"

"Sure."

"Well I'm driving by and he's standing there beside his pickup. He waved me down, so I pulled over to see what was up. Then he pointed to his stock tank, which was shot full of holes."

It wasn't the first time we'd had reports about this sort of vandalism. "How recent?"

"Must have just happened, because water was still leaking out. So probably last night. But that's not the only thing."

"What?"

"On the side of the tank facing the road there's a big drawing of a coiled up rattlesnake. It's black and maybe sprayed on."

"What do you mean?"

"I mean the thing's really well-done, not haphazard at all, like whoever did it was using a pattern or a stencil."

We'd both heard stories about people shooting holes in water tanks so border crossers couldn't drink from them, and we had seen the evidence. But the snake stencil was something new. All at once it seemed like my whole life was revolving around snakes. I may have mentioned they are not my favorite subject.

"Did you get pictures?"

Larry shook his head. "No. Damn. Want me to go back?"

"That's probably a good idea."

Larry had just left when my cell phone buzzed to life. I recognized the sheriff's personal number. Sometimes we talked at the beginning of the week, even if nothing much was happening, just so he could get caught up on events in my corner of the county. It soon became clear this was not one of those occasions.

"We got a call down here this morning from an acquaintance of yours."

"Who?"

"Harlo Henshaw."

Uh oh.

The sheriff then proceeded to describe what had happened the night before at the Santa Rita Saloon, according to Henshaw and his buddies.

"Well, Luis, it was a little more complicated than that."

"Complicated how?"

I took my time explaining the circumstances leading up to Sally Benton's action with the beer pitcher, and how it ended up. The sheriff listened without interruption, but apparently he was not totally happy. "I think maybe you should have another talk with him, try to calm him down a little. I did my best, but he seemed pretty hot."

"I'm not sure it will do any good."

"Maybe not, but do it anyway. And while we're on the subject, I have a question. To your knowledge, has the man or his little band of brothers broken any laws?"

I thought about Gus Barlow's water tank. "Not to my knowledge."

"Then I guess about all we can do is keep an eye out. But I don't like the feel of this Border Posse group. Don't like it at all. Some of my patrol deputies have run into them down in the San Raphael Valley, but we haven't been able to catch them doing anything except driving back and forth along the border."

I had an idea. It had been a while since the sheriff and I had met in person, and such meetings had proven useful in the past. "I believe Harlo Henshaw operates a little pawnshop on the north side of Nogales. Maybe I'll take a drive down there today. And while I'm at it, could I drop by your office afterwards? There are a couple of aspects of the Slawson killing I'd like to go over."

"Good idea. Try to be here by noon. I'll have Mary get us some lunch."

~ ~ ~

Harlo Henshaw's place turned out to be a bigger operation than I had expected. Signage across the front told prospective customers that it was a full-service pawnshop, including guns, but you also could borrow cash against your car title or a forthcoming paycheck. Then you could wire the money home for an additional fee, if you wanted to. The building was unpainted cinderblock, and there were bars across the front door and all the windows. A faded green dumpster sat off to one side, filled to the bursting point. Sparse mesquite grew on the rocky slope behind the store, their thorny branches festooned with windblown trash.

As I walked in, Henshaw was standing behind a glass-topped counter that ran the full length of the back wall. There was just a single room for customers, but a closed windowless door behind the counter opened to something that might have been a storage room. The whole place smelled of stale tobacco smoke. The store was empty except for the two of us, which probably was a good thing.

The man didn't look happy to see me. I took off my regulation gray Stetson, walked over to where Harlo was standing, and said good morning. He took one last puff and stubbed out his cigarette in an ashtray already filled with butts. He avoided eye contact, drummed his fingers on the glass countertop, and kept silent. Apparently the ball was in my court.

"I thought maybe we should talk about last night."

That brought his eyes up. "What about it?"

"I've spoken to the sheriff, and I know you called down there."

"Damned right I did."

"I thought we had things straightened out. I mean, Sally Benton probably was out of line when she spilled the beer on you, but she did apologize."

Harlo shook his head. "You should have arrested her. It was an unprovoked assault, and I have my rights."

This was going to get tricky. "Well, sure you've got rights, and it's my job to protect them. But a little common sense on your part – a little common decency, really – and none of this would have happened in the first place."

The man had the gall to look wounded. "And just what is it we did that was so bad?"

"You mean other than insulting at least half the people in Frenchy's place last night? Gimme a break." Henshaw started to say something, but I held up my hand. "Look, Harlo, we all know there are big problems along the border. Some bad things are happening, especially about drugs. Sheriff Mendoza knows it, I know it, and the Border Patrol knows it. We're all doing what we can. And we appreciate help from the public when it comes in an appropriate form. But groups like yours – this Border Posse or whatever it is – you're making our job harder, not easier, even if what you do might be legal."

"Harder how?"

"Well for starters, by hassling people just for how they look or where they come from."

Harlo Henshaw actually grinned. "We know about that partner of yours, Larry somebody. What is it, like he's Pancho and you're Cisco? Oh, and we also know about your girlfriend."

Where the hell did that come from? I gave him my best tough-guy lawman stare, until he finally broke it off and looked down at his boots. "Well you keep safe, Harlo. And stay inside the law, or we'll be seeing more of each other than you're gonna like."

Then I put on my hat, turned on my heels, and walked out.

~ ~ ~

Nogales was crowded with mid-day traffic as I made my way across town to departmental headquarters. I parked out back in the shade of a big palo verde, locked up the Blazer, and went in through a side door that had a key code for employees.

Mary Gonzales was on duty in her usual receptionist spot, from which she filtered the sheriff's calls and visitors with a long-practiced efficiency. She looked up from her computer screen and smiled as I approached. "Morning, Cal. He's in and you're expected. Lunch should be here shortly. Coffee in the mean time?"

"No, thanks. Already had my quota for the day."

Photos of sheriffs past and present hung on the wall behind Mary's desk. The ones including Luis were group shots posed at various social functions. Everybody was smiling for the camera, and lots of hands were being shaken. One of them caught my eye, and I moved in for a closer look. The sheriff was front and center along with a dark-haired woman I did not recognize. But there was one familiar face in the group standing behind them. It was J.L. Minkston.

Sheriff Luis Mendoza stood up out of a big leather swivel chair as I came through. His narrow craggy face was only a couple of shades paler than the mahogany desktop that separated us. His black hair was turning gray at the temples, and it was a little thinner on top than I had remembered. He fell short of my six feet by an inch or so, but he probably outweighed me by at least thirty pounds.

In my experience the sheriff usually wore a suit to work, but today he was in uniform. However, he had loosened his brown tie, and his regulation dress jacket with a shiny gold star on the breast pocket hung on a rack just inside the door. His desktop was clean and empty, except for a phone, a coffee cup, and three photographs. I recognized his wife, Serena, in one. Another one included four young adults and three children that probably were his children and grandchildren. The third photo was a group of young girls in their confirmation dresses. One of them looked familiar, but it took me a while to realize that it was a much younger Maria.

The back wall of the sheriff's office was mostly glass, affording a view south to the hills of Nogales, Sonora. They shimmered in the noontime sun, partly obscured by a brown haze. He pointed toward one of two straight-backed chairs on my side of the desk.

"Morning, Cal. Have a seat."

"Morning sir. Have I interrupted something?"

He looked momentarily puzzled. "No, why?" Then he got it. "Oh, you mean the uniform? That's for a Rotary event this afternoon. We've got plenty of time."

I took this as an opportunity. "Speaking of such things, I couldn't help but notice a new photo on your outer wall."

"Which one?"

"It's you shaking hands with a woman I don't know, but there's a neighbor of mine in the group standing behind you. His name is J.L. Minkston."

"Is the woman short, with curly black hair?"

"Uh huh."

"That's Rosa Lopez. She's president of the Chamber of Commerce. They were holding a fund-raising luncheon for our widows and orphans group a couple of weeks ago. Gave us a nice check. But this other fellow – Minkston did you say? – I'm not sure I know him. Why do you ask?"

"Just curious. Apparently he's starting up some sort of new development out near Elgin. When I introduced myself the other day he said you two had already met."

Luis nodded. "Oh sure, I remember now. He stood up at the luncheon and made a little speech about that. You know, when everybody went around the room talking about what they were up to? Sounded like he had big plans. He introduced himself after the meeting broke up, but that's all there was to it. In any event, why should this be a matter of concern for the sheriff's department?"

"Probably isn't. It's just that there's something odd about the guy. I can't really put my finger on it. He's been talking to people in the valley about selling their land, or maybe going partners with him, and I know for a fact that some of them are not too happy about it. So I just thought I'd ask."

The sheriff looked skeptical, and I didn't blame him. He's a very smart man, good at reading people, and he must have sensed that I wasn't telling him the whole story. Frenchy Vullmers had more than hinted that Andy Slawson's death might convince Aunt Grace to sell her property next to the Mustangs. But the possible link between Minkston and the Slawson murder was tentative at best, so I decided to drop the subject for now.

There was a knock on the door and Mary Gonzales came in with our lunch. She laid a big round tray on the sheriff's desk and lifted off a linen towel that had been covering two plates of steaming chile rellenos, a pot of cowboy beans, a stack of flour tortillas, and a pitcher of fruit punch. It looked and smelled delicious.

Luis and I ate and made small talk for the next twenty minutes or so. His wife Serena is Maria's godmother, so there was a natural connection between us that extended beyond the strictly professional. Also, he had attended Elgin school as a boy and knew the village well, including Aunt Grace. He asked me two things during our meal. First, how was she holding up? Second, when were Maria and I going to get married?

I ducked the second question. "Under the circumstances, Aunt Grace seems to be doing pretty well. She's a tough lady."

The sheriff chuckled and rolled his eyes. "Boy did I learn that the hard way back in Elgin School. Please give her my best." I was relieved but not surprised he had the courtesy not to push me any further about Maria. Instead he punched a button on his phone and requested that Mary clear away our thoroughly depleted lunch plates. I took that as a sign it was time to get back to business, and I was right.

It wasn't thirty seconds after Mary had left when there was a knock on the door, and in walked Joe Ortega, head of the department's criminal investigations unit. I had met Joe lots of time before, and we had worked together on several cases. Now that I had been promoted to detective, he technically was my boss. He seemed competent enough, but there was something about the man that had always put me off.

Joe was in his mid-forties, about my height, with close-cropped light brown hair and a neatly trimmed beard. He wore tan slacks, a short-sleeved white shirt, and a metallic blue tie. He definitely did not look happy.

I stood up and we shook.

Luis invited us to sit. "Cal, you know I like to let you manage things up in your end of the county as much as possible, especially now that you hold the rank of detective?"

"Right."

"But still I think it would be a good idea if you

brought Joe up to speed on recent developments in your district, so he doesn't have to hear them second hand through the department's gossip mill."

This wasn't like the sheriff, and I recognized a jab when I heard one. "Uh sure, that's fine. Where would you like me to start?"

"Well, let's start with this Border Posse situation. How did it go this morning with their head guy? Name's Henshaw, right?"

"Right. Not all that great. He was pretty hostile. But I really don't think he's gonna make any more trouble about the other night."

Ortega turned in my direction. "The other night?"

I explained about the incident with the beer pitcher at the Santa Rita.

Luis shifted in his chair. "So you're suggesting what?"

"That we just sit tight, at least as far as the incident with Sally Benton is concerned. But I am worried about some of the other things those boys may be up to."

"Such as?"

I decided to share my suspicions about who might have been shooting holes in stock tanks in the county, including the one last night over at Gus Barlow's place.

Ortega look skeptical. "But you've got no proof, right?"

"Right. At this point the only thing I know for sure is that last week they trespassed in Moss Winslow's vineyard, and more or less threatened his field hands. I know it because I was there. But that seems fairly minor. And you say they haven't done anything illegal down along the border?"

The sheriff shook his head. "Not that we know of."

"What about Border Patrol? Have they complained?"

"I haven't heard anything. Joe, what about you?"

"Nope."

The sheriff shrugged. "So I guess we're just stuck. It makes me nervous, because I have a feeling something bad is going to happen, and it seems like we should be doing something to prevent it."

I decided to bring up the snake thing. I told the sheriff and Ortega about the pseudo-Mexican flag being dragged around by the Border Posse, and about the stencil on Gus Barlow's water tank. "And then there's Andy Slawson, who gets killed by an actual snake."

Ortega did the skeptical look again. Apparently it was one of his specialties. "You think there's a connection?"

"I think there might be, yes. Seems like a coincidence otherwise."

"Well it seems like a stretch to me. But in any event, where do we go from here? I mean about the Slawson killing. Do you have any new leads?"

"Not a lead exactly, but there is one angle I'd like to pursue. It might help if we knew exactly where that Mojave rattlesnake came from, and how it compares to others in the area in terms of overall appearance."

"Is that possible?"

"It might be." I proceeded to tell the sheriff and Ortega about Maria's plan to take the dead snake, or what was left of it, up to Hazel Smith at the university.

Luis Mendoza made shuffling noises with his feet, which meant it was time to be wrapping things up. He confirmed that by looking at his watch. "Okay then, you go ahead and see that snake lady."

Joe Ortega clearly wanted more information, and I didn't blame him since we hadn't yet discussed the case in much detail. "You're sure this Andy Slawson was murdered, right? That somebody put that snake in the mailbox deliberately?"

"Don't see how it could have happened any other way."

"But if I'm hearing you correctly, you really have no solid leads as to who might be behind the whole incident?"

"I have some ideas, but no, there's nothing concrete."

The sheriff stood up, walked across the room, and pulled on his uniform jacket. "I gotta go now, but why don't the two of you stay here and chat. Take all the time you need."

Joe Ortega was not ready for the sheriff to leave, because he'd been saving something. I'd already noticed he was carrying a folded-up newspaper when he walked in. Now he laid it out on the sheriff's desk. It was the latest edition of the *Tucson Gazette*, and a big front-page headline read as follows:

TROUBLE IN PARADISE

Snakes, Space Aliens, and Vigilantes in the Sonoita Valley

The byline said Percy Butterfield. Luis Mendoza rarely gets ruffled, but one thing he hates is bad publicity. I knew I'd just stepped in it, and to make matters worse Joe Ortega was there to gloat.

The sheriff scanned the article, apparently until he came to the part where Butterfield began to quote me. Then he looked up and almost literally growled. "What the hell, Cal? When did you talk to this man? And why? You know he's got a reputation."

"Yeah, sorry about that. I thought it would be all right as long as I stuck to the facts already made public. Looks like he did some more digging on his own."

Luis might have accepted that, but Joe Ortega didn't give him a chance. "You know we have a press officer for this sort of thing, and for just this sort of reason. So now let's see what we've got here. We have a murder with no leads, not even a clear idea as to the intended victim, and now all this really terrific publicity. Great. Just great."

Joe tried to stomp out of the room, I suppose for effect, but the sheriff wouldn't let him. "Come on Joe, sit back down. There's nothing to be gained by fighting. What's done is done. Now let's get on with the case. I've gotta go now, but I'm ordering you two to stay here and work together. The best way to get rid of a clown like Butterfield is to solve the damn case."

I was grateful for the support from Luis, but fully aware of the damage I had done to our working relationship.

After Luis left Joe and I turned our chairs so that we were facing each other rather than the unoccupied side of the sheriff's desk. It was awkward as hell, but apparently Joe decided just to get on with things. "So Cal, tell me just how this snake ID project might help solve your case? Seems kinda far-fetched to me."

I explained how the snake might have come from somewhere in the low desert, which could link to Andy Slawson's prior entanglements with gangs and drugs in Tucson. "So learning something about that snake's particular type might help us direct our investigation down there as opposed to up around Sonoita.

"And then there's one other possibility. Whoever used that snake on Andy might be keeping others like it around for future dirty work."

Ortega shifted uneasily in his chair. "But I still don't see why anybody would want to do such a thing, even once, let alone more than once. As I see it, there are two problems with this whole thing. First, there's no guarantee the guy that gets killed is the intended victim. And second, even if the perp could arrange that, most people actually survive snakebites, don't they?"

"I've thought about that. But I can think of one explanation. Suppose somebody just wanted to harass a bunch of folks without necessarily killing any of them? A batch of snakes placed strategically around the county might be just the ticket."

Ortega got it. "The Border Posse, right?

"It's possible. Not that we have any proof."

"And they might be planning more of these things."

"Again, it's possible."

"Sounds like things are getting pretty complicated up your way, or at least they could be. Sure you don't want some help? I have detectives available."

I knew he was anxious to make a turf grab, and now with the Butterfield story the likelihood of that happening had increased significantly. "Please just give me a little more time. Right now I'm not even sure what the help could do. With Larry Hernandez handling routine patrols out of the Sonoita Station, I'm pretty much at liberty to concentrate on the Slawson case." I thought but didn't add: "For all the good it's doing."

Then I had an idea. "But there are a couple of other angles where I could use your help." I proceeded to tell Joe Ortega about J.L. Minkston and Ambrose Pendleton, and asked if he could have somebody look into both of their backgrounds.

Ortega agreed, but understandably he wanted to know what possible connection there might be to the Slawson killing.

I had to admit it was a stretch. "In terms of Pendleton, the only real connection is that he has a rattlesnake collection, and that he might be trafficking in rare species. How that ties to Slawson, at this point I have no idea. But it would be interesting to learn what we can about the man's financial situation. He comes across as a poor little rich kid, but that might not be the case."

"And what about Minkston?"

"The link there is a bit more plausible, but only

just. It seems he has been after local landowners to sell out, or to go into partnership with him on his development deals. Some of his activities seem to be bordering on harassment."

"You mean like harassing them with snakes?"

I had to admit it all sounded a bit crazy, but then so did everything else about this case. Ortega ended our meeting by promising to put his people on tracking down the backgrounds of Minkston and Pendleton, and to make sure all patrol deputies kept an eye out for the Border Posse folks. I decided my meeting with Joe Ortega could have gone a whole lot worse.

Chapter 12

It had been a long day at the office, so to speak. My ego had been wounded down at headquarters, and I was looking forward to a quiet evening at home with Maria. I had settled on the patio, ready to take my first sip of *Bohemia*, when she reminded me that it was the second Tuesday of the month and time for the regular meeting of the Elgin Nature Club.

"Do we have to? What's the program anyway?"

"I know you don't usually go, but I think we should out of respect for Aunt Grace. And besides you might be interested in tonight's talk, in light of all that's been happening."

I had no idea what she was talking about. The Nature Club was more her deal than mine, although I was aware that Aunt Grace was president and basically ran the whole thing. They met one evening a month at the fairgrounds pavilion in Sonoita, sometimes just to chat but usually to hear an invited speaker. Grace also led frequent but less regular field trips around the region, with themes ranging from geology to wildflowers to birds of prey, depending on the season. Maria was on the club's e-mail list, and she kept track of all their scheduled events.

"So who's tonight's speaker?"

"I can't remember his name, but we met him at Andy Slawson's funeral service. Ambrose somebody? He's talking about snakes."

The monthly meeting of the Elgin Nature Club suddenly got more interesting. "Rattlesnakes in particular?"

"I think so. Why?"

So much for a quiet evening at home. "Oh, it's just something Dan McCall said to me the other day about Pendleton. He suspects the man may be involved in the illegal capture and sale of rare species."

"Huh."

I took another sip of my *Bohemia*. "So when does this thing start anyway?"

Maria rose from her chair. "Seven-thirty. We have a couple of burritos left over from last night. I'll go heat 'em up."

~ ~ ~

About fifty people already had assembled at the fairgrounds by the time we showed up. Aunt Grace was there of course, along with Frenchy Vullmers. Apparently his assignment was coffee and refreshments. He was busy laying out cups and plates of chips and cookies on a big table at the back of the room. I was surprised to see Al Treutline in the group, because he didn't strike me as the nature type.

I recognized Ambrose Pendleton, who was up in the front of the room with Aunt Grace. They had already set up a screen and were working to boot up a projector. We obviously were going to be treated to a slide show. Also, three wire cages were sitting on the floor behind the speaker's podium, so apparently part of the presentation was going to be live. I decided not to go up for a closer look, and instead joined Frenchy at the refreshments table. A big urn of freshly brewed coffee smelled so good that it tempted me into a cup, even though I usually avoided caffeine after dinner. I'd been having enough trouble sleeping lately, but decided to take a chance. Who knew, maybe I'd stay awake long enough that Maria and I would have an evening together after all.

Frenchy and I exchanged greetings, and I asked about Aunt Grace.

"I think she's doing well, Cal. And thank you for coming tonight. This little club is dear to her heart, and I know she is gratified to see such a fine turnout."

I couldn't help asking about Pendleton. "Is he a regular club member?"

Frenchy was polite as always, but I sensed this might have been a sore subject. "I believe he is new to the valley. Perhaps it is a bit early to tell."

Sometimes the job of a deputy sheriff was to be less than polite. "To early to tell what?"

"Ah, well, the young man appears to have – how do you say – some rough edges?"

I wanted to push further, but at that point President Slawson called the meeting to order and requested we all take our seats. I caught Maria's eye, and we found a place together on the second row.

Aunt Grace began by thanking everyone for coming, and reminding everybody about the upcoming field trip a week from Saturday. The theme was going to be identification of fall grasses, and there was a sign-up sheet in the back along with a handout that included pen-and-ink drawings of some of the common species. A Forest Service employee who was an expert on the local flora would be leading the trip.

After dispensing with some technical business about membership dues (five dollars per year) and passing around a list for people to put their contact information, Aunt Grace got directly to the night's program. Her introduction was brief and to the point. Mr. Pendleton was relatively new to the valley, having recently graduated from an eastern ivy league school with a degree in conservation biology. He aspired to be an environmental writer, and he already was working on a book about organic gardening. But his real passion was reptiles, and that would be the topic of his talk this evening.

Grace looked up from her notes. "So please help me welcome Mr. Ambrose Pendleton."

The audience applauded politely, as the man rose from his chair in the front row and walked to the front of the room. "Thank you, Ms. Slawson, for the kind invitation, and thank you all for coming. And please call me Brose."

The evening started off smoothly enough. Pendleton began by pointing out that the Sonoita Valley was home to such a wide variety of native reptiles as to be a place deserving the very highest conservation efforts. Nobody in the Elgin Nature Club was going to disagree with that. He then went on to describe, with some examples, the unique role each of those species played in the grasslands, savannahs, and riparian woodlands that made up the natural ecosystems of the region. Again, there wasn't a naysayer in the crowd.

Then it came time for show-and-tell, and that's when things began to get dicey.

First, Pendleton slid the three cages up to a spot between the podium and the front row of folding chairs. These, he explained, held the three most common rattlesnakes in the valley, the black-tailed, Mojave, and western diamondback. As if on cue, they all began to rattle. Then he opened the front of each cage, "so we could all have a better view," as he went on to describe their key attributes.

Looking back on the whole episode, and from what Maria had taught me, he had it spot-on about the differences between the three species in terms of both their appearance and habitat preferences. However, the guests probably weren't learning very much, because Pendleton had barely gotten started by the time each of the three snakes began to emerge from its cage and slither in the general direction of the audience. A Mojave rattlesnake was in the lead, heading right for Al Treutline, who was sitting in the center of the front row. Al quickly rose to his feet and fled to the side of the room. More and more people followed, as a wave of alarm spread through the crowd from front to back.

At first Ambrose Pendleton continued his lecture unperturbed, almost as if he'd expected something like this to happen. He only stopped, someplace between the black-tailed and the western diamondback, when a child screamed and bolted from the hall. By that time Frenchy and Maria and I had come up to the front of the room. I wasn't sure exactly what any of us planned to do, but we never got the chance because Pendleton took charge. "No, no, folks. Don't be alarmed. These animals are peaceful; they have no desire to harm you. They are your friends. And besides, I milked their venom glands just yesterday."

Like that was going to make a big difference.

While the audience continued its retreat, Pendleton set about the business of returning each of the snakes to its respective cage. To me that was the spookiest part of all, because he simply picked up each of the animals with his bare hands – albeit quickly and by its tail. Given all the hissing and buzzing that went on, I doubt that any of the members of Elgin Nature Club were buying into the idea that those three serpents were 'our friends,' at least on this particular night.

Once the snakes were safely back in their cages, a clearly shaken Aunt Grace attempted to restore order. She exhorted all present to return to their seats, and reminded us that the slide show portion of the evening was still to come. Only about half the audience took her advice because the other half had already left. Maria and I decided to stick it out, and in retrospect that probably was a good thing.

Before Aunt Grace turned the podium back to Pendleton, she fixed him with a stare that was familiar to all of us who had been her pupils: try a stunt like that again, and you're gone.

The slides came up, the lights went down, and the presentation resumed. I expected there would be more pictures of reptiles, and perhaps the places where they lived. Boy was I wrong. The first slide was of the whole of the Sonoita Valley, taken from a northeastern vantage point, most likely somewhere up in the Mustangs. Pendleton more or less repeated his comment about the conservation value of the place in terms of its biological diversity. So far, so good. But the next three slides were shots of a vineyard that looked a lot like Moss Winslow's, including one that showed somebody walking down a row of grape plants wearing a backpack-style chemical sprayer.

Pendleton was silent for a few seconds, letting the images sink in before he started up. "Now a lot of you probably think that these new vineyards in the valley are a good thing, adding to the local economy and all. But these places are evil, folks, pure and simple. Think about the groundwater being sucked up for irrigation. And then there's the pesticides! These places are all about pollution!" Pendleton paused for effect. There was a fire burning in the man's eyes that I could see even in the relative darkness of the meeting hall. "So if you care at all about our valley, this simply has to stop!"

I thought Frenchy Vullmers was going to jump out of his chair, but Pendleton held up his hand. "But there's more folks, lots more." And with that he went to the next slide, which showed a fence line separating an operating cattle ranch from an adjacent property not being grazed. I wasn't sure where it had been taken, but evidently he'd found a ranch that was being stocked pretty heavily because the grasses on the grazed side of the fence were unusually sparse and short. "And the evils of grazing are not just about cows, either." He pushed the remote control, and there was a picture of Maria's goats in their corral. I knew some members of the Elgin Nature Club were ranchers and that they were still in the audience, including Sally Benton. But before she or anybody else could object, Pendleton pressed the remote again.

The next image showed J.L. Minkston's little real estate trailer, with all the fluttering flags and pennants, and the sign about Mustang Estates. "And this – well, *this* – may be the greatest sin of all." The next series of slides were of houses and barns and horses and suburban lawns. As far as I could tell, none had been taken in the Sonoita Valley.

Evidently Ambrose Pendleton III had come to his punch line. "And so if we in the Elgin Nature Club, if we really mean it, we've got to take action. *All* of this environmental degradation has simply got to stop, and it has to stop now!" He paused for effect, or maybe it was for an applause that was never going to happen.

"So. Any questions?"

The room remained silent. After it had become clear that there would be no questions, but only a stunned silence, Aunt Grace rose to her feet and moved to the front of the hall. Ever the gracious host, she first thanked our speaker and then thanked everyone for coming. She concluded with a reminder about the upcoming field trip, and mercifully brought the meeting to a close.

Chapter 13

J.L. Minkston

Later that same night the first cold front of the fall came down out of the Rocky Mountains. It got as far as the Mogollon Rim in northern Arizona before it stalled out. Temperatures dipped below freezing in Flagstaff, and it snowed on the San Francisco Peaks, but the same front brought nothing to the Sonoita Valley except a gusty wind.

It was well past midnight, and J.L. Minkston could not sleep. He was not disturbed by the wind, nor even aware of it. The only sound he could hear inside his rambling estate of simulated adobe and insulated glass was that of a pump circulating water in his swimming pool. His wife Joyce had gone off to their condo in Maui, and their two girls were away at college. J.L. liked that fine. He enjoyed the quiet, and the chance it gave him to concentrate on business. This fall there was much business to be done, so as usual he was stewing instead of sleeping. Finally he gave up, slipped on a robe, and padded out into the darkened living room. The tile floor was cool on his bare feet.

J.L. Minkston frowned at his image reflected in a sliding door that led out to the pool. He had been trim and hard during his days as a college athlete, but now his mid-section had grown thick and soft. The doctors in Tucson were after him about cholesterol and booze, but he was too worried about other things to pay much attention. Maybe in two or three months, when everything had worked out, he could concentrate on getting back into shape.

The developer moved closer to the window and gazed

out across the plain from his vantage point in the foothills of the Whetstone Mountains. The lights of Sonoita winked in the distance. He could make out his nearly completed shopping plaza, along with Al Treutline's gas station and a few of the homes scattered over the hills south and east of town.

J.L. Minkston had a dream. In his mind's eye there was something much larger out there, and it was something grand. In his dream the village of Elgin had become the real town in the valley. It had a hotel and a golf course, a civic center with a museum, and a theater. People would come from all over to enjoy the country and the climate. They would buy his houses, eat in his restaurant, stay in his hotel, and join his country club. They'd even ride horses at his dude ranch. "Warm in winter, green in summer," read the brochures put out by Minkston Enterprises. The brochures didn't mention how hot and dry it was in June, nor did they say anything about the wind or the rattlesnakes.

In the beginning Moss Winslow couldn't wait to get involved in J.L.'s dream, and Minkston welcomed him on board because he needed the man's ranch and water. But he couldn't raise the money Moss wanted for the place, so a partnership was the only way.

Moss Winslow had turned out to be a dreamer like J.L., but he had no business sense at all. If only he had been content to run his livestock on what was left of the ranch, and let J.L. take care of the rest. Minkston especially regretted that Moss had planted that ridiculous vineyard. It had cost both of them a bundle, and so far they hadn't produced anything worth putting into a bottle. In short, Moss Winslow was an idiot.

Most of the people in Sonoita knew little or nothing about Minkston Enterprises, and he hoped it stayed that way. If any of them found out about Barstow or

Grand Junction, it could mean real trouble. For one thing, they had no idea just how close he was to the edge. They might be fooled by his big house and fancy car, but right now all his property was mortgaged at least once. The banks were being patient because they had bought into his dream, and they stood to gain or lose almost as much as J.L. himself. The whole scheme depended on selling those parcels at Mustang Estates within the year, and finding some new investors who had land. But so far the lots weren't moving nearly fast enough, and now the county was getting itchy about well permits. If that got out, the whole thing could fall apart.

J.L. Minkston knew exactly what it would take to make his dream a reality. He could take care of Moss Winslow, no problem. In fact, he had already started. Sally Benton was refusing to budge, so that was a dead end. The keys to success lay elsewhere. J.L. Minkston knew his dream had only one real limit. That limit was water, and he knew just the people who had it. If only he could persuade them to sell out or go partners.

Chapter 14

It had been a windy night. This may have had something to do with my lack of sleep, but it wasn't the biggest part. Mostly I'd been stewing about the Slawson case. The sheriff had made no bones about it. He was less than pleased with my progress. Not that I blamed him exactly, but I suspected another player was bending his ear and that was Joe Ortega, head of the department's criminal investigations unit. If and when the sheriff pulled me off the case it would go directly to Joe, with me in a supporting role at best.

By the time I dragged myself out of bed and had a quick shower, Maria already had the coffee going and had finished milking the goats. Our appointment with Dr. Hazel Smith was set for anytime between nine and noon, but evidently Maria was anxious to get on with the day. The remains of one particular Mojave rattlesnake would be the focus of our meeting, and she already had it loaded into a cooler that was standing just inside the front door, ready to go.

Maria had thrown a couple pieces of bread in the toaster. Evidently breakfast was going to be an abbreviated affair. She turned from the counter as I entered the room. "You look disheveled."

I poured myself a cup of coffee. "Yeah, I feel disheveled. But this caffeine should help. It was a short night."

She gave me a look. "But an interesting one, no?"

She had me there. We had not yet had a chance to talk about Ambrose Pendleton ('call me Brose'), or about his disjointed presentation to the Elgin Nature Club, because the night quickly had moved in another direction. In fact, things got started as soon as we left the fairgrounds, and it reminded me that riding with girlfriends had gotten less interesting since the arrival of bucket seats. She grumbled about a stiff neck afterwards, but I guess Maria liked snakes even more than I imagined. No other explanation came to mind. It might be worth keeping one around the house if they were that much of a turn-on. Almost.

Maria finished the last of her third cup of coffee, and pushed back from the table. "I think that guy's nuts."

"You mean Ambrose Pendleton?"

"Who else? I felt sorry for Aunt Grace. Here she was expecting a nice informed talk about reptiles, and instead everybody got lectured about how we're all environmental sinners of one sort or another."

"I wonder what that man does for a living."

"Maybe nothing at all. Didn't Aunt Grace say he was an aspiring writer? Isn't that usually another word for unemployed? Maybe he's some kind of a trust child."

I chewed and swallowed one last bite of toast. "Well for sure the man's got no tact. It was bad enough when he let those snakes loose, but then he managed to insult nearly everybody in the room. I mean your goats stay in their little corral and barn, so you're not really a rancher. And you sure aren't a farmer. But we both live in a house, so I guess by his definition that makes us part of the exurban horde supposedly over-running the valley."

Maria nodded, thoughtful now. "He's right, of course. Anybody living here does so at the expense of other plants and creatures that could be using the same space. We need to be mindful about that, and do our best to minimize our impacts. Don't you agree?"

Who could disagree with that?

Maria rose from the table. "Well, we'd better hit the road. I want to get there in plenty of time, just so Dr. Smith understands we're serious about this snake business. Maybe we'll learn something useful today."

I had my doubts, but it didn't seem like the right time to share them. "Hope so."

We loaded our herpetological cargo into the Blazer, and headed out. It was cool, clear, and too early for wind. The sun had just broken over the Huachucas, and the angled light illuminated the grasses in bright golds and reds. I was reminded again why fall was my favorite time of the year.

We drove west to Sonoita, then followed 83 north to the interstate. It was a drive I had taken many times, but the landscape transitions along the way never grew dull. First, open grasslands gave way to mesquite and then to oak savannahs as we crested the low hills at the north rim of the valley. The oaks were evergreen, with dense compact leaves and spreading crowns. These scattered trees would add a rich green texture to the grasslands all through the coming winter.

Maria crossed herself as we passed mile marker forty-four, just north of the pass. It was the place where her husband Tony Obregon had died in a motorcycle accident twelve years ago. He'd been one of my best friends and I missed him too, but it must have been worse for Maria. I could see the pain in her eyes.

Once over the pass, the highway began its twisting descent down into the cacti and scrub of the true Sonoran Desert. We followed 83 north until it merged with I-10, and then headed west. Traffic already was getting heavy by the time we reached the suburban fringes of Tucson.

Hazel Smith was a full-fledged member of the University of Arizona faculty, but her office and laboratory were part of a campus outpost called

Tumamoc Hill. Maria had been there before, and she knew exactly where to get us off the interstate and then drive efficiently through the tangled streets of southern Tucson. Soon we had left the city behind and were following a steep winding road up the side of the hill itself. The drive afforded us a clear view north across metropolitan downtown. The Santa Catalina Mountains rose in the background, only partially obscured by a brown cloud that likely would build over the city as the day went on.

The Tumamoc Hill research facility included a cluster of buildings embedded in classic Sonoran Desert vegetation, including numerous tall saguaro cacti. We parked in a visitors' spot and walked the short distance over to a stone building that housed Dr. Smith's office and laboratory. Maria explained it was the oldest structure on the Hill. Our drive from Sonoita had taken less than two hours, but already the mid-morning heat was noticeable. I carried the snake.

The wooden door to the Smith laboratory was the tall old-fashioned kind, with lots of glass and a brass knob. We walked in and were greeted by a smiling woman named Rosie, evidently the receptionist. "Hi, Maria. My, it's good to see you. And you must be Deputy Creede?" We also were greeted with an all-too-familiar buzz coming from one of several glass terraria sitting on a bench along one wall. Rosie caught my look. "And please excuse Jake. He's the house diamondback, and for some reason he's edgy today."

I held up the cooler. "Maybe Jake doesn't like the smell of a dead cousin. But it sure looks like we've come to the right place."

Rosie laughed and pointed Maria to a door leading off the west end of the laboratory. "Hazel's expecting you."

Maria led the way back to an office that appeared

to be a combination storeroom, recycling center, and art gallery. There were four chairs in the room. A distinguished looking middle-aged woman sat in one, with her back to a window that opened out onto a well-tended desert garden. Two of the remaining chairs were empty, but the third was piled high with file folders. The herpetologist rose from behind her cluttered oak desk to hug Maria, and then she reached over her shoulder to shake my hand. She wore high-top leather boots with her jeans tucked inside. Her bright Navajo over-blouse was a little bleached out by the sun, as was her grey-streaked ash blond hair.

"Maria, it certainly is good to see you. And this must be Deputy Creede? Welcome, Deputy."

"Pleased to meet you, Dr. Smith. Maria has said lots of good things about you." I handed over the freezer chest, which she eagerly accepted and placed on her desk.

"So this is the snake that did the dirty deed? Oh, and please call me Hazel. We keep things informal on the Hill. It's one of several reasons I like it better up here than down ... *there.*" She looked over her shoulder, back toward downtown Tucson, in the center of which lay the main campus of the University of Arizona.

Maria nodded in agreement. "I can see why you like it up here. Though sometimes it was a little frustrating because you weren't on campus much except during formal class time."

Hazel Smith's blue eyes almost twinkled. "But as I recall, it didn't slow you down. Over the years, I found that the serious students always managed to find their way up here. And anyway, they really didn't give me a choice."

I could sense confusion on Maria's part, so I asked the question for her. "Choice?"

"Oh, this wasn't my idea, Deputy. The department

head made the decision for me. He claimed it was on account of my snakes. He said they were a danger to others." The herpetologist laughed and shook her head. "But I don't think that was the real reason. The fact is I can be a pain in the rear, especially at faculty meetings. He really wanted to get rid of me, but I already had tenure, so this was the best he could do. And I must say it worked. I hardly ever go down there."

I was anxious to get to the business at hand, and evidently so was she. With the facial expression of a kid at Christmas, she removed the lid from the freezer chest and lifted out the snake that had killed Andy Slawson. She pulled a pair of reading glasses down off her forehead and gave the carcass a close inspection, seemingly oblivious to the smells of putrefaction I could detect even from across the room. "Oh ho, what have we here! It is, of course, a Mojave, but you already knew that. You're here for more details, right? Come into the lab and I'll show you my morgue."

We entered a small side room next to Hazel's office. The walls were lined with shelves filled with gallon jars holding the bodies of preserved snakes. In the middle of the room under a hanging light fixture was a desk with a complicated microscope and camera set-up. In contrast to her office, Hazel's morgue was well ordered and extremely tidy.

She laid our snake on the table, and turned to me. "Maria told me something about your case. I understand this snake killed a boy, but I'm not exactly sure why you believe a crime was committed, or how you think I might be able to help."

I explained the circumstances of Andy Slawson's death, and why I was certain that someone had placed the snake in Moss Winslow's mailbox deliberately. "I'm not sure you can help, really. But Maria thought if we could figure out where that snake came from, then maybe that would give us some idea about who was responsible."

Dr. Smith nodded. "Well, it is a fact that local populations of rattlesnakes often have distinctive markings. And as you can see we have a pretty good reference collection here. So I can make some comparisons and maybe come up with something." She picked up the snake and gave it another close look, especially around what was left of its head. "And I must say, there is something familiar about this gal."

She put down the snake, turned back to me, and raised a skeptical eyebrow. "So that's not what's bothering me. My question is, even if we can trace your specimen to a particular spot, how might that lead you to your killer?"

"Maybe it won't. But I can think of at least one possibility. I understand that Mojave rattlesnakes live down here in the desert as well as in the grasslands around Sonoita. We know that the victim lived in Tucson until recently, and that he'd gotten tangled up with drugs and gangs. So maybe somebody from down here had a motive, caught one in his back yard, and brought it down with him. It could help guide our investigation if you can tell me whether our murder weapon came from the desert or the grassland."

Hazel Smith nodded. "We almost certainly can do that. In fact, I'm prepared to say right now that this is not a desert specimen. And with a little more work we may be able to track her down to a particular canyon or drainage, although I'm still not sure how that is going to help you all that much."

I was more than prepared to share in Dr. Smith's pessimism. Then another thought occurred to me, and it was one that ultimately proved fateful. "Let me ask you this. If we found someone keeping another snake, or maybe even a group of snakes, could you tell me if this one came from the same population?"

"Most likely. And as Maria knows, rattlesnakes tend to gather together in winter in protected places called hibernacula, where they help keep each other warm. So if somebody knew what they were doing, at the right time of year it would be possible to collect a whole bunch of them relatively easily."

Maria clearly got where this was headed. "So if we found somebody with snakes just like this one in their possession, we'd have our killer, right? "

I nodded. "Well, that would be the good news."

"And the bad news?"

"Maybe our killer hasn't finished the job?"

This possibility seemed to galvanize Hazel Smith into action. "So I'd like to keep her for a while, if that's okay with you."

Maria spoke for the both of us. "Sure, that's why we came. Pickle him and keep him as long as you need."

"It's not a him, it's a her."

I wondered how she knew that already. "Dr. Smith, I'll need you to sign a chain of custody form if you are going to keep the snake. Then at some point please provide us with notes on the procedures you will be using to make the identification. If this case goes to trial, the prosecutors will admit the snake into evidence and have you testify as an expert witness."

"Of course. But there's one more thing. I have a pretty good reference collection here in the lab, mostly pickled and some frozen, but it may take some field work to pin things down more precisely." She turned to Maria. "Is there any chance we could go out together? Say in the next week or so? You know the area better than I do."

Maria quickly volunteered me as well. "Sure, we'd love to. Maybe Sunday, when I don't have to work?"

I was pleased to be included, but mindful of the

sheriff's desire to get on with things. "Any chance we could make it sooner? Maria, what about taking one of your vacation days?"

We settled on Friday.

Hazel Smith placed the snake back in the cooler. "A student of mine, Willie Sanchez, is studying the systematics of crotalines using DNA profiling. His project is still in its early stages, but he's already found some good genetic sequences that might help us nail down the location of your specimen even further. Anyway, I'll see you on Friday. What should I bring?"

I took an educated guess that 'crotaline' meant rattlesnake in herp-speak, and made a mental note to ask Maria about it later. "Just whatever you normally carry in the field, I guess. We'll take the department Blazer. What time would you like to get started?"

"Well, rattlesnakes like to sleep in, especially by this time of year when the morning temperatures are below their comfort level. Of course by now most of them should be denned up for the winter, so we'll be looking for places where they can find shelter. As I recall there are lots of caves in the Mustang Mountains. That's near you, right? So that probably would be a good place to start. Are we going to have any trouble getting up there?"

"The talus slopes below those limestone cliffs are too rough for a vehicle, so we'll only be able to drive part of the way. We could take horses, I suppose, but it's such rough terrain I would prefer just to walk, if that's okay with you."

Hazel Smith's blue eyes flashed. "Don't let the gray hair fool you, Deputy. I've been hiking the Arizona backcountry for more years than you've been on this planet. So let's just see if you can keep up."

Maria stifled a laugh and shot me a look. Clearly I had stepped in it. Snappy comebacks seemed like a really bad idea, and none came to mind in any event. "Okay then, we'll see you on Friday. Just come to the sheriff's office in Sonoita. You can't miss it. We're right at the junction of state Highways 82 and 83. Say about nine o'clock? Will the snakes be up by then?"

All right, so I guess that was sort of a snappy comeback. But I must have gotten away with it, because the herpetologist grinned and her eyes morphed from glare to twinkle. "See you then, Deputy. I'm looking forward to it."

Chapter 15

"**Y**ou know Mom and Dad are going to ask about our supposedly impending marriage, right?"

Maria and I were on our way down I-19 toward Green Valley, a retirement community south of Tucson where my parents had lived for the past four years. I knew the subject of our relationship would come up, because it always did with them. "So all I'm saying is, this time let's have our story ready."

I knew it was a touchy subject. The flash flood of the past summer had put things on hold, supposedly because Maria and I were too busy refurbishing the damaged Obregon homestead. Maybe so, maybe not. After all, how much time did it really take to get married?

Maria had been staring silently out the window, apparently contemplating the desert lands that were part of the Tohono O'odham Nation between Tucson and Green Valley. Finally, she turned toward me. "I thought we agreed to wait until we got the house and the dairy fixed up."

"Yeah, I know we did, it's just that..."

"So that's the story, okay? And I'll handle it with your parents. You just follow my lead. Or better yet, don't say anything at all."

We rode in silence the rest of the way.

Harold and Doris Creede lived in a modest patio home with tan stucco walls and a red tile roof, built tastefully into a natural desert landscape in Green Valley. It was one of the things I liked best about this community, especially compared to some in the Southwest where the development plan was to obliterate most of the native vegetation and replace it with lawns and swimming pools.

We were seated outside in the shade of a huge mesquite, watching Gambel's quail and mourning doves at a bird feeder that Dad filled religiously every day. Maria had presented Mom with a gift of her goat cheese, which was graciously accepted. It was mid-afternoon, and we were enjoying iced tea and snacks. I had declined Dad's invitation to join him in a beer, because I was in uniform, on duty, and driving a county vehicle.

Maria was true to her word, and she didn't even wait for a prompt. "Before you ask, we haven't yet set a date yet for our wedding, and of course we'll not do so without first consulting both of you and also my parents."

I had to give Mom credit, because her question wasn't about when but where. Maria explained that we hoped to have the ceremony at our house, but it would be performed by Father Peter from the church in Nogales. All of this was news to me, but I had my orders.

Dad, bless his heart, changed the subject. "Well, what's new in Sonoita? I'm glad we leased out the Pitchfork and moved up here, but we still miss the place, don't we Doris? And seeing you two is about the only time we get to catch up."

I decided to fill them in about Andy Slawson, but only with those details that I knew were public knowledge.

Dad clearly was puzzled. "So you have no idea who might have put that snake in Moss Winslow's mailbox?" He shook his head in puzzlement. "Whoever did that, well, it just doesn't make sense. I mean how could they have known who it would end up biting? Hell, it could just as easily have been Moss as that

Slawson boy."

It was my mother who first realized an even more ominous possibility. "Oh dear God, Cal, it could even have been intended for Maria!"

"I know, Mom, and don't think it hasn't crossed my mind."

Maria was having none of it. "I just can't imagine why anybody would do that. But don't worry, I'm being really careful these days when I open any of the boxes on my route."

Dad had a question about Winslow. "So how is Mossy taking all this? You know we went to school together, and I've known him pretty much all my life."

"I guess he's doing okay, but he has been acting sort of strange lately."

"Strange how?"

I told him about his obsession with flying saucers and such.

Dad nodded. "Yeah, but there's nothing new about that. I remember he was interested in rockets and space and things like that clear back when we were kids. He was a hard worker, helping out with the family ranch, especially in the summer. But he always was sort of a loner. He never married as far as I know, and I think he's become something of a recluse."

I was anxious to learn more. "Well, maybe, but it seems like he's still pretty busy with the ranch. He's also gotten into the grape business, and he's involved in some way with a new developer in the valley, although apparently there's some trouble about that."

"What developer?"

"His name's Minkston."

Dad had been about to take a swallow of beer. Instead, he laid down his glass so abruptly it rattled the glass-topped patio table that separated us. "*J.L. Minkston?*"

"Yeah, why?"

"Because he's been around before, that's why. I'm surprised you don't remember."

My mother shook her head. "No Harold, he couldn't have. It happened when Cal was overseas, and I don't think we've ever mentioned it since he came back. Especially because nothing ever came of it."

"Came of what, Mom?"

"Well, he wanted to start a big new development in the valley. He had all these grand plans about houses and condos and a golf course, and I don't know what all."

"But you say nothing ever came of it? Why not?"

"Because he wanted to buy the Pitchfork Ranch, and we weren't interested."

My father interrupted. "Not exactly buy the ranch, Doris. He didn't have the money for that. No, he wanted us to go into some sort of partnership. We would put up the land, he would build the actual development, and we'd share in the profits. And boy how he talked up those profits. We were going to get rich."

This was beginning to sound familiar. "Obviously you didn't go along. Why not?"

Dad looked disappointed. I didn't really blame him, but it was something that had to be asked. He sure had a ready answer, and in it he displayed a level of sarcasm I had rarely if ever seen before. "Well, let's see now. You mean besides the fact that we love that place, and the fact that we would never sell it, even part of it, without your consent? Okay, then how about the fact that J.L. Minkston is a sleazy money-grubbing con-artist."

I must admit I had pretty much come to the same conclusion based on my limited interactions with Minkston over the past week. But I knew my father to be a temperate man, and not usually one to be overly critical. "It sounds like you may know something that I should know."

"You bet I do. To be honest, when he first approached us we thought about it – not to give up the whole ranch, of course, but maybe a part of it. It could have given us, and you by the way, a level of financial security we might never realize any other way. But before we made any sort of commitment, I had a lawyer friend of mine up in Tucson do a little digging. It was Tom Cole, and what he found was alarming to say the least."

"Alarming in what way?"

"Turns out the Sonoita deal was far from Minkston's first rodeo. And to stick with that particular analogy, it turns out he's come up short of the full eight seconds way more often than he's actually finished the ride."

"Leaving partners and creditors like you holding the bag?"

"You got it. Oh I guess some of his developments have worked out, but others haven't. Overall, his track record was bad enough that Tom advised us to lay off. Fortunately, we hadn't signed anything, and so that's just what we did."

"And what about Minkston? I mean, did he try to get anybody else in the valley involved?"

"Not that I know of. I think he just went away." My father shook his head. "And now you say he's back? Huh."

"Do you happen to remember where any of Minkston's failed developments happened?"

"Let's see. This was a while back, and none of it is first hand because all of it came through Tom. But I'm thinking some of them were in southern California, and at least one was someplace in western Colorado. Maybe

Grand Junction? I can't remember for sure."

Maria, who had just been sitting there the whole time, suddenly interjected herself into the conversation. "You know that Minkston guy came sniffing around the Obregon homestead, don't you?"

I had not heard that from her, although Minkston himself had suggested as much the other day. "When was that?"

"Oh, maybe a month ago. I think it was on a Sunday. You were off somewhere, doing deputy sheriff business I suppose."

"What did he say?"

"It was pretty much the same story he gave your parents, I guess. We could be partners in the development, with me providing the land and water. I'd make way more money than I ever could with what he called my 'little goat operation.' Mostly he was interested in my water, because he kept going on about that particular angle. I think he must have figured out how hard it can be to find ground water around Elgin."

My mother asked the question that was on my lips. "So what did you tell him, dear?"

"I told him to drop dead, of course. Well, not in so many words, but I expect he got the message."

Knowing Maria, I was sure he had.

It already was late in the afternoon. I knew Maria was anxious to get back to her goats, and so I had just one more question for my father. "Do you happen to know if any of Minkston's failed developments resulted in civil or criminal charges?"

"Couldn't say. But you could probably find out. After all, you're a deputy sheriff, and one recently promoted to detective if I remember correctly." Then he winked at my mother.

Chapter 16

Larry Hernandez and I were in the office the next morning, catching up on some routine paperwork, when the telephone rang. I recognized Sally Benton's name on the caller ID.

"Sheriff's Department, Deputy Creede speaking."

"Morning, Cal. This is Sally Benton."

We hadn't spoken since the incident with the beer pitcher at the Santa Rita Saloon. "Morning, Sally. Listen, if you're calling about the other night..."

"No, it's not that, though I do apologize again for letting my emotions get the better of me. That guy Henshaw and his buddies are a real piece of work. I probably would have just let it slide if it weren't for the bartender and those nice people from Nogales having to hear the man shoot his mouth off like that."

"I understand, and so does the sheriff. We can't officially condone what you did, but neither are we going to do anything about it."

"Well, that's a relief. Thank you."

I trusted Sally Benton, so I took a chance. "Off the record Sally, I like your style. You've got guts. But you said there's something else?"

"There is. Felix Martinez, my foreman, was riding fence yesterday down in Lyle Canyon, and he came across something you need to see."

"What's that?"

"Well, I'm no expert, but it looks like somebody is growing marijuana on my place. And not a small amount, either."

This certainly wasn't the first time the department had learned about such activities in the Sonoita Valley.

Most of it had involved small-scale stuff, often just a handful of plants supposedly grown for personal medical uses. But if somebody was raising marijuana on Sally Benton's property without her knowledge or permission, that would take things to a higher level.

"You say this is down in Lyle Canyon?"

"That's right. There's a spring that comes bubbling up out of a rocky ledge on the west side of the wash, about a mile upstream from my north property line. Somebody has diverted the water so that it spreads across the rows of plants."

"You say 'rows' plural? About how many plants did you see?"

"Well, I didn't count 'em, but there must have been at least fifty."

"If I came out there, could you show me?"

"You bet."

Sally Benton's place, the V-9 Ranch, included about 15,000 acres on the west slope of the Huachuca Mountains. It was mostly mesquite-grassland, except for the Lyle Canyon streambed that included riparian trees along with tall sacaton grass growing in the floodplain.

I told Larry what was up, and left him in charge of the office. The drive over to Sally's house took about thirty minutes. She lived in an elegant one-story white adobe with a red tile roof, immediately adjacent to the Lyle Canyon floodplain. A three-foot wall surrounded her house, with landscaping that consisted of various cacti and other succulents, along with a half-dozen well-tended mesquite trees. The wall arched up over a gate made of intricately carved mesquite planks. That is where I pulled the Blazer to a stop.

Sally must have been watching, because she didn't even give me a chance to get out of the vehicle. She came out her front door and pointed to a three-car garage east of the house. "Shall we take my Land Rover? There's a pretty good road that follows the canyon down as far as the spring."

I shook my head and waved her over. "No, might as well take my Blazer. This definitely counts as official business."

For about two miles we followed a well marked two-track that skirted the edge of the sacaton grass. Occasionally we drove under a canopy consisting mostly of tall spreading sycamores, along with a few velvet ash and cottonwood trees. Then Sally pointed to a small drainage that fed into the main canyon from the west.

"The spring is up there at the head of that ravine."

I could see tire tracks leading in that direction. "It probably would be best if we walked from here, if that's all right with you."

"Of course, but it's not a hard drive. Felix and I didn't have any trouble yesterday."

"So you drove in?"

"Sure, why not?" Then Sally got it. "Oh shit. Sorry. You're thinking we might have destroyed evidence?"

That's exactly what I was thinking, but there was no point in chastising Sally after the fact. "No problem. I'll just need to get casts of the tire treads on whatever vehicle you drove, so we can distinguish them from any others we find at the site."

It took us about ten minutes to walk up the drainage. The scene was much as Sally had described it. A small but steady flow of water emerged from the rocks at the head of the ravine, and somebody had dug a trench directing the water to the head of a relatively level field with fine soil about fifty yards below the spring. It was here that someone had planted the crop. The plants were in five rows, each being watered by a different fork that had been dug off the main ditch.

There were two signs that the field was being carefully tended. First, the whole thing was free of any plants besides the marijuana, and there was no way that could happen without regular weeding. Second, I could see that the total flow from the spring was insufficient to irrigate all five rows at the same time. Somebody had to be moving the water around pretty regularly to sustain all those plants.

I asked Sally to wait in the shade of a nearby cottonwood while I inspected the area for evidence. It turned out there was good news and bad news in terms of catching whoever was running his or her own pot operation on the V-9 Ranch. The good news was that the person or persons were coming here often to weed and to water, so we had a chance of catching them in the act. The not so good news was that they were being very careful about it. I could see tire impressions adjacent to the field, but they were in knee-high grass and so there would be no chance for tread casts. Also, there were no footprints evident either in the field itself or in the surrounding area. The growers obviously swept up after every visit.

I joined Sally under the cottonwood.

"What do you want to do, Cal? Shall I have Felix just tear the whole thing up?"

"Absolutely not. This is a serious operation here, and we need to catch whoever is behind it."

"How are you going to do that?"

"For starters, have you seen any strange vehicles coming or going on your place?"

"I asked Felix about that, but neither of us remembers any, at least not recently. Of course the V-9 is a big spread, and there's more than one way to get to this spring."

"Well, keep an eye out, and give me or Larry Hernandez a call if you do see anything. In the meantime I think we'll go with a plan that relies less on luck."

"What's that?"

"With your permission, I'd like to install a couple of motion-activated cameras in the trees around here. They'll provide a good overview of the whole place, but we can hide them in the branches so the growers hopefully won't see them."

Sally Benton liked the idea, as did the sheriff when I called him. He also told me they had several of those cameras available at headquarters down in Nogales, and that Larry Hernandez knew all about them.

And that was how we came to launch Operation Potwatch. The name wasn't my idea. Larry got credit for that.

~ ~ ~

The snakes had departed their mountain cave at the end of March, when spring had come to southeastern Arizona. Following an ancient ritual they radiated like spokes of a giant wheel out into the grasslands below, each on an individual quest for mice or rats to replenish fat reserves that had been depleted over the winter. Only when this was accomplished would they begin the return journey, using the positions of the sun and the stars to find the way home. Getting back into the cave was essential in order to survive the coming winter, but so were a full belly and a good layer of body fat.

One of the older snakes had searched in vain for most of the summer without finding food. It wasn't until September that she finally came upon a population of silky pocket mice. They were small, and she ate several over a ten-day period. It was scarcely sufficient, but the time had come to get back before the first killing frost. She was the last of her group to begin the homeward migration, and the last to complete the journey.

The snake made her way slowly but deliberately up through the rocky debris on the familiar slope until she came to the cave. It was the middle of October, and something was terribly wrong. There were freshly broken rocks scattered around the entrance, and strange odors inside the cave she did not recognize. Worst of all, there were no others, and they all should have returned by now. Survival would be uncertain without the added warmth of their bodies. She searched into the farthest reaches of the cave, but found none of her companions. Finally she found a corner that was littered with old skins, where at least the smells were familiar. She coiled there, and waited to die.

Chapter 17

Maria and I were having a breakfast Friday morning that was both leisurely and plentiful. Dr. Hazel Smith wasn't due to meet us in town until nine o'clock because, as she put it, the snakes would be sleeping in. That explained the leisurely part. The plentiful part had to do with the significant amount of hiking we would be doing that day, in pursuit of rattlesnake dens in the Mustang Mountains.

Maria had made enough chorizo and eggs for three because we had company. She had invited Aunt Grace to join us for breakfast and then to go along on the field trip. She had accepted with enthusiasm. Neither of us was certain Grace would be up to all the climbing we'd be doing, but nothing said she had to go everywhere we did. It would be a good chance for her to get out in the field again, and perhaps she would feel involved in the search for her nephew's killer.

The goats had been fed and watered, and we were enjoying a second cup of coffee with plenty of time left before we needed to leave for Sonoita. One part of me was anxious to get Aunt Grace's take on Ambrose Pendleton, especially in light of his strange performance at the Nature Club meeting earlier in the week. Still, I was reluctant to bring it up because I suspected she was embarrassed about the whole episode. Fortunately, she solved the problem for me.

Grace took one last swallow of coffee and pushed back from our kitchen table. "Thanks, Maria, for a good meal. I suppose we'll need to be heading to town soon, but before we go I wanted to apologize for the other night."

I decided it was politic to play dumb. "The other night?"

"You know, at the Nature Club meeting. I had no idea that Ambrose Pendleton was going to let those animals loose in front of everybody, and then carry on that way about our collective environmental sinfulness. I wouldn't have invited him in the first place if I'd known what he had in mind. He told me it was just going to be a slide show about reptiles."

"Have you ever seen his collection, Aunt Grace? Have you been to his home?"

"No, never. Why do you ask?"

"Oh, I just wondered what all he had in his possession. It has to be more than just those three snakes he brought the other night."

Maria apparently decided to change the subject. "We all appreciate what you do for the Nature Club, Aunt Grace. The programs and field trips you put together are terrific."

She nodded and blushed. "Thank you my dear, that's very kind of you. But the club is something I really enjoy. You know I majored in biology at the university at the same time I was getting my teaching credential. Actually, my particular emphasis was in botany, and I have maintained a life-long interest in plants. I'm still active in that area. It helps to stay busy, especially now that Andy's gone."

I wanted to know more, because of what Frenchy Vullmers had said the other night about his potential partnership with Aunt Grace in the grape business. "Active in what way?"

"Two ways actually. First, you may have heard that we – that's Mr. Vieumilliers and I – we are making plans to start up a little vineyard on my property."

"I had heard that, yes. But there's more?"

"Oh yes indeed. I've been active for quite some time

in the field of forensic botany. That's the use of plant evidence in criminal cases."

I had heard of the field, and in fact I had used it to help solve a recent case of livestock rustling. But I had no idea Aunt Grace was involved in such things. "What sort of work do you do, and for whom?"

"Well, lots of things. But for example, sometimes I help identify plant remains in the stomachs of murder victims. Pima County had a recent case where the medical examiner, a lady named Dr. Gail Tanner, wanted to know the contents of a victim's last meal."

Maria was looking a little pale. "So that's what you do? Dig around in people's stomach contents?"

Grace Slawson laughed. "It's not as bad as it sounds, Maria. They usually prepare slides for me, or send me preserved samples. Then I look at them under the microscope and identify the cell types. Did you know that each of our plant foods has a unique cell structure?"

I wanted to know more. "Does the work ever take you into the field?"

"Oh, indeed. Last year, for example, I helped trace the movements of a pickup truck driven by drug smugglers. There were some unusual seeds stuck in the tire treads and I was able to trace them to plants growing in a wetland where the Border Patrol had found a body. I did that work for a Patrol agent and for Sergeant Ortega, who works for Luis down in Nogales. I expect you know him."

I made a mental note to keep Aunt Grace in mind for any future work involving plants. I also wanted to ask her about any dealings she'd had with J.L. Minkston. Was J.L. after her land, as Frenchy Vullmers had suggested the other night at the Santa Rita Saloon?

"What can you tell me about a man named J.L. Minkston?"

Her face darkened, and she hesitated before replying. "That man? We - that is, Patrice and I - we have found him to be most unpleasant."

I was interested to learn that she was on a first-name basis with the owner of the Santa Rita Saloon, but even more interested in her reaction to my question about Minkston. "If you don't mind my asking, unpleasant in what way?" I had my suspicions, of course.

"Well, as you probably know, he is trying to do some big real estate development right here in Elgin. Some of it has already started, but I guess he needs more land and water to make the whole thing happen."

"Has he made you some kind of offer?"

Grace shook her head emphatically. "No, he has not. I didn't give him a chance. Of course that was before Andy."

Her voice trailed off, and I remembered what Frenchy had said about how she envisioned the vineyard project as something for her nephew.

I glanced up at the clock on the wall above Maria's refrigerator. "Well, it's time for us to be getting in to Sonoita, Aunt Grace. But you let me know if Mr. Minkston bothers you any more about this, okay?"

~ ~ ~

It was a real crowd in our little one-room office. I asked Larry Hernandez to sit in on the briefing Hazel Smith was giving us about the upcoming snake hunt. So that made five of us, including Maria, Aunt Grace, and me. Larry wasn't going along, but I wanted him up to speed on the investigation. He was grumped about it, of course, but his assignment that day, in addition to keeping an eye on things around town, was to drive to Nogales and pick up the cameras we were going to install next to Sally Benton's marijuana field.

Dr. Smith was standing behind my desk, with a map of the valley rolled out before her. "Mojave rattlesnakes could be anywhere around here of course. But by this time of year they all should be in hibernacula, or at least well on the way back from their summer feeding grounds."

Larry frowned. "Hiber ... what?"

The herpetologist smiled. "Sorry. That's jargon for the dens these animals seek out to spend the winter. It turns out they are very loyal to those places because the mass of their bodies tangled together is critical to surviving in the cold."

Aunt Grace nodded. "So if we find one snake today, we're likely to find a whole lot of them?"

"Exactly," said Dr. Smith, pointing to a particular spot on the map. "And from what Maria and Cal have told me, a good place to start would be at the base of the limestone cliffs right here in the Mustang Mountains, because they have lots of caves. If we strike out there, then we'll expand our search. I assume we have access?"

I'd already made the necessary arrangements. "The Mustangs are a mix of public and private land, but I've cleared things with the local landowners. We can go pretty much anywhere we want. Shall we get started?"

We loaded ourselves into the county Blazer and drove east out of town on route 82. Maria rode shotgun, with Hazel Smith and Aunt Grace in the back seat. The cargo area behind them was stuffed with a large collection of field gear, including four backpacks, a cooler that Dr. Smith already had provisioned with dry ice, two devices for catching snakes, a camera, and abundant snacks and water.

I turned off 82 and drove south on a county road that ran along the western flank of the Mustang Mountains. The sun already had risen well above their distinctive jagged skyline, into a clear and cloudless sky. Although it was mid-morning the air retained a crisp feeling that I have always associated with fall.

Our destination was the old Waterford Ranch, now

largely part of a Bureau of Land Management property that ran from the county road east up into the Mustangs. I turned left off the pavement onto an access road and stopped. Maria's job was to get out, open the Texas gate, and then close it behind us. We followed a two track from there as it curved southeast across an alluvial outwash. The flats were dominated by a dense stand of Lehmann lovegrass, a species that had been introduced from southern Africa in the 1940s, supposedly as a means of restoring degraded rangelands. Because it was less palatable to livestock than the native grasses, Lehmann's had spread rapidly across the Sonoita Valley, much to the chagrin of the same ranchers it was supposed to have helped.

We followed the trail as far as the base of the mountains, where it split in two. The right fork was better traveled, and it led up to the red rocks, oaks, and junipers on Mustang Peak. But our destination was to the left, toward the gray limestone cliffs that formed the northern part of the range. There were caves at the base of those cliffs, and it was in these, or at least near them, that we hoped and expected to find Mojave rattlesnakes. By now the grasses had largely given way to a dense stand of wait-a-minute bushes, so-called because of their curved thorns. These were mixed with even nastier shin-daggers, a small yucca whose blades were stiff and sharp enough to puncture a tire, to say nothing of your leg.

I drove carefully up the two-track as far as seemed prudent, and then it was time to hike. We got out, loaded up our backpacks with the day's gear, and headed north up a steep talus slope that stopped at the base of the cliffs ahead.

We reached the nearest cave in about an hour. I was soaked with sweat, my once-pressed uniform shirt now thoroughly limp. I wondered, not for the first time, how Maria had managed to remain so cool looking after being out in the fierce Arizona sun. Dr. Smith and Aunt Grace seemed relatively composed as well. The only casualty so far was me. At one point I managed to stab myself on a shin-dagger yucca. It hurt like hell.

Hazel handed me her device for handling rattlesnakes, a four-foot long pole with a noose at one end and a handle for tightening the noose on the other. She called it a snake grabber. I appreciated the fact that the professor obviously used caution when handling such dangerous animals. It certainly contrasted favorably with the recent behavior of Ambrose Pendleton, and also with some of the 'experts' I had seen on television wildlife programs.

Hazel pulled a miner's lantern out of her pack and strapped it around her head. Then she turned on the lamp and proceeded into the cave. "Follow me," she said over her shoulder. "If we run into any live animals I'll have you come up with the grabber."

The cave was only about five feet high, and we all had to walk at an awkward bent angle. Hazel kept working her way farther back into the cave, but after fifteen minutes she still had found no live animals. She did find a handful of snakeskins, which she put in a plastic bag. The cave had a distinctive smell. The odor was familiar somehow, but I couldn't place why. I asked Hazel about it and she surprised me with her answer.

"So you're smelling something in here?"

"Yeah, sort of sharp and musty."

"Now that's interesting, Deputy. It might be the snakes."

"How so?"

"Well, some people claim that confined places where rattlesnakes congregate take on a distinctive odor. Personally, I've never smelled it, and so I'm skeptical. But maybe some people's noses are more sensitive than others."

At Dr. Smith's suggestion, we all exited and moved east along the base of the cliff to the next cave. It was by far the biggest, with some well-preserved pictographs lining its walls. I was pleased that no one had added any graffiti to the ancient artwork, but once again we were disappointed not to find any snakes.

We moved quickly on toward the third and smallest cave along this particular stretch of cliff face. Hazel Smith perked up. "This seems more likely. Snakes like the security of a tight space, and those other places were too wide."

We all heard the familiar hiss at about the same time, and stopped short.

"Sounds like we've got something here," said Hazel.

Two large Mojave rattlesnakes were coiled just inside the entrance to the cave. "I was hoping this would happen. Sometimes the animals will stick around the entrance of their dens to soak up the sun, before winter really shuts them down. Now let's go see what these boys look like."

The snakes were buzzing furiously by now, and I was decidedly uncomfortable about the prospect of a closer encounter. "How do we do that? I mean, how do you get close enough to tell if they're like the one that bit Andy? Do you want me to shoot one?"

Unlike me, Hazel Smith obviously was unperturbed. "No, please don't do that." She handed me the noose and pointed to the closest snake. "Just hook that noose around the snake's body, as close as possible right behind the head, and hold it down. I'll take a look at the scale patterns, and if it looks right then we'll take the next step."

I wondered what that next step would be. "You

have a lot of confidence in me, Dr. Smith. I'm not very experienced at this sort of thing."

"Would you rather have Maria do it?"

Guess who was thrilled with the invitation. "Sure, let me do it, Cal."

Talk about being on the spot. "No. No, I'll be all right. I can handle this."

I reached out tentatively toward the larger of the two snakes, secured the animal just behind its head, and then held on as it flailed its body in what I hoped was a vain attempt to escape. After about thirty seconds the snake calmed, and Hazel bent down for a closer look. I marveled at her composure.

In less than a minute she stood back up and shook her head. "No, something's wrong here. I think we may be at the wrong place. I may have tricked myself with the scale patterns. These are close to the one that you got out of the mailbox, but not nearly close enough. Still, I think we'd better kill it, and I'll take it back to the lab for some DNA work."

I was secretly relieved to learn that we didn't have to take a live snake anywhere. "How should I do that?"

"Do what?"

"Kill it. Do you want me to shoot it?"

The herpetologist looked both surprised and distressed. "Good grief, no. That's how you almost ruined ... ah, I mean that's how you damaged the last one. No, just hang on and stay out of my way."

She must have seen the look on my face. "This shouldn't take more than five minutes or so." With that she removed a good-sized billy club from her pack, then quickly moved in and gave the animal two sharp raps directly on top of its head.

Five minutes, maybe. It seemed like a lifetime to me before the heavy body of that particular old Mojave rattlesnake finally stopped flailing and twitching. Even then, I was relieved when Dr. Smith continued to use the noose to load the snake into her backpack.

Everyone was so engrossed in the process of securing the first snake that none of us noticed that the second animal had disappeared, presumably having moved back out of reach inside the cave entrance.

Aunt Grace had been her usual composed self through the whole collecting ordeal, until it was all over. Then she chuckled and said something about the virtues of being a botanist. Hazel Smith swung the pack and its contents up over her shoulder, and stood up. "That's a good start, but we're going to need more data. Let's spread out along this cliff face and see if we can find any more."

Grace looked distressed. "You mean we're going to kill more of them?"

Hazel shook her head. "No, that won't be necessary. I just wanted one for my reference collection back at Tumamoc. If we find any more, I'll just take photographs, and then collect a bit of tissue off their bellies for Willy's DNA work. He won't need much, but it is important that we get some idea about the amount of genetic variation in this population."

Over the course of the next three hours we captured, photographed, and took tissue samples from four more snakes, all at or near the mouths of smaller pockets in the limestone. I found the process of handling the live snakes even more harrowing than dealing with the one we had killed. After one of us had noosed the head and pressed it to the ground, somebody else had to hold the tail to keep the body still enough so Dr. Smith could reach down with a scalpel and tweezers and get her tissue sample. The tail-holding part was particularly spooky, but Maria let me off the hook by volunteering. She seemed unfazed by the whole thing.

There was only one close call that day. We had been separated for about an hour, each working different sections of the cliff and adjoining talus, when I heard someone exclaim "Oh my!" about a hundred yards off to my right. I looked up to see Aunt Grace sprawled awkwardly on her back in a tangle of wait-a-minute shrubs. By the time I reached her, she already was back on her feet, picking thorns out of her arms. Maria and Hazel had been farther off to the west, but they had heard the commotion and quickly headed our way.

I could hear a snake buzzing from somewhere back up the slope. "What happened?"

Aunt Grace clearly was flustered, but apparently more worried about the thorns than the snake. "Well, Cal, this is embarrassing, but I stepped on that snake before I even saw it. And it startled me so, the next thing I knew I was down here on my back."

"Are you all right? I mean the snake didn't get you, did it?"

Grace hesitated. "I don't think so."

By this time Hazel had joined us, with Maria close behind. The herpetologist bent down in front of Grace. "Actually, it did get you. See those wet spots on your jeans? That's venom." She pulled up Aunt Grace's right pant leg to reveal a sturdy leather hiking boot. There was no sign of a puncture. "That was a close call, but it looks like you're in the clear. Now let's go get that snake."

That made two, with three to go before we called it a morning.

Back at the vehicle, we unloaded our gear and put the one whole snake and the tissue samples in the cooler for transport back to Tucson. But before closing things up Hazel Smith stuck her nose down inside the cooler and looked again at the dead animal. "No, something's definitely wrong here. I don't think we've got the right population. I need to get back and reexamine the snake that killed the boy and consult my collection again. Maybe by Monday Willie will have turned up something with the DNA. He's been comparing the snake you gave me with others from this area already in our collection. He said he thought he'd have results in a day or two. But I'm pretty sure we'll need to do more fieldwork, no matter what. So when can we go out again?"

I was puzzled by something. "Shouldn't we look around here some more? There's lots of the day left, and other places in the Mustangs we could check."

Hazel shook her head. "We could I suppose. But everything tells me we aren't close enough here."

"You mean the snake that killed Andy might not have come from around here at all?"

"That's right. It certainly didn't come from the low desert, you can be sure of that. But it might have come from another valley or mountain range in this part of the state. Those are the places we need to start looking."

Maria clearly she didn't want to miss out on anything. "Wednesday's my regular day off. Maybe you could come back then? And I've got an idea, Cal. Aren't there some limestone cliffs up in the Whetstone Mountains? Maybe we could try over there."

The Whetstones were the next range north of the Mustangs. There were some caves in those mountains, so that is where we did look, and where we hit the jackpot in ways none of us could have guessed at the time.

Chapter 18
J.L. Minkston

It made a forlorn and seemingly endless day, sitting alone in that little half-baked trailer, waiting for customers who never came along. J.L. Minkston had run ads in the Tucson and Nogales papers, but to little avail. The parcels that comprised Mustang Estates just weren't moving, and he was getting closer to the financial edge with each passing day. He needed more land, and especially more water, and he needed them soon. Since he couldn't actually afford to buy any of either, the whole enterprise depended on finding some new partners.

Moss Winslow already was in the bag and that was the one bright spot. The old fart didn't know it yet but that damned vineyard of his was doomed. J.L. was sure it was only a matter of time before Moss gave up and agreed to let him use all the land and, most importantly, all the water.

He'd gotten lucky on that one. There had been an article in the paper about a vineyard outside Tucson that had become infected with something called Pierce's Disease, a deadly bacterium that was spread from one plant to another by insects. He'd found out where the vineyard was and grabbed a bunch of the sickest plants under the cover of darkness. Then he'd hired the stupid kid that did yard work for him to sneak over and stick them in the middle of one of Winslow's carefully tended rows of grapes. J.L. had driven by there just the other day, and a bunch of the vines already were starting to look bad.

The problem was that the Winslow Ranch included

plenty of land but only one decent well. And besides, the man was so land-poor he had nothing else to contribute. Sally Benton had all the land and water and money in the world, but there were two problems. First, her place was way over in Lyle Canyon, and second she was so rich there was no way he could tempt her into a partnership. Also, he'd done some snooping and found out she had no direct descendants. Instead she'd left her estate, including all of the V-9 Ranch, to a local land trust. There was no way those ecology wackos would go along with a real estate development, even if he got lucky and Sally croaked in time.

Grace Slawson had an ideal property in terms of both location and water. He had hoped she might be willing to get involved after that nephew of hers had died from a snakebite. And it might have worked out except for that friend of hers, Frenchy Somebody-or-Another, who ran the Santa Rita Saloon. J.L. could tell right away that he was a tough guy, and he had Grace Slawson's back. So that possibility seemed like another dead end.

There was only one remaining property that was in the right place with the right water. It belonged to a lady named Maria Obregon. Minkston knew she had a serious boyfriend who also happened to be the local deputy sheriff, so he needed to be careful. But he had a plan, and it just might work. And really, there was no other choice. He locked up the office and headed for town. There was something he needed to buy at the local feed store.

Chapter 19

It was one of those phone calls that every peace officer dreads. Larry and I were in the office Saturday morning, getting ready to take the motion-activated cameras over to the marijuana field on Sally Benton's place. The phone rang and I picked up in the usual manner.

"Sheriff's office, Deputy Creede speaking."

"Hello, Mr. Creede? This is Vicky McCall, Dan's wife? We met the other day at the church service?"

"Of course, Vicky. How are you? How's Dan?"

"Well, that's what I'm calling about. I'm wondering if by any chance you've seen or talked to him recently."

This did not sound good. "No, no I haven't Vicky. Is something wrong?"

"I hope not. It's just that I haven't heard from him for the last two days. He didn't come home last night, which isn't like him at all. I tried both his cell and radio a bunch of times, but he never answered. So I'm really, really worried."

"Did you check with Game and Fish? Maybe he's on a special assignment or something."

"Of course I did. They haven't heard from him either. They said they're sending somebody down to drive his regular circuit in Santa Cruz County, but I was hoping you might be able to help out as well."

"Of course. Can you give me a description of the vehicle he was driving? I'll notify headquarters down in Nogales, and they'll get the information out to all our patrol deputies."

"Just his usual department pickup I suppose. I think it's gray. And you'll look too?"

"Of course, Vicky. And don't worry. I'm sure he's just

had a breakdown or something. I expect he'll turn up real soon."

That sounded lame even to me, but I couldn't think of anything else to say.

People go missing all the time, mostly for reasons that turn out to be of no concern to a deputy sheriff. But this one felt different. First, from what I knew Dan was a loyal family man, a devout Mormon, with a wife and two young kids at home. I thought it very unlikely he would just leave with no explanation. Second, like me, he was a sworn officer, albeit one whose duties were largely restricted to enforcement of state game laws.

Larry wanted an explanation as soon as I hung up, but I put him off. There were two calls I needed to make right away. First, I contacted the Game and Fish office up in Tucson and got the make and model of the vehicle assigned to Dan McCall. Then I called dispatch in Nogales and had them put out a BOLO for Dan's vehicle. Only then did I bring Larry up to speed, and suggest a plan for the day. "You got those cameras, right?"

"Yep."

"Then I suggest we head over to Sally's place and set 'em up. That crop looked pretty mature to me, and it would be a really bad thing if we missed the harvest."

Larry frowned. "Why don't you do that while I start looking for Dan? We could do it the other way around, but I don't even know where that field is on the Benton place."

He had a point. "I suppose we could do it that way. But I don't know for sure how these cameras work. Any chance somebody from the Nogales property store gave you instructions? You know, the kind somebody past his teenage years can actually understand? I'm not exactly a tech wizard when it comes to this sort of stuff."

Larry picked up one of the cameras. "Let me show you. It's pretty simple, really. And you're heading over toward Lyle Canyon, right? So maybe I'll go on patrol down as far as Lake Patagonia, then work my way back up along the east slope of the Santa Ritas."

"Sounds like a plan. I expect some of the boys from Nogales will be covering the border area. So after I'm finished at Sally's, I think I'll take a drive down along the west side of the Huachucas. I have a suspicion about this."

"What sort of a suspicion?"

"That Dan might have had a reason to be working up high."

"Why?"

"Oh, just something he said the other day about rattlesnakes that live in the mountains."

Larry spent the next ten minutes showing me how to set up the motion-activated cameras, and then we went our separate ways.

I kept my eye out for an Arizona Game and Fish pickup on the way over to the V-9, but there was no sign. In fact, the ride over to Sally's place was completely uneventful until I got all the way down to the marijuana field. Then there was a big surprise.

Just under half the crop had disappeared since Sally and I had been there two days earlier. I got out of the Blazer and walked the whole area, looking for anything the growers might have left behind. Once again it was obvious that they were being very careful, because nothing turned up. There may have been some new tire tracks in the grass, but none that left usable impressions.

It took me about an hour to get the cameras set up. I selected juniper trees, one on each side of the field, for two reasons. First, the dense green foliage did a good job of hiding the cameras. Second, junipers are evergreen, so there was no chance the cameras would be exposed after leaf fall. I just hoped the motion sensors worked.

Now it was time to start looking for Dan McCall, or at least for his vehicle. I drove back north up Lyle Canyon until Sally's two-track met the county road that connected Fort Huachuca on the east with state Highway 83 to the west. I turned left and drove as far as the west gate to the fort, where I stopped to ask the guard if she had seen any vehicles belonging to Game and Fish. The woman didn't think so, so I turned around and followed the road south to its junction with 83.

My plan was to take 83 south along the west flank of the Huachucas, with side trips up into the mountains wherever access permitted. If my hunch was right and Dan had been looking for somebody poaching rare rattlesnakes, he likely would have done the same thing because those particular species were confined largely to the higher elevations. I knew some of the mountain roads crossed into Cochise County, but I decided this was an emergency and they could be notified afterwards if anything turned up.

The first opportunity came just a little ways beyond the Canelo Ranger Station, where a gravel road led up into Brushy Canyon. I followed this for several miles, until it more or less petered out. There was no sign of Dan's truck, although the high country up there was beginning to look like snake habitat – pine mixed with oak on some of the north-facing slopes, with lots of rocky outcrops.

I retraced my steps back down out of the mountains, and then followed the Lyle Canyon road south until it merged with 83. The last big canyon before the whole place turned into Mexico was Sunnyside, named after an old mining and religious community now almost completely gone. There was a good road at this point that ran pretty much straight up into the mountains. I followed the canyon upstream, past the old ghost town itself, until I came to a small pond formed by a trickling aquifer that must have kept the place alive back in the old days. The area was heavily wooded, including oak and pine on both the flats and adjacent slopes.

I drove on until the road became little more than a couple of ruts. I was about to turn back when my radio crackled to life.

"Sonoita Two this is Sonoita One, come in."

I knew it was Larry. His signal was scratchy but clear enough. "Sonoita One. What's up?"

"I found him, Cal. You'd better get over here. It's not good."

"What's your ten-twenty?"

"I'm up in the Santa Ritas, south of the ridge off the Gardner Canyon Road. The body's lying halfway in and halfway out of a little creek. It's near an old mine."

"You sure it's him? You sure he'd dead?"

"Ten-four on both, Cal. And there's a big gray Dodge Ram pickup with the Game and Fish quail logo on the side. Oh, and his sidearm is missing."

Jesus. "Ten-four. I'm on my way. You probably should drive out and meet me on the Gardner Canyon Road. Otherwise I'm not sure how I'll find the place."

Before Larry had a chance to reply, we were interrupted by a contact from Nogales dispatch, who obviously had been monitoring our conversation. I told them to call off the BOLO for Dan, and then requested a crime scene unit asap. I also asked them to contact Arizona Game and Fish, because I knew they'd want to be in on it. Larry suggested that rather than leave the body alone he would drive back and mark the junction point off the Gardner Canyon Road with yellow tape. He said it would be easy to follow from there because there was only one road.

Then he had another suggestion. "On your way over here you might want to see if Grace Slawson is available."

"But why?"

"Didn't I hear you say she was a botanist?"

"Ten-four. But explain please?"

"Because there's some weird looking plants in the water where I just found Dan's body."

I took me the better part of an hour and a half to round up Aunt Grace and get to the scene of the accident or crime or whatever it was. Fortunately she was home and anxious to help. I called Maria on my cell on the drive across the valley, told her what was happening, and that I didn't know when I'd be home. She was understandably distressed, but I asked her not to contact Vicky McCall. It was too early, and besides I guessed that Game and Fish probably would want to do that when the time was right. God, but this was going to be awful.

By the time Grace and I pulled up next to Larry's Jeep, someone else from Game and Fish already was there. Larry introduced me to Laura Floyd, out of their Tucson office. She was tall like Maria, but curvier, with wavy brown hair and hazel eyes. Laura told me she had confirmed the identity of the body, not that I had any doubts. The young woman was ashen-faced as she walked over to her truck and got on the radio, presumably to make the necessary call back to headquarters. I was surprised when Larry got into the cab with her. It seemed like they already knew each other.

Aunt Grace and I walked the short distance over to the creek and looked down at the mortal remains of Dan McCall. His legs and feet were in the water, but the head and torso were on the bank, face-up. A closer inspection of the body revealed two things. First, a large dark pool of blood had spread from the base of his skull out into the mud and grass. Second, his holster was empty. I moved in to check for vital signs, found none, and immediately backed away.

I turned to Aunt Grace, who stood silently at my side. "We don't want to get in close until the forensics team from Nogales arrives, but I was wondering what you could tell me about the overall scene, in terms of the vegetation."

She looked around appraisingly. "We're in the middle of a typical pine-oak woodland, so nothing special there. There are hundreds of places like this all over the Santa Ritas. But this creek is another matter. I'm guessing maybe that's why you asked for me?"

"It is. Any permanent water is rare enough in these hills. But Larry noticed that this one has some sort of green plant growing all along the bank. And it looks like some of the leaves are stuck to Dan's – uh, I mean to the victim's – blue jeans and boots. Do you have any idea what it might be?"

"You've got good eyes, deputy. And Larry did the right thing by asking for me. Actually that's not a flowering plant, it's a fern, and those are called fronds instead of leaves. But you're right, ferns are not at all common in these parts. So if we can find any of it associated with a perp's clothing, or even his vehicle, that could be valuable evidence."

Perp? Either Aunt Grace was addicted to T.V. cop shows, which I very much doubted, or she was a more experienced real life crime fighter than I'd thought.

"Would it be all right if I collected some? I mean, before your forensics people get here? We don't want these fronds to dry out before I have a chance to properly protect them."

"You bet. Just be sure not to touch anything else."

Grace shot me a look that brought back memories of times when I'd said something foolish in her classroom. Then she bent down to take a closer look at the plant material clinging to the dead man's pants and boots. "You know this fern looks a little odd."

"Odd how?"

"Like maybe I've seen the genus but not this particular species. We should be able to pin it down exactly with a little microscopic work. I've got the right setup over at Elgin School."

This had me curious. "What does this have to do with the school?"

"Oh, didn't you know about the grant we got to set up a biology lab over there? It must have been after your time. Anyway, I often use that equipment when I'm working on a case. Sometimes the students help out, and it's a big deal for them. Other times I go after hours."

Aunt Grace walked back to the Blazer and pulled two objects out of the back hatch. I recognized a standard daypack as one, but the other was something foreign. It was a bundle of blotters and folded sheets of newsprint, about six inches thick, sandwiched between two lattice frames made out of narrow strips of wood. Adjustable canvas straps held the whole thing together.

Curiosity got the better of me. "What's that?"

"It's a plant press, Cal, a standard piece of botanical field equipment. I'm surprised you've never seen one. I'm sure Maria would know what it is."

"My major was English literature, Grace. I don't think it was the sort of thing my professors had lying around their offices."

That got a smile but not a laugh, which was understandable given the circumstances.

Aunt Grace laid her gear down beside Dan McCall's body, and set to work. First she extracted a bound gray notebook and some tweezers out of her daypack. Then she took the plant press apart and spread several sheets of newsprint out on the grass. I noticed the press also held sheets of corrugated cardboard in addition to the blotters. Using the tweezers, she peeled off a piece of fern frond that had been plastered against one leg of Dan's jeans, and carefully laid it out flat on one of the sheets of paper. Then she wrote a number on the newsprint and the same number on a page in her notebook. She repeated this process a half dozen times, collecting fronds from more clothing and also from the streamside and muddy ground near Dan's body.

Having finished the collection, Aunt Grace extracted six evidence labels from her daypack, writing down one of the numbers, as well as the date, time, and location on each label. She then signed each label and laid it on the sheet of newsprint with the corresponding number. Once this was completed, she folded the newsprint sheets in half and sandwiched them between the blotters and pieces of corrugated cardboard, "to soak up the moisture," as she explained. Finally, she placed the stack of papers, blotters, and cardboard back inside the wooden frame of the plant press, and tightened the straps.

Having completed her work with the plants themselves, Aunt Grace turned her attention back to the notebook. She annotated each collection number with information about its location, including a general description of the underlying soils and surrounding vegetation, and a list of all people present at the scene.

We discussed whether I should take charge of the specimens as evidence, but decided against it. She had lots of work to do in the lab, and it would be inconvenient for her to sign the collection out from an evidence room every time she wanted to work on it, especially if they ended up down in Nogales.

Aunt Grace explained what would happen next. "When these specimens dry I'll glue them onto proper herbarium sheets, along with the labels of course. Then I'll get down to the critical business of figuring out exactly what species of fern we have here."

She had just finished up with the ferns when I heard the sound of a vehicle approaching from somewhere back down the mountain. Shortly after that a white van with a sheriff's department logo pulled up next to my Blazer. Joe Ortega was driving, and with him was Julie Benevides, the woman who had handled the Andy Slawson crime scene. We assembled under the shade of an Emory oak, and I made introductions because I wasn't sure whether Joe and Julie had met either Aunt Grace or Laura Floyd. I had forgotten that Grace had done some forensics work previously for Joe Ortega, so it turned out they already knew each other.

Joe took charge once the introductions were completed. He instructed Julie to begin her analysis of the crime scene along the creek, while he assigned himself to Dan McCall's pickup. He asked the rest of us to sit tight. Ortega finished up with the truck in about a half hour, and then joined Larry, Laura, and me near the body, where we all stood around watching Julie still at work. I asked Joe what he'd found.

He shrugged. "The truck was unlocked, which suggests that the victim had not moved very far before he encountered whatever happened here. I didn't find anything of particular interest inside, but we're going to want to impound it down in Nogales for a more complete look. Laura, I assume the department is okay with that?"

She nodded her ascent. "So you'll be looking for prints?"

"Sure, that and anything else we might be able to trace to the killer, assuming there was one."

That didn't please Laura at all. She started to object, but Joe put his hand up. "Let's just wait and see what Julie has to say." Then he asked Larry how he'd happened to find the body and the degree to which he might already have disturbed the area. I could tell it rankled Larry a bit, but he was right to ask. Larry explained that Dan had not been moved, and I confirmed that Aunt Grace and I had done nothing except to collect some ferns associated with the body.

Joe still didn't like it. "Couldn't you have waited on that?"

Aunt Grace came to my rescue. "I was anxious to get those specimens secured in my press before they dried out. And we didn't know how long it would be until you got here, Sergeant. In any event, I touched nothing but the plants themselves, and then only with tweezers."

It took Julie Benevides another half-hour of measuring and photographing before she rejoined our group. Joe asked the obvious questions. "What did you find? Any ideas as to cause of death?"

The young woman shrugged her shapely shoulders. "We probably should wait for the coroner's report before going public with anything. But it looks like blunt force trauma to the base of the skull. And it could have been accidental."

That seemed unlikely to me. "Why do you say that?"

"Two reasons. First, when I rolled the body over I noticed the skull was resting against a jagged rock partly buried in the ground. Second, all the blood around suggests the body has not been moved since the impact."

I wanted to make sure I understood her logic. "So you're thinking maybe somebody got into a shoving match with the victim, and he fell back against the rock?"

"That would be consistent with the evidence.

There's lots of disturbance to the area, which suggests the victim may have been engaged in some sort of physical altercation."

Ortega wanted more details. "Any evidence from the disturbed ground that we could use? Like footprints maybe?"

Julie shook her head. "No, sorry. But I did find something else on the body that could complicate the picture."

Aunt Grace had been standing aside, seemingly disengaged in the conversation, but this apparently got her attention. "What's that, my dear?"

"There are two punctures on the inside of the victim's right forearm, about a quarter-inch apart. They look like fang marks from a rattlesnake, except they're real close together. And the right arm is swollen somewhat compared to the other."

We all wanted to see that, especially Joe Ortega, who walked immediately over to the body and bent down for a closer look. "So maybe this game warden got bit by a baby rattler?"

Julie shrugged. "Well, that's one possibility I suppose."

I could think of another explanation, and it was one that played directly to Dan McCall's reason for being all the way over here above Gardner Canyon in the first place.

Two tasks remained at the scene. One was to load Dan's remains into a body bag for transport back to Nogales. The second was to scour the whole area for any relevant evidence, including Dan's missing sidearm. Julie and Larry took care of the body, while Aunt Grace, Laura, and I combed the area. Joe used a metal detector in hopes of finding the weapon. We started at the creek banks and moved out, bagging and labeling anything of obvious human origin.

The search proved frustrating not for a lack of evidence, but because of too much. Lots of people had been there before us, most likely a mix of hikers, campers, and hunters. We collected everything from empty tin cans and cigarette butts to spent cartridge shells and broken pieces of glass, eventually filling three thirty-gallon black plastic garbage bags. Most of the stuff we collected looked old, and it was going to be a daunting task to sort the whole mess out. I had my doubts it would get us much of anywhere because none of it seemed obviously attributable to either the victim or his possible killer. It was something that had to be done, but I was glad the job would fall to the forensics people at headquarters and not to Larry or me. We had plenty on our plate as it was.

One thing we did not find was Dan's weapon, despite the fact that Joe Ortega had worked the whole area with his metal detector. Laura Floyd volunteered that she could get us the make, model, and serial number from Game and Fish. "It probably was a Glock forty caliber, just like mine."

Joe nodded his thanks. "It'll be a long shot putting that information out to local gun dealers and pawnshops, but we've got nothing to lose I suppose. Still, my bet is that our killer will just hang on to it, assuming he took it in the first place."

Two other sorts of evidence that could have done us some good were tire tracks or footprints, but these proved nearly useless. The immediate vicinity of the creek was heavily disturbed, but the grass was so thick that no tracks or prints were evident. The two-track itself was more promising, though very rocky. The problem was we'd pretty much blown it by our own arrival. The road was a jumble of footprints and tread marks, most of which were ours. It was a mistake that Joe Ortega predictably grumbled about, but he'd been just as careless as the rest of us.

In the end, we made casts of a variety of footprints and tread marks that didn't seem to match anything we'd been wearing or driving. I held out more hope for Aunt Grace's little fern collection than for anything else. As it turned out, that was the deal.

Chapter 20

Maria and I had finished eating dinner, and I was washing up the dishes while she was outside fussing with the goats. It had been a very long day and I was pretty much wiped out. There would be lots to do tomorrow, especially about Dan McCall. But for now I just needed to crash and re-group, and maybe spend a little personal time with Maria, which had been all too infrequent lately.

Then the phone rang and it was Larry. He was out at the McCall's place, and apparently Vicky wanted to see me. So much for down time.

I'd never been to the game warden's home before, but Maria knew where it was because of her mail route. She was handy that way, among others. She readily agreed to come along, and I knew it wasn't just to provide directions.

In my present condition I just wanted to drive in silence, but Maria wanted to talk. "That's just so tragic about Dan McCall. I mean with his wife and those two little kids left behind."

"I know. I'm just glad you'll be there with me tonight. You're better at this sort of thing than I am. It's going to be awkward as hell."

Maria shook her head. "I heard they're Mormon, so at least Vicky should be strong in her faith."

"Yes, but still..."

"She'll need comfort from others. And that's why we need to be there."

Lots of people must have had the same idea because the place was crowded. The McCalls lived in a small frame house nestled among the oaks west of 83 about five miles north of Sonoita. I recognized Larry's Jeep and two Arizona Game and Fish pickups in front of the house, among the half-dozen vehicles already there. It was nearly dark now, and on the cool side. The clear sky was thick with stars, with just a hint of a reddish evening glow at the crest of the Santa Ritas. There was no wind. The tragedy playing out inside the house belied the tranquility of the scene.

Maria and I made our way up onto a front porch cluttered with children's toys, including a tricycle, a wagon, and a small swing set. Larry came over as soon as we walked in the front door. I saw Vicky on a couch in the living room, huddled with a tall man and a woman I did not recognize. Her face was drawn and tear-streaked, but I also sensed that she was in control. There were three men wearing Game and Fish uniforms in the crowded room. I immediately recognized Aunt Grace, who was in a far corner deep in conversation with Laura Floyd. Maria walked directly to where Vicky was seated, while Larry took me aside.

"She's seen the body, Cal. Laura and I drove her down to Nogales this afternoon."

"Must have been tough."

Larry nodded. "It was, but Laura was great, and their bishop met us there. That's him on the couch with Vicky, along with his wife."

I wanted to know how it was that Larry and Laura seemed to be spending so much time together, but this didn't seem like the right moment. "You said Vicky wants to see me? Do you know what about?" I was prepared to offer sympathy and whatever comfort I could. I just hoped she didn't want too many details about the crime scene.

"Not for sure, Cal. But I think it may have something to do with Dan's recent activities."

As soon as it was tactfully possible, I made my way

over beside Maria, who had pulled a chair up next to the couch where Vicky was sitting. It was one of the most awkward moments of my life, right next to a handful of phone calls I'd made from Afghanistan back home to grieving family members.

At the police academy they'd taught us to say 'I'm so sorry for your loss' under circumstances like these. It was trite, but I said it anyway because I meant it and couldn't think of anything better.

Vicky McCall was magnanimous, to say the least. Perhaps it was her faith. If so, it was something to be envied. She looked up, her blue eyes clear and her gaze direct. "Thank you, Mr. Creede. You are most kind. And let me introduce you to our bishop, John Bellingham, and his wife Gretta?"

I shook both their hands, and then turned my attention back to Vicky. "Please call me Cal. And Deputy Hernandez said you wanted to speak to me?"

"Yes I do."

She rose from the couch, made excuses to the bishop and his wife, and directed me down the hall into what obviously was a child's bedroom. It was a cheery place, with bright wallpaper done up in balloons and animals. There was sports equipment everywhere, including bats, balls, and a miniature basketball hoop attached to one wall. She must have sensed my discomfort. "The boys are at a neighbor's, so we can talk here. They don't know anything yet, except that their daddy's had an accident."

"Of course, Vicky. How can I help you?"

She hesitated, but only for a split second. "I need to know, Cal. Did he suffer?"

There was only one way to answer that question, whatever the truth. "No, I don't think so. It must have been quick."

Was that the right thing to say? My experience was

way too limited. I wished Maria had been there to coach me, especially because it turned out Vicky wanted to know more. "They let me see him at the morgue, but not the back of his head, which is where I guess..."

Her voice trailed off, and I could sense the real agony she was facing. "You were right there, Cal. You must have seen how it was."

Clearly the ball was in my court, and I decided a woman this brave deserved at least some measure of the truth. I reached out and put my arm on her shoulder. "He fell, Vicky. He fell backwards, and it looked like he hit his head on a rock. So he must have been knocked unconscious right away, even if..."

Vicky McCall pulled away, and for the first time showed signs of anger layered over her grief. She'd caught me trying to soft pedal something, and she knew it. "That can't be the way it was. I mean it's not like he fell off a cliff or something. He was just lying next to a little stream, right? So somebody had to push him. Had to push him hard."

"You're right."

"I don't want just to be right. I want to know who did this!"

I made an attempt to approach her, but again she backed off. "I don't need your comfort, Cal. There's plenty of people out there who will take care of that, or at least try. Just as soon as I can have his body, the boys and I are moving back up to Kingman. That's where our families are. What I need from you is justice."

"That's what we all want, Vicky – me, the sheriff, deputy Hernandez, the whole department. I'm sure his colleagues at Game and Fish do as well. They have resources too. And you have my word, we'll find whoever is responsible."

"Do you have any suspects?"

I knew this was coming, but it was not an easy question to answer. "Perhaps, but at this stage of our investigation I'd rather not speculate. I hope you understand." Again, a bunch of platitudes. And again, naturally, she knew it.

"Okay, I guess I understand your position. So I'll leave you with just one word. Well, two actually. Ambrose Pendleton."

Dan and Vicky McCall must have kept few secrets. But how much did she know, and could it help our case? I decided to bring her into the loop just far enough so I could probe for anything Dan might have shared.

Unfortunately, it didn't help. Apparently all Dan knew was what he'd already told me. Pendleton collected snakes and other herps, but there was no solid evidence that he'd been dealing in rare species. That was what Dan had been looking for along that little creek over above Gardner Canyon. Apparently he'd found it.

If I was right, in addition to being an environmental wacko and a dealer in illegal reptiles, Ambrose Pendleton was a stone cold killer. Now all I had to do was prove it.

Chapter 21

"The goats aren't right."

Maria and I were having chorizo and scrambled eggs for breakfast. It was dawn on the Sonoita Plain, and the first rays of the rising sun had just bathed the Mustang Mountains in a pink glow. I swallowed the last of my second cup of coffee and laid the cup back down on the kitchen table. "What do you mean, not right?"

"Well, for one thing my new billy Ferdinand has a big bruise on his thigh that I'm pretty sure wasn't there yesterday. And the girls were way crabbier than usual during the milking this morning, like it hurt when I touched their udders."

"Are you going to call Dr. Pike?" Tim Pike was the local large animal veterinarian. I knew that Maria liked and trusted the man.

"I will if things get any worse. I'm just glad it's Sunday, so I can stick around and keep any eye on things instead of doing the mail route."

I pushed back from the table. "Well, I'd like to take the day off too, but Larry and I made plans to meet at the office, in light of recent developments."

Maria shook her head. "I know. That's just so tragic about Dan McCall. I still can't get over it. Do you have any idea how this might have happened?"

"Nothing specific at this point."

She shot me a look that I had come to recognize. "But...?"

"But maybe it has something to do with endangered rattlesnakes."

"Snakes again? Seems like everything about your job keeps coming around to snakes these days."

"No kidding. And you know they're not one of my favorite subjects."

I reminded Maria about the last conversation we'd had with Dan McCall in the parking lot after the Slawson funeral.

"So you think the fellow he was talking about, the snake collector guy who gave that awful talk at the Nature Club, that he might be involved? What was his name?"

"Ambrose Pendleton. And yes, that's a possibility. But don't go blabbing it around because at this point I don't have a nickel's worth of evidence."

This did not amuse my fiancée at all. "Since when have you known me to go blabbing things around, *caro*?"

At least she still liked me. "Well never, of course. Sorry. This whole episode has got me on edge. One thing's for sure, though. Dan's death just moved to the top of my list."

"Even ahead of Andy Slawson? And what about that marijuana plantation on Sally Benton's place you were telling me about?"

"I suppose Andy and Dan are sort of tied." I'd actually forgotten about the marijuana, which shows what a complicated mess my professional life had become lately.

~ ~ ~

I was not surprised to find Larry Hernandez already in the office when I arrived a half hour later. It *was* surprising to find Laura Floyd sitting in my chair, which she had pulled over to his side of our shared desk. Something about their reaction as I walked told me their conversation had been something other than strictly professional.

She jumped up as soon as she recognized who I was. "Good morning Deputy. Larry and I – that is, Deputy Hernandez and I – we were just talking about the McCall case. My boss up in Tucson has assigned me to Dan's district, at least for the time being, and I'm supposed to provide liaison between Game and Fish and your department."

"That's good Laura. Let's get started. And please call me Cal." I pulled over a third chair in the office – one for guests – and we all sat. "So Larry, any word from the sheriff? I haven't talked to him or anybody else from Nogales since yesterday."

"Yeah, he checked in just after I got here. Said they were transporting Dan's body up to Pima County so their M.E. could take a look. Said he'll get back to us as soon as they learn anything."

"Any further word from forensics?"

"I asked about that. But apparently there's nothing besides what we learned from Julie out at the site."

I turned my attention to Laura. "What about at your end? Does anybody from Game and Fish have any idea just what Dan might have been doing over in Gardner Canyon?" I had my own theory, of course, but I was anxious to hear the department's official take, assuming there was one.

Laura explained that nobody knew anything for sure. "But Dan had been working on a case of illegal trafficking in endangered reptiles."

This certainly fit with my last conversation with the man, and with his widow. "Any suspects?"

Her answer surprised me. "Two, actually. One is a local guy who apparently keeps a large snake collection in his home."

"That would be Ambrose Pendleton?"

Laura nodded.

"And the other?"

"It's somebody who runs a pet store up in Phoenix. I can't remember his name. Apparently the stuff he has on display is all legal, but there are suspicions about what might be in his back room."

"Enough suspicions for a search warrant?"

"Apparently not, and that's the problem. They tried some sort of a sting operation, but he didn't fall for it. So the whole thing's in limbo."

I remembered the man I'd seen eating dinner with Pendleton at the Santa Rita just six days earlier. "That man who owns the pet shop, do you know what he looks like? Could you get me a photo?"

Laura Floyd asked Larry for a piece of paper, and then made herself a note that she folded into her shirt pocket. "I can't give you a description, but I'm pretty sure we can get you a photo."

"Good. Make that a top priority. I just might have seen this person a few days ago with Pendleton in the Santa Rita Saloon. If we can put Pendleton and this dealer together in the Sonoita area, that might be enough for a warrant to search Pendleton's place."

Larry looked skeptical. "Even if they can't tie the dealer to anything illegal?"

He had a point. "Well, maybe something will break on that end. Who knows, maybe the guy would rat out Pendleton as part of a plea deal. Let's hope so. In the meantime, what else have we got?"

All was quiet for a time in the Sonoita substation of the Santa Cruz County Sheriff's Department. It was Larry who eventually broke the silence.

"Well, here's one idea I had. You're trying to track down the local identity of the Mojave rattler that killed Andy Slawson, right?"

"Right."

"And you've got this lady up at the university who is helping out, right?"

"Right again."

"So maybe you should ask this Ambrose fellow to help out."

"You mean have the two of them work together?"

"You got it. And then maybe it could happen that

the reptile lady from the university ended up in Pendleton's house. You know, while they consulted together or something? And maybe she'd get the chance to snoop around a little?"

Laura Floyd immediately caught the flaws in Larry's plan. "But even if she did find something like a rare rattlesnake, I see two problems. First, wouldn't a good lawyer figure out how to quash it as an illegal search? And second, just because you found a snake, how would it tie to Dan's murder?"

Her points were well taken, but I thought there might be a way around both of them. First, if the man I saw with Pendleton at the Santa Rita turned out to be the reptile dealer from Phoenix, that might be enough for the sheriff to get us a search warrant for Pendleton's place. Then we could get Hazel in there legally to help. Luis had a way of making near-magical things happen when the occasion demanded. Second, once inside we might find something even more interesting than a snake in Pendleton's house or vehicle, assuming Aunt Grace was on the right track about that fern or whatever it was she found next to Dan's body.

I decided to bring the meeting to a close. "Okay, Laura, I assume you need to go about your usual game wardening, but try to get me a photo of that pet dealer in Phoenix as soon as possible. And Larry, stick around for a just a bit. We need to talk about another case."

The Game and Fish lady was barely out the door before Larry beat me to the punch. "You're wondering about Laura and me, right?"

"Well, not that it's any of my business, but yeah, sure, I guess I am a bit curious. You knew each other before yesterday?"

"We did. I met her about a year ago when we both were taking a self-defense class up in Tucson. We hit it off right away, and one thing led to another. So we sort of, uh, dated for about six months, before she got sent up to the Kingman office, which was her first assignment with Game and Fish. Then we lost touch, up until yesterday."

"And now it's back on?"

Larry shrugged and grinned. "Maybe. I'll keep you posted." It was clear he wanted to change the subject. "So you wanted to talk about another case?"

"Yeah, it's about the deal with Sally Benton's pot plantation."

"You got over there yesterday and set up the cameras, right?"

"Yep, and there have been developments. Since my first visit somebody came in and harvested a bunch of the plants."

"Want me to go check it out? I'm gonna need directions."

"No, let's wait a day or two, then I'll drive over there with you. In the mean time I need to get back in touch with Hazel Smith up at the university, see if she's figured out any more about the snake that killed Andy. Last time we talked she was pretty sure it didn't come from the Mustangs, so we may need to widen our search."

Larry stood up to leave. "Anything else for today? Otherwise, I'll do a patrol around the valley and then maybe head home."

"Sounds good. I'll talk to you tomorrow."

"You gonna follow up on getting that Dr. Smith into Pendleton's house?"

"You bet. As soon as I talk to the sheriff."

Chapter 22

Normally I wouldn't bother Sheriff Mendoza on a Sunday, but since he'd already called the office I assumed he was open for business. He answered his cell on the first ring, and I could hear road noise in the background.

"Is this a good time to talk?"

"Actually, I'm heading up your way. There's a pancake breakfast fundraiser for the Patagonia Boy Scouts. I get invited to these things all the time. Boring as hell, but good for public relations. With an election on the horizon, Mary usually signs me up without even asking."

"You want me to come down?"

"Not unless you're desperate to rub elbows with some local glad-handers, which I suspect is more my deal than yours. Just sit tight and expect me at your office in about an hour and a half."

"I'll be here. And be sure to enjoy those pancakes."

There was no reply. Trying to be funny with the boss rarely paid off. You'd think I would have learned that by now.

I called Maria to ask about the goats, and she sounded really worried.

"Now one of my nannies has a bruise too. I called Dr. Pike. He's tending to a sick heifer over at the V-9, but he said he'll get here as soon as possible."

"Did you describe the symptoms?"

"Sure, but he didn't say anything except that I should keep my herd as quiet as possible."

"Okay, good. Let me know what you find out. I've got to stay at the office for a while. The sheriff's on his way up."

There was time to kill, so I fired up the office computer for a little search. One topic of interest was the Border Posse, but that drew a blank. Evidently none of those special fellows was into websites. There were a couple of links to articles about the posse in the Nogales paper, but they didn't tell me anything I didn't already know. Next I typed in 'Ambrose Pendleton.' All that got was an address in one of the ranchette developments east of town. Other than in the phone book Mr. Pendleton apparently did not exist, at least in the files of the two major search engines I tried.

'J.L. Minkston' was another matter. There were two hits in addition to the usual address leads, both related to bankruptcies. The first referred to a corporation called Grand Mesa Enterprises, Inc., based in Grand Junction, Colorado. Minkston was listed as president and, as far as I could tell, the sole officer of the corporation. It had declared bankruptcy in 2005. The second was a document describing the financial demise of another business, Golden West Acres, Inc., with an address in Barstow, California, which if I remembered correctly was somewhere out in the Mojave Desert. According to the filing, Golden West had sunk out of sight in 2010.

I typed in the names of both the Grand Mesa and Golden West corporations, found links to two websites, but they wouldn't open. Evidently J.L. Minkston knew how to burn his electronic bridges. I was about to start a search for his newly launched Mustang Estates, when the office phone rang. It was Maria.

"Hello, Cal? It's my goats! They're all real sick and one's already dead!"

I was stunned. "Is Dr. Pike there? Does he know what happened?"

"Yes, yes, he's here. And he thinks he's figured it out. Apparently somebody put rat poison in their grain! He found some strange-looking little pellets mixed in with the oats and barley. He won't know for sure until he gets it analyzed, but he's pretty sure that's what happened."

"I thought you said the goats had bruises, like they'd been hit or something."

"Dr. Pike says no, or at least it's very unlikely. What happens, the rat poison causes blood thinning. Then they can bleed internally even from a minor event, such as when they bump up against each other in the corral."

"Is there anything he can do?"

"Yes, he's giving all the animals some kind of vitamin shots. Apparently it can reverse the effects."

"So they'll be okay?"

"He thinks so."

"And what about the one that died?"

"That was Ferdinand, my new billy!"

"I know Maria. I'm so sorry. How did he die?"

I could hear Maria stifling a sob. "He's … he's not sure, but it might have been some sort of massive internal hemorrhage. He's taking Fernando back to his lab for an autopsy. Not that it matters. Oh, Cal, this is *all* my fault! I should have seen something was wrong in the grain. Maybe I've got no business trying to run a dairy at all!"

This had to stop. "Now that's nonsense, and you know it. You'd do anything for those animals. They're lucky to have you."

"You mean like Fernando? How lucky was he?"

"I don't want you to beat yourself up over this anymore. I'll be home as soon as I can."

Obviously, Maria was on the ragged edge. In light of what she'd told me about Tim Pike's discovery, it likely would fall to the sheriff's department to figure out who had put her there.

~ ~ ~

"So now it's five cases, actually."

"Five? I know about the Border Posse, the

marijuana field, and of course the deaths of the Slawson boy and now, of all things, warden McCall. By my count that makes four, which is bad enough. And now you've got another one?"

The sheriff was in my office, in Larry's chair. He'd dropped a big file folder on the desktop between us, and it was clear he'd come to talk. We were having coffee. I told him about Maria's goats.

He almost dropped his cup. "Jesús! And you think it was deliberate?"

"Seems likely. There's no way she could have put the poison in the grain by accident. Hell, as far as I know we don't even have any of that stuff around the place. Maria doesn't believe in it."

Luis Mendoza sighed audibly. I knew he cared deeply about my fiancée.

I pointed to the file folder. "What's that?"

"Joe Ortega brought it by, said you had asked him to look into the backgrounds of Ambrose Pendleton and that Minkston fellow. From what I can tell he came up with some interesting information. You should take a look."

"I will. But the bottom line?"

"About Pendleton, turns out he has a record. He got busted on a weapons charge and also for domestic violence back east. Apparently it was related to an ex-wife. Looks like you were right about his being a trust child. His dad is some big stockbroker type from Connecticut, evidently with the right connections, because he did no jail time for either felony."

"When was this?"

"Five years ago."

"Anything since?"

"Nothing criminal that we know of, but his finances might be shaky. We can't get into his bank account without a court order, and there's not enough evidence for that. No evidence, really. But Joe did find that the man hasn't been paying either utilities or property taxes since he moved out here. So maybe he's been cut off, like you suggested."

I told Luis about Dan McCall's suspicions that Pendleton was trafficking in illegal snakes, and the possible link with an unscrupulous reptile dealer in Phoenix. I also floated the idea of arranging a search of the man's house. "So now, in light of Dan's death, maybe you could get a judge to sign a warrant, ideally not just for his financial records but also his residence?"

The sheriff frowned. "It might be a bit of a stretch, but I'll see what I can do. It sure would help, though, if you could tighten the link with the dealer."

"I may have seen them together at the Santa Rita Saloon the other night, but we're waiting on a photo ID of the man."

"Good. Keep me posted."

"Will do. Meanwhile, what about Minkston?"

Luis drained his coffee and nodded. "We've got stuff there, for sure. Looks like he's a pretty shady character." He then proceeded to tell me about his real estate developments in Colorado and California. I already knew something about these from my web search just an hour earlier, but evidently Joe Ortega and his team had dug a lot deeper. Not only had the man gone bankrupt twice, but there were serious complaints about shoddy workmanship, the bilking of sub-contractors, even attempts to bribe county building inspectors.

"Was he ever prosecuted?"

"They tried to get him on a bribery charge, but it didn't stick. Oh, and here's another interesting tidbit. Apparently this isn't Minkston's first appearance in our part of the world."

"Yeah, I know about that from my parents. He tried a few years back to get them involved in developing the Pitchfork Ranch. Fortunately they didn't bite."

"Good for them." The sheriff pointed again to the file folder. "So take a look at those papers, I suppose. But here's the thing. Looks like this Minkston is a real sleaze ball, but that doesn't make him a violent criminal. Do you really suspect he's behind any of the stuff you've got going around here?"

I sensed we had come to the real reason for the sheriff's visit. "Only that he has motive."

"Motive how?"

"I think he's desperate to find partners in his local real estate ventures."

"And?"

"And maybe he'd go to all sorts of lengths to get people to cooperate."

"What sorts of lengths? Just hypothetically speaking, of course, but I really need to understand your thinking here, Cal."

"Well, suppose he wanted to get hold of somebody's land and water, but that somebody had other plans. If he could do something to derail those plans, then maybe that somebody would be willing to sell out."

The sheriff's forehead wrinkled. "Can you name any of these possible somebodies?"

I could think of three, each of whom had in some way been the victim of recent violence or misfortune. "Sure. Aunt Grace Slawson, Moss Winslow, and now Maria. We know for a fact that Minkston has approached each of them about going partners. We also know Grace and Maria turned him down cold. Only Winslow has gone along with it, and apparently now even he's getting cold feet."

"So you think the Slawson kid dying might change

Aunt Grace's mind about her land? Or that Maria might want to get out because of what just happened to her goats?"

"My guess about Maria? No way in hell. But with Aunt Grace I'm not so sure. Apparently she and Frenchy Vullmers – he owns the Santa Rita – they planned to set up a vineyard on her place. Frenchy tells me it was mostly for Andy, and now that he's gone, maybe her plans are gone too."

"Doesn't sound like the Aunt Grace I knew back in my Elgin School days, but I see your point."

The sheriff got up from his chair and poured himself another cup of coffee. I was anxious to get home to Maria, but evidently we weren't finished. He sat back down and cleared his throat. I could sense something big was coming.

"You've got all these open cases going on right now. It's looks like a real shit storm, to put it bluntly. So I have two questions. First, do you need some help from Nogales? You know Joe Ortega's on my case about this. Second, do you think all of these things happening at once is just a coincidence, or might they be related in some way?"

I decided to answer his second question first. "There are two possible links. One is Minkston, which we've already talked about. I can't figure him for Dan McCall's death, but for the Slawson killing and Maria's goats there definitely is a connection. And maybe even for Sally Benton's pot field, assuming he needs cash bad enough."

"And the other link?"

"Rattlesnakes."

"And that's where Pendleton comes in? I can see him for McCall, assuming you're right about his snake business. But Slawson? What motive could he have for that?"

"It's tenuous as hell, but maybe that snake in Moss Winslow's mailbox was intended for somebody else."

"Like who?"

"Like maybe Winslow himself. We haven't discussed it yet, but it looks like Pendleton may be some sort of serious environmental wacko." I told the sheriff about the man's bizarre performance at the Elgin Nature Club meeting.

"Really? You think the man's *that* nuts?"

"At this point I'm not sure what to think, Luis. But while we're at it, there's another possible snake connection we need to consider."

"What's that?"

"The Border Posse." I described their battle flag with the snake on it, and the snake stencil on Gus Barlow's shot-up water tank, and their protest at the Winslow Ranch about supposed illegal workers.

The sheriff sighed again, and then actually bent over and put his head in his hands. I had never seen him do anything remotely like that. It seemed like forever, but eventually he looked back up and spoke bluntly and directly.

"You've got a real mess on your hands, Cal. And I'm sorry to say it, but you're not getting much of anywhere. You can have a few more days I suppose, but then I'll have no choice but to take some of this off your plate and hand it over to Joe Ortega. Maybe even all of it, if you don't turn things around pretty fast."

I knew this was coming, and I didn't blame him.

Neither of us could see it that Sunday afternoon, but the fog presently hanging over the Sonoita Substation of the Santa Cruz County Sheriff's Department was about to lift. The real reason the sheriff would need to call in outside help wasn't because I was getting nowhere. It was because, in one case, I'd gone too far.

Chapter 23

The weather turned awful that afternoon. Perhaps it was a portent of things to come. Rain in Arizona is a blessing, so that wasn't it. Instead it was the wind, which started to blow out of the northeast just after noon. It was one of those incessant window-rattling sort of winds, usually more typical of March than October in this part of the world. Apparently the thing was widespread because the evening news showed big sand storms over Phoenix as well as other parts of the low desert. Good grass cover held much of the soil in place in the Sonoita Valley, but even here the air had turned a dusty yellow-brown by sunset.

Maria and I had finished our dinner and I volunteered to clean up solo in light of her recent trauma. By the time I was done washing the dishes I could feel grit on my teeth, and the cloth I used to wipe down the countertops was coated with a thin muddy grime. The old Obregon adobe was a solid structure, but evidently the window frames weren't all that tight.

I've noticed before that wind makes people edgy, as if Maria didn't already have ample reason to fret. Tonight she was nearly inconsolable about her goats, and it didn't seem to make much difference what I did or said in my attempts to ease her pain. For one thing, she seemed convinced that the whole thing had been her fault.

"I should have noticed the odd pellets mixed in with the grain."

We were on the couch together, and I took her hand. "It was nearly dark when you went out to the barn this morning. I wouldn't have seen it either."

"I should have called the vet earlier, and then maybe Ferdinand wouldn't have died."

"You said it looked like an ordinary bruise. Don't those sorts of things happen all the time?"

And then the worst one. "Maybe I should just give it up. Maybe it isn't right to hold down a full-time job with the post office and then try to run a dairy."

"Maybe that's what somebody has in mind."

This seemed to bring Maria out of her trance. She wiped away a tear and turned her head toward mine. "What do you mean?"

"What I mean is, that poison didn't get mixed in with your grain by accident. Somebody put it there. Can you think of anybody who might want you to give it up? The dairy, that is?"

She shook her head. "If I had to give up my goats, I'm not sure I'd even want to go on living out here, just staring at those empty corrals."

"That's just my point."

"But who could...?" And then she got it. "You think that man, that Minkston fellow, that he might have done this?"

"He's been after you to go partners on a land development deal, right?"

"Yes, and he's been persistent and obnoxious about it. But I just can't imagine him doing such a thing. Could he really be that *evil*?"

I shared her skepticism, but only up to a point. "We've been digging into the man's history. Turns out he's been involved in some pretty shady deals. It looks like he has no scruples when it comes to making money at other peoples' expense."

"So what do we do now?"

"That's between me and the sheriff. But I do have some questions. First, just to narrow things down, can you think of anybody else who might have done this?"

"Like who?"

"Oh I don't know, somebody on your mail route with a grudge perhaps?"

Maria shook her head. "Nobody comes to mind. What else?"

"Have you ever seen Minkston snooping around the place? Has he ever come to see you?"

"No, he just keeps calling my cell. But you know we're both gone a lot, so he'd have plenty of opportunity. Don't you see that's what I'm saying? If only I'd been around here full time, this wouldn't have happened, whoever it was!"

She started to cry again, but regained her composure after about a minute. "So what else? It's getting late, and I should go check on my animals. And then tomorrow I need to get into town and buy some new grain at the feed store."

That sounded better. At least she was making plans. "Do you still have some of that contaminated grain, or did Dr. Pike take it all?"

"He didn't take it all. Why?"

"Because I'll make the grain run for you tomorrow, and I'll take some of those pellets with me. Maybe the folks at the feed store will remember somebody who recently bought a whole lot of rat poison."

The wind blew all night, and neither of us slept well. But the morning dawned calm, and there were no additional goat casualties overnight. We both set off to work with our hopes and plans more or less intact. I've said before that Maria Obregon is one tough lady.

Chapter 24

Larry and I had agreed to meet at the office first thing on Monday, and as usual the drive in took me past J.L. Minkston's trailer-cum-office. In light of the previous night's wind, I'd half expected to discover that his signs and little flags had all blown away.

It was much worse than that, because the whole damn thing had tipped over. Evidently the man hadn't bothered to use any sort of tie-downs. He was standing beside his sad little trailer, literally scratching his head, as I pulled off the county road. Fortunately, if that is the right word, the trailer had fallen with the door side down. What must have been a god-awful scrambled mess was confined inside rather than scattered over half the county. The other good news was that the trailer looked relatively intact, despite its recent tumble.

Minkston was understandably shaken. "Good thing you came by, deputy. Can you believe this? I know you folks can get some wind down here, but this is ridiculous!"

I was tempted to remind him about the county ordinance regarding tie-downs for mobile homes, and the reason for it. But that seemed like rubbing salt in his wound, so I let it go. "That sure enough was a stiff one yesterday."

"Damned right it was. So, do you think we can get this thing back up on its feet?"

"You mean the two of us?" He must have been kidding. "No way, but let me call Ernie's Auto Service down in Patagonia. I'm pretty sure he has a wrecker that can do the job for you."

"Thanks, that would be great."

Maria's parents, Ernesto and Cecilia Contreras, owned Ernie's Auto Service. She picked up when I called. Ernie was out fixing a flat for somebody, but she said he could be there in less than two hours. I gave Minkston the good news and got back in the Blazer. I suppose I should have felt sorry for the man, but given what I knew about his plans for my favorite part of the world, it just wasn't in me.

~ ~ ~

Larry wondered what had taken me so long. I caught him up on things over coffee, including the situation with Maria's goats. For a while he just sat there in silence, staring out our little window. He did have something to look at, because the Mustang Mountains were stunningly clear beneath a crystal blue sky scrubbed clean by the overnight wind. Eventually he pivoted in his chair and made eye contact.

"Cal, just what in hell is going on around here, anyway? Seems like it's just one mess after another. And what's worse, we don't seem to be getting anywhere with any of it."

I nodded in acknowledgment of this fundamental truth. "The sheriff said exactly that when he was up here yesterday. Made me itchy, but I know he's right."

"He came to see you on a Sunday?"

"There was some sort of pancake breakfast fundraiser in Patagonia, so then he just came on up. He brought along some paperwork on the stuff Joe Ortega had dug up about Ambrose Pendleton and J.L. Minkston."

"Any of it useful?"

"Yep." I filled him in on the details.

Larry put down his coffee cup. "Well, that's some good news I suppose. So, did you ask him about a search warrant?"

"You mean for Pendleton? Yeah, but the sheriff was skeptical."

"Maybe I can help with that. Laura Floyd called last night. Said she expected by today to have a photo of that reptile dealer up in Phoenix we were talking about."

I was impressed with how quickly the Game and Fish agent was acting on my request. "So she'll send it to us by e-mail?"

Larry fidgeted. "Well, actually, she had another idea."

"What's that?"

"Tonight's that two-fers deal at the Santa Rita, right?"

I'd almost forgotten it was Monday, and I really wanted to spend the evening with Maria instead of babysitting the Regulars at Frenchy's place. It did not take a genius to figure out where Larry was headed. "So you're volunteering for two-fers night, with Laura in tow?"

"She said she'd trade you the photos for a steak dinner."

I was about to tweak Larry about his newfound girlfriend, when the telephone rang. It was one of those coincidences that are spooky in hindsight. I picked up in the usual way. "Santa Cruz County Sheriff's Department, Deputy Creede speaking."

It was a woman's voice, and a familiar one. "Hello Cal? This is Hazel Smith up at the university, and I think I have some good news about that Mojave rattlesnake of yours."

Amidst all the recent chaos I'd nearly forgotten about her. "I'm glad it's good news because we could use some around here. Tell me what you found."

"We definitely can rule out those caves in the Mustang Mountains as the source of your snake. Willy has run a bunch of DNA analyses, and they just don't match up."

This actually did not sound like good news, and I told her so.

"Just be patient young man, and let me finish."

Properly chastised, I apologized and asked her to continue.

"You may remember that we have a pretty extensive collection here in my lab. So Willy has been running his tests on Mojaves we've collected from all over southeastern Arizona. Mostly they weren't even close, but we had one big hit. Have you ever heard of French Joe Canyon? It's in the Whetstone Mountains."

I knew the Whetstones were the next range north of the Mustangs, and I'd seen the sign pointing to French Joe Canyon, but I'd never been up there.

"So you think the snake that bit Andy Slawson came from French Joe?"

"Seems likely, but we need to get more specimens."

It sounded like another snake collecting trip was in my future. Not my favorite activity for sure, but at this point any possible break in my stack of unsolved cases would be welcome. I crossed my fingers and asked the critical question. "Are you able to go?"

Thankfully she said yes. "But the rest of my week's getting complicated. Any chance you could make it as early as tomorrow? And tell Maria she'd be welcome. Oh, and by the way, it's gonna be one helluva hike from the end of the road up to the cave, so wear your hiking shoes."

"I'm not sure about Maria, but I'll be there. And I've got an idea. I could bring two horses. Do you ride?"

"Of course I do. That's a great idea."

"Where and when do we meet?"

Dr. Smith gave me directions to the place on state route 90 where a two-track leads west up into the Whetstones, about half way between Huachuca City and Benson. This made it out of my jurisdiction, but I decided there was no need to notify Cochise County. I liked and admired their sheriff, and I knew she and Luis were tight. But officially this was just a university-sponsored collecting trip, and I was sure Hazel carried all the necessary permits. I would just be along as a field assistant, pulling the horse trailer with my old Jeep Cherokee rather than with the county Blazer.

I'd grown up with two good horses on the Pitchfork Ranch, Bluster and Spike, and I used to ride a lot before my parents rented out the place and moved up to Green Valley. I was prepared to let them go at that point, but the renters had kindly agreed to board them with the rest of their stock. Maria and I rode occasionally, sometimes to help with their roundups.

Bluster was a buckskin mare. She was very smart but a bit headstrong. Spike was a black gelding with a white blaze, and more reliable. I decided it would be best if Hazel rode Spike. If Maria wanted to come along I'd have to find another mount, but that didn't seem likely because it was going to be a workday. Even if she decided to take the day off, I was pretty sure she'd use it to stay home and fuss over the goats.

When Larry and I looked back on it, we both agreed these next days were when the dam finally started to break.

Chapter 25

After I got off the phone with Dr. Smith, Larry and I made our plans for the rest of the day. I asked him to check with both the local feed store and hardware store, to find out if anybody had been buying rat poison lately, and I gave him the sample from Maria's barn for comparison. There was no guarantee our perp had purchased the bad stuff locally, or that there would be a paper trail in any case, but it was someplace to start.

"Once that's done, then go drive your routine patrols."

"Got it. And just so I know, where will you be today?"

"Over at the V-9. I think it's time to check on those cameras. At the very least we need to make sure last night's wind didn't rearrange things out there."

It turned out there had been big developments at Sally Benton's marijuana field. For one thing, it was gone. For another, one of the cameras had blown down. It was lying on the ground right at the base of the tree. The good news was it appeared to be intact, and the second camera had remained in place. Hopefully we had some images of whoever had done the harvest.

I inspected the whole area, but found nothing more of interest. The grower or growers were careful people, but somehow they had missed the cameras. There was no cell service on this relatively remote part of Sally Benton's ranch, but the radio worked. I contacted Larry and told him to meet me in the office in an hour. Given my relative naivety when it came to tech stuff, he was the one who would open the cameras and download whatever treasures they might contain.

Once back in town, my first stop was at the post office. I hoped Maria would be there loading up the day's mail for delivery, and I wanted to make sure she was doing all right. But she had already left by the time I got there, and she didn't answer her cell when I called. It would have to wait. Maybe she would come by the office over lunch, if she wasn't at home worrying over the goats.

~ ~ ~

It would be an understatement to say we hit the jackpot that day. Both cameras were intact and filled with images. Larry made fast and efficient work of downloading the files. He shot me a look when I reminded him to be sure everything was backed-up.

Evidently they had come at dawn two days earlier. The light was low but sufficient. The first image Larry pulled up on the screen showed four different figures out in the field. They were in motion and a bit blurry, and it happened that none of them was facing either camera. Still, I thought one looked familiar. Larry kept scrolling, and it was on the sixth image that things came clear. Staring straight at the camera and carrying a bundle of marijuana was mister Border Posse himself, Harlo Henshaw.

I called the sheriff, who naturally was tickled pink. "Well I'll be damned. Couldn't have happened to a nicer guy. How do you want to proceed?"

I'd thought about that. "We could just pick him up of course, along with anybody else we can identify from those images. But I have another idea. Maybe Henshaw's pawnshop is where they keep the stuff. Perhaps they even sell it out of there. Could you send somebody under cover to attempt a purchase? Then we could get them for dealing as well as growing, if that makes a difference."

The sheriff liked the idea. "We probably should get the feds in on it anyway, and they have lots of undercover people who could attempt the buy."

"You mean Drug Enforcement?"

"Sure. I try to stay tight with the D.E.A. folks, and I owe them a couple of favors as it is. I'll get back to you when we have the thing set up."

"Probably should do it soon, before they do whatever they normally do with their stuff. This can't be the first time."

"I'll get right on it, Cal, and I'll keep you in the loop. Once we've made the buy, and assuming it's a hit, then we'll raid the place. I assume you might want to be in on that?"

"Damn straight."

I got off the phone with the sheriff, and filled Larry in on the plan.

"When do you think they might make their move?"

"Sheriff didn't say, but probably in the next couple of days. Once they catch Henshaw attempting a sale, then we'll take down the whole operation. Want to go along?"

"Wouldn't miss it." He paused, and I could tell something else was troubling Larry. "Aren't you going to ask me what I found out this morning while you were doing the big marijuana bust?"

In the midst of all the excitement about the Border Posse and Operation Potwatch, I had temporarily forgotten about the rat poison. "Oh yeah, sure. Sorry about that. What happened?"

"Well, nobody seems to have bought any of the stuff lately at the hardware store, or at least the kid behind the counter didn't think so. We might go back later, when the owner is around."

"And the feed store?"

"More luck there. It turns out Myrtle Schwartz, who runs the place, keeps meticulous records of such things. She's had three customers in there in the past ten days looking for rodent poison. Two local women she knew.

They bought only one small package each, apparently both muttering about mice in their pantries. But the third customer was a man, and he bought several boxes. Apparently it annoyed Myrtle because it pretty much ran her out of the stuff."

"Did she know the man?"

"She thought he looked familiar, but she couldn't give me a name. And there was no paper record because he paid cash."

"I guess maybe we'd better take some photos over there and give her some sort of virtual line-up."

It took Larry and me about an hour to come up with a good array of photographs. One was an image of J.L. Minkston that I managed to find on the internet, and six were total strangers that we thought looked something like him in terms of age and general appearance.

Myrtle Schwartz was an old-time resident of Sonoita, and she knew pretty much everybody in the valley. She seemed anxious to help, but it was a bust. She spent several minutes looking at our lineup and then shook her head. "Nope. None of these is even close."

"Can you describe the man?"

"Well, I'm not much good at this sort of thing, but let's see." She paused and looked again at the images that still lay on the counter in front of her. "Okay, then, here's what I can tell you. First, the man was much younger than any of these."

"How much younger?"

"Oh, I'd say he was in his late twenties or thereabouts."

"And can you tell me anything about his looks?"

"You mean like distinctive features?"

"Sure. Anything like that could help."

Myrtle thought some more, and then her

expression brightened. "Yes, I do remember something. Three things, actually. First, he was tall – well over six feet I'd say, and sort of on the thin side. Second, he had long curly hair. I remember that because I don't like long hair on a man. My Raymond, before he died, he always kept his hair short and neatly-trimmed." She pointed to Larry. "Sort of like you, young man. Now it's not that I have anything against hippies necessarily, but it's just that..."

I judged that Myrtle needed to be interrupted at this point, in order to keep her on track. "And you said there were three things about the man?"

"What? Oh yes, Mr. Creede. The third thing was his beard."

"What sort of a beard?"

"It was – I can't remember what you call it – but it wasn't a big beard. It was short and just around his mouth and chin."

"Like a goatee?"

Her face brightened in recognition. "Yes, that's it. It was a goatee. I'm sure of it."

I thanked Myrtle Schwartz for her help and said we might be back later. She asked what this was all about, but I put her off with the usual mumbo jumbo about it being just a routine investigation.

I queried Larry on our short walk back to the office, which was only a long block from the feed store. "What do you think? Did her description ring any bells?"

He shook his head. "No, not really. You?"

"Could be, but it doesn't make any sense.

"Who?"

"She gave a pretty good description of Ambrose Pendleton."

"You mean the snake guy? What could he possibly care about Maria's goats?"

"Damned if I know. But we'd better get a picture of Pendleton over to her just to make sure."

Chapter 26

The next day started out uneventfully, but it didn't end up that way.

Maria was quiet, even somber, at breakfast. The goats were doing okay, all except for Ferdinand of course. But still I couldn't fault her mood, nor was I surprised when she turned down Hazel Smith's invitation to come along on our trip up into the Whetstones. I knew she was worried that whoever poisoned her grain might come around again, and maybe try something even worse.

"I just can't understand why anybody would do this, Cal."

"Me neither." I decided not to mention our discovery about who had been buying rat poison in Sonoita. It was all too speculative at this point. Still, I couldn't help wondering about Ambrose Pendleton, whose trail seemed to be showing up in all sorts of places these days. Were his environmental views so extreme he might resort to something like this? I mean, sure, Maria's goats were exotic livestock, but their impacts were damned near negligible on the Obregon homestead, to say nothing of the whole valley.

I gave Maria a smooch and loaded my daypack with water and a few snacks. "See you some time this afternoon. It may be a long day by the time we get back down out of the mountains and I get the horses corralled and curried."

Tom Foley was foreman at the Pitchfork Ranch, and I'd called ahead the night before. I still nominally kept a one-room apartment in the bunkhouse, but now that Maria and I had become a permanent item it mainly served as a storage area for my tack. Tom already had the horses saddled when I pulled my Jeep into the ranch yard. We hitched up a two-horse trailer and loaded Spike and Bluster. As usual Bluster nipped at Spike across the partition, just to show him who was in charge.

I drove east out of Sonoita on State Route 82, passing between the Mustang Mountains on the south and the much larger Whetstone range to the north. A sprawling Santa Fe style adobe was tucked into a small arroyo at the southern base of the Whetstones. A mailbox at the end of the gravel drive leading back to the house had 'Minkston' painted on the side in big black letters. I was impressed by the size and obvious quality of the home, in contrast to the man's sorry little office.

It was about 8:30 by the time I came to the crossroads of 82 and 90, at which point I turned left and drove north along the eastern flank of the Whetstones. Hazel Smith was waiting for me about nine miles north of the junction, where a sign and cattle guard marked the beginning of a rough two-track that led up into French Joe Canyon. Hazel was standing outside a new Toyota, which she had parked just inside the cattle guard. I drove in far enough to clear the horse trailer, then stopped and got out.

She waved and smiled. "Morning, Deputy. Looks like we're ready to ride."

"That we are, ma'am." I took off my Stetson and shook her hand. She was dressed in the same field gear she'd worn for our recent trip up into the Mustangs, including one of those big floppy canvas hats with a flap that covered the nape of her neck. The only difference from the other day was that this time her boots were meant for riding instead of hiking.

We agreed it made sense to take just one vehicle into the mountains, which obviously was going to be my

Cherokee. She took her collecting gear out of the Toyota, locked it up, and then loaded herself and her stuff in beside me. "This could be a long day and an interesting one. I suggest it will work better if we keep things informal. Is that all right with you?"

I wasn't sure what she was driving at. "Sure, I suppose so, but what exactly does that mean?"

"That means that I'm Hazel and you're Cal. Okay?"

"You bet."

The road leading up into French Joe Canyon was deeply rutted from the previous summer's rain, and it was narrow in spots where the creosote brush had crowded in. At one time this alluvial outwash probably had been an open grassland like most of the Sonoita Valley. But shrubs had long since replaced most of the grasses, probably because of the combined influence of relatively poor soils and historically abusive livestock grazing.

We drove west into a gusty wind that was strong enough to rock both the Jeep and my horse trailer. Dust billowed up behind us, but it was carried off by the wind almost immediately. In less than a mile we came to a fork in the road, and Hazel pointed left. From there we ran south for about another mile. Then the road turned back west again, following a dry creek bed up into the mountains themselves. We drove until we broke out into a dramatic bowl surrounded on three sides by high cliffs.

Hazel pointed toward a small cluster of trees at the far end of a grassy flat. "That's as far as we should go in your Jeep. From there on it's horseback."

I off-loaded Spike and Bluster while Hazel assembled her gear into a good-sized pack, which we then hung over the horn of Spike's saddle. I offered to help her get on board the old boy, but she declined and then swung herself easily up into the seat. I mounted

187

Bluster and moved in beside her. She pointed north toward a steep south-facing cliff. "I don't know if you can see it from here, but there's a line of caves along there, just above the rubble line. That's where we collected the Mojave that Willy matched to your mailbox critter, so that's our goal for today."

"You mean to collect more specimens?"

"Or at least to get tissue samples. Like I said, the snake we got from there was a very close match to the animal you say bit that boy – Andy, was it? – but we need to get more data." Hazel had pivoted in her saddle so that she was looking right at me. "But I still don't understand just how this is going to help with your case."

"It might not Dr. Smith – I mean Hazel – but what I'm hoping is that we might find some evidence of who's been up there recently."

"Well okay, then. But it still seems like a long shot."

Sometimes a long shot pays off, as we were both about to learn.

It took us better than two hours to reach the base of the cliff. There was no trail and the terrain was both steep and cluttered with rocks and brush. The horses were breathing heavily and covered in sweat by the time we dismounted next to the entrance of a large cave. I tied Spike and Bluster to an isolated scraggly juniper that provided the only shade in the area. Then I gave each of them a drink from a canteen I always carry while riding.

The valley of the San Pedro River spread out below us to the east. The riverbed itself was marked by a ribbon of green and gold cottonwoods about ten miles distant. Fall was here, but the trees still hadn't lost all their leaves. The Dragoon and Mule mountains marked the eastern edge of the valley, but they were partially obscured by a brownish haze, probably from dust being stirred-up by the persistent wind.

Hazel Smith wasted no time. She dug a snake noose out of her pack, along with a miner's headlamp. She replaced her canvas hat with the lamp and headed directly for the cave, calling back over her shoulder as she walked. "There's a flashlight in there for you. Get it out, bring the pack, and follow me."

By the time I got loaded up Hazel already had a good lead, and I expected to see her disappear inside the cave before I even got there. Instead she stopped short just outside the entrance. "Well I'll be damned."

"What is it?"

"Come see for yourself. Looks like somebody's been here before us."

I came lumbering right up of course, but I couldn't see anything obvious. It looked pretty much like an ordinary cave, and I said as much.

Hazel was quick to offer an explanation. "It's the rocks. They've been disturbed. The entrance was filled with them the last time I was here. Somebody's moved them aside, probably to make for easier access." She pointed to some large boulders at either side of the cave opening. "See how fresh those surfaces are? No lichens. No oxidation. They've been turned over, and some are broken in half. And it happened pretty recently."

With that she plunged inside, leaving me to follow as best I could. I carried the flashlight in one hand and all her gear in the other, except for the collecting noose she already had mobilized.

Despite my best efforts to keep up, Dr. Smith had gotten well ahead of me when I heard the all-too-familiar hiss of a rattler coming from somewhere farther back in the cave. That was followed immediately by a "Holy Mary, Jesus, and Joseph!"

That didn't sound very professorial, nor did it sound like somebody I knew from experience was naturally calm around snakes. But who else could have been back there? Then pretty soon here came Hazel with a rattlesnake. It was a big one, but it hung limp and nearly motionless from the end of her noose.

Apparently she felt the need to apologize for her outburst, and in the dim light cast by her lamp I thought I could detect a hint of a blush. "Sorry about that, Cal. But you need to see what's back there."

I wasn't thrilled with the idea. "More snakes, right?"

She shook her head, which caused the light from her headlamp to danced eerily around the pocked walls of the cave. It made the whole thing even creepier. "Should have been, but there aren't any."

"What then?"

"The place is all torn up. You need to go take a look while I deal with this snake."

With that Hazel Smith walked out toward the shaft of sunlight angling into the cave entrance, while I cautiously made my way farther back into the gloom.

It seemed like forever, but I'd probably walked no more than a hundred feet before I came upon an area that showed sign of recent disturbance. Even in the weak beam of my flashlight I could make out a pile of shed snakeskins. The whole area showed signs of disturbance, including scuffmarks on the floor and a dark stain on one wall that could have been blood. There was a dank acrid smell to the place that I thought might have been from the blood. I took a camera out of the pack and photographed the whole scene.

I spent the next half hour exploring the back end of that cave. I cautiously dug down through the pile of snakeskins, looking for any evidence that might lead to the identity of the previous intruder. Nothing turned up. Whoever had been there before us evidently had made a serious effort not to leave any traces. I did manage to scrape some of the possible blood off the wall with my pocketknife and put it in an evidence bag. I had no way of knowing if it was snake blood or human blood, but it was worth a look anyway.

I had pretty much given up hope, and was about to walk back out into the sunlight, when the beam from my flashlight picked up a glint off something half buried in rubble just inside the cave entrance. It was an aluminum soda can. I pulled on a pair of latex gloves and dropped the can into an evidence bag. Then I rejoined Hazel, who was in the process of securing her own evidence, which included a snake that now appeared to be dead, along with a whole bunch of shed skins.

She was quick to offer an explanation. "I decided to put the poor thing out of its misery. It was two-thirds dead already, and it never would have made it through the winter alone like that."

The horses became agitated when we hung our packs and their newly acquired contents over the saddle horns. But they let us mount up without objection, almost as if they were anxious to be rid of the place.

We almost certainly had hit some kind of a jackpot up there in the Whetstones. I was convinced by now that somebody down on the Sonoita Plain had a room full of snakes, and that Andy Slawson's death was not going to be the end of it. But that same somebody had been very careful. Unless the stain on the cave wall turned out to be human blood, or there were prints we could lift off that lone soda can, I could see no path to finding our killer other than finding that room.

Despite our apparent success, a strange feeling washed over me as we made our way slowly back down to the little clearing where I had left the Jeep. I'd had this feeling before – that something familiar was right in front of me, yet somehow just beyond my reach. It had been there on the morning we explored the caves in the Mustangs, and then again this very day up in French Joe Canyon. But why had it come over me in these places? I had never been to either one before. Both places were about rattlesnakes, and God knows this case was about snakes. My whole life seemed to be about snakes anymore. But what were those rattlers trying to tell me? And what sort of a detective sits around waiting for a message from a dead snake?

Chapter 27

It was late afternoon before I got back to the office. Larry had called on the radio as Hazel and I were making our way down out of French Joe Canyon. He wanted to make sure I didn't go straight home after returning Spike and Bluster to the Pitchfork Ranch. Apparently something was up, and it was important that I come by the office.

The lady herpetologist and I parted company back at the highway, she with her snake and a bunch of shed skins and me with the soda can and possible blood evidence from the cave up in the Whetstones. Her parting words were that she would get Willy to work on the new snake tissue right away, with a promise to get back to me by the end of the week.

I was anxious to tell Larry what we'd found in the cave, but he didn't give me the chance. Instead, he pointed to a manila folder on my side of the desk. "Take a look in there and tell me if you recognize him."

There were three photos, none of them first-rate. They all were of the same person, but taken from different angles and distances as he moved along an urban sidewalk. The place did not look familiar, but the man did.

Larry caught my look of recognition. "Laura gave me those last night when we were at dinner. It's the dealer in rare reptiles outside his store in Phoenix. Name's Roscoe Danforth. I take it he looks familiar?"

I nodded. "These photos aren't the best, but I'm virtually certain that's the man I saw last week with Ambrose Pendleton at the Santa Rita Saloon."

"That's good, because Laura says the Game and

Fish brass are anxious to move on both of them."

"You mean for dealing in endangered herps, or for the murder of Dan McCall, or both?"

Larry shrugged. "She didn't say. But maybe with your ID we could get a warrant to search Pendleton's house on the pretext of looking for those rare rattlers. And then who knows what might turn up."

"Right. Let's get Laura in here tomorrow. Then maybe we can set up a conference call with her boss and ours, and work out a plan. In the meantime, let me tell you about today."

I reached down into my daypack to give Larry a show and tell, but once again he waved me off. "There's something else you need to know about."

"What?"

"The sheriff called about two hours ago. There have been some big developments on the marijuana front. He wants you to call him."

I was going to do that anyway, to ask him about a couple of things, but the Border Posse hadn't been one of them. Instead, I wanted to learn the status of the McCall autopsy, to request his help with the evidence from French Joe Canyon, and maybe to set up the conference call with Game and Fish that Larry and I had just discussed.

It seemed like everything was happening all at once. Still, that was way better than nothing happening at all.

The sheriff picked up on the first ring, and he had news. "So they sent an undercover D.E.A. guy out to Henshaw's pawnshop this morning? He was wired up for the transaction, and he came away with something like a kilo of marijuana."

"Wow. So now you're gonna raid the place?"

"Yes, but it's more complicated than that. Better, actually."

This sounded interesting. "Better how?"

The sheriff gave a little chuckle, which was something I'd heard him attempt only rarely. "You know those little protest events the Border Posse boys like to have? Well, it turns out they have one scheduled for tomorrow for your fairgrounds, and we made sure they got their permit."

I wasn't sure why this made things better, but Luis had no trouble clearing that up. "Most likely when we raided Henshaw's pawnshop, the other Posse members would be elsewhere, right? Probably they'd be scattered all over the county, and for sure they'd lay low once they found out about the raid. So we might never know who all was involved in the drug business besides Henshaw himself, unless we could ID some from the camera images you got at the field."

"Yeah, and as I recall most of the pictures were pretty unclear."

"Exactly. So anyway, here's the plan. One team will hit the pawnshop, mostly the D.E.A. folks along with Joe Ortega. At the same time another team, mostly us and including me, will round up everybody at the fairgrounds. That way we'll get all of the Posse at the same time, or at least most of them."

I thought of one obvious catch. "But maybe they're not all involved."

"Sure, but we can sort that out later. We'll have no trouble keeping all of them in custody at least for a day or two on probable cause."

"And get 'em separated before they have a chance to coordinate their stories."

"Exactly. So anyway, Cal, I assume you and Larry will want to be in on this?"

Just for the symmetry of it, we agreed that Larry would join the pawnshop team, while I did the fairgrounds. Luis told me both events would occur at noon sharp, and Larry would need to drive down to a rendezvous point a mile south of the shop about eleven. My assignment was to alert everybody when the Posse was in place. Then I'd walk down the road to the fairgrounds entrance at just the right time and pretend to be interested in their protest.

Before letting the sheriff go, I made sure to come back to my original list of questions. In response I learned that preliminary autopsy results on Dan McCall could not absolutely rule out accidental death. However, the M.E. thought it unlikely because damage to the base of his skull was more severe than ought to have occurred from a simple fall. In addition, the marks on the victim's forearm definitely were from a snakebite, but the amount of swelling made it extremely unlikely the bite figured in his death.

"Did the M.E. say when she might release the body? McCall's widow must be distraught enough as it is."

"Joe made the call, so I'm not sure. Want me to check?"

"That would be great, thanks. Maria and I both know Vicky. She's a great gal and they have two nice young kids. They're Mormon, originally from someplace up in the northern part of the state. Kingman, as I recall. I think Vicky plans to move back up there to be with family."

"That's probably a good thing. Terrible tragedy." The sheriff paused. "So anything else? I've got to get organized for tomorrow."

"Two things, actually, but they shouldn't take long." I proceeded to catch Luis up on my find from the cave above French Joe Canyon, and to request his help doing forensics analysis on the possible evidence. He agreed to pick up the samples after the raid at the fairgrounds the next day.

Next, I told the sheriff about my photo ID of

Roscoe Danforth, the reptile dealer who'd been with Pendleton at the Santa Rita. Did he think with that evidence we might get a search warrant for Pendleton's house? The sheriff replied it seemed likely, and he agreed with the plan Larry and I had made for a conference call with Game and Fish. Maybe we could do it tomorrow after our adventure with the Border Posse had come to what we hoped and expected would be a successful conclusion.

With that the sheriff was gone, and I turned back to Larry, who clearly was struggling to figure out what was up based on half of a phone conversation.

"Maybe you should have put that call on the speaker phone? Am I about to be involved in something?"

I gave him a sheepish nod. "Would if I knew how. Show me some time, will you? But anyway here's the deal."

Once fully updated, and in light of the hour, Larry got ready to leave. He seemed in a hurry, and I expected he had plans. "Be sure to tell Laura we may need to meet here late tomorrow. You know, about a possible search of Pendleton's place?" Larry was a pretty sensible and sensitive guy. I'm sure that's the reason he didn't feign any sort of crap about who it was he might or might not be seeing that night.

Larry had just left, and I was about to follow him, when the door opened and in walked Moss Winslow. He didn't look happy.

"Good afternoon, Moss."

"Nothin' good about it."

I expected he was here to grumble about my lack of progress on the Andy Slawson case, but that wasn't it.

I asked him what was up.

"It's about my grapes. They're all dying."

"I'm really sorry to hear that."

Winslow pulled out Larry's chair and sat. "Yeah, well, I didn't come here for sympathy. I came for justice. Somebody's killed my vines, and it was deliberate."

"How do you know that?"

"You may have noticed they weren't looking good the last time you were out at my place? Well, it only got worse, so I called the university and they sent out some professor who's an expert. He took one look and apparently knew right away. He said I have something called Pierce's disease. Nearly always fatal, and there's not much you can do to stop it once your vineyard is infected. All you can do is tear out your vines and maybe burn 'em before it spreads to other folks' fields."

"I surely am sorry, Moss."

"Yeah, you said that already. But that's not the worst part."

Moss got quiet and fixed me with a level stare. Apparently I was supposed to ask him about the worst part, so I did.

"What's the worst part, Moss?"

"When the professor was out looking at my vines, he found something odd. He said a half dozen of the plants weren't like the others because they were a completely different strain. And they were the sickest of all. In fact, most of them were completely dead. He pulled one up and it hardly had any roots. It was like somebody had just stuck them in the ground."

"So you think somebody planted diseased vines in among your healthy ones?"

"Don't see how it could have happened any other way. And that's where you come in, 'cause that was a crime sure as we're sittin' here."

He had a point. "Any idea who might have done this, Moss?"

"Too many ideas, maybe." Winslow paused, maybe

for effect, while he made a big production out of wiping his bifocals with a red bandana he'd pulled out of his hip pocket. "Could have been my field hands, I suppose, but that doesn't seem likely 'cause I pay 'em good and what would be their motive?"

"So that leaves...?"

"Should be obvious to a bright young man like you."

A couple of possibilities had occurred to me, but it seemed like a good idea to let Moss volunteer his without prejudice. "Maybe, maybe not. Why don't you just spell it out?"

This didn't seem to please him, because he fidgeted a while before responding. "Well, okay then. There's two things. First, there's that snake collector guy I heard about. Ambrose somebody? I understand he had bad things to say about my vineyard at some meeting the other night. He even showed pictures of my place and then talked about how growing grapes was bad for the ecosystem, whatever the hell that means."

"How did you hear about that?"

"Can't remember, but why does that matter?" Moss snapped his fingers. "And say, I hadn't thought about this before, but if he keeps a bunch of snakes around his house, you don't suppose he's the one put that Mojave in my mailbox, do you? And then maybe when that didn't work because it got Andy Slawson and not me, then he decided to kill my grapes instead?"

"We've got no evidence for any of that."

"Yeah? Well maybe you should look a little harder."

"We're looking at everything we can, Moss. But what was your other idea?"

"My other idea is J.L. Minkston." Moss stopped to clear his throat, and I could tell the man was close to choking up. "And you know why? 'Cause Minkston's been after me to ditch the whole vineyard idea so he can use all my land and all my water for his damned development."

"Can he do that, Moss? I mean, without your permission?"

"Yeah, I think so. Apparently it's in our contract."

"Apparently?"

With that Winslow got sheepish instead of just mad. "Yeah, I sort of forgot to read all the fine print. And guess who just pointed out all the parts I'd skipped over the first time?"

"So Minkston's been out to your place recently?"

"Yep, two days ago. You shoulda seen the man gloat. He practically had dollar signs in his eyes. So anyway, what are you going to do about it?"

That was a good question. "I'll talk to both Ambrose Pendleton and J.L. Minkston, of course. But they'll most likely deny everything."

Moss Winslow flared again. "Sure, and then what? Then you'll just sit here doing nothing?"

"We're following some leads, Moss. There has been some progress."

"Progress how?"

It was a close call whether to bring the man up to speed on our search for the source of the snake. Something told me to hold back. "I'm not at liberty to go into details just yet. Not until we have more firm evidence. You'll just have to accept my word that we are moving forward with the case. And I will look into the business about your grapes, too."

"So this 'moving forward' of yours better get results pretty soon, or maybe there's another way to deal with things."

I did not like the sound of this. "What other way is that?"

"I've got connections, you know."

"Connections?"

He pointed skyward, just like before. "With them. They can make things happen in ways you wouldn't even understand."

Uh oh.

Chapter 28

The Border Posse roundup didn't go exactly as planned. Some parts worked better than others, and we had one close call.

Larry headed off about mid-morning for his rendezvous with the Nogales team preparing to raid Henshaw's pawnshop. I was the lynchpin for the whole operation, because it was my job to notify both Larry and the sheriff once the Posse boys were set up for their demonstration in Sonoita. Then I would walk over on the pretext of checking for their permit. That would be the signal for the sheriff and his team to block off Highway 83 both north and south of the fairgrounds entrance, just in case any of the demonstrators tried something stupid.

Harlo and his little group arrived right on schedule, about 11:30, and started setting up their array of flags and nasty signs. I was about to get on the radio and put everything in motion, when who should walk into the office but Aunt Grace. She was about the last person I wanted to give the bum's rush, but her timing couldn't have been worse.

She was pleasant as always. "Good morning, Cal. There are a couple of things I'd like to discuss, if you've got a minute."

"Only just, Aunt Grace. And I'm sorry about that, because I wanted to talk to you as well. Unfortunately, there's something I've gotta do that can't wait."

"Well, then, I'll come back another time."

"No, it's all right. Come in and sit. But you said a minute, and I'll be holding you to it."

She took Larry's chair on the opposite side of our

desk, and got right down to business. "It's about that fern we collected off Dan McCall's body over in Gardner Canyon."

"Yes?"

"Well, I had real trouble figuring out the species because it just didn't fit the descriptions in any of my books. And so yesterday I took it up to the herbarium at the university. I think there's good news."

I could always use good news. "And?"

"And it looks like we collected a very rare species. In fact, based on all their records, which are substantial, it hasn't been seen in the Santa Ritas or anywhere else in Arizona for over a century."

I got it. "And so if we can find that fern associated with the possible killer or his property..."

"Exactly. So I just thought you'd like to know. Anyway I'm headed over to Patrice's place now. He's working in the kitchen today, and I agreed to help out. It's some sort of a new recipe."

Aunt Grace stood up as if to leave, but I stopped her. Time was of the essence on this particular morning. But there was one more question I just had to ask, and it had nothing to do with ferns. I rose from my own chair, walked over and looked out the door. The Border Posse was still there, apparently just putting the finishing touches on their setup. I judged we had maybe five minutes before a crowd started to assemble. And we definitely wanted to wrap this thing up before any innocent bystanders came around.

"Before you go, Aunt Grace, I wanted to ask you about something. It's a bit personal, if you don't mind."

"I suppose not, Cal. What is it?"

"Is it true that you and Frenchy Vullmers, uh, I mean that you and Patrice are going into the grape business?"

She looked relieved. "Why yes, as a matter of fact

we are. He thinks my place is just right for some particular varietals that he knows about, and..."

"What I mean is, now that Andy is gone, I just wondered if..."

Aunt Grace put up her hand and gave me a quick nod that said she understood. It seemed to be a day for interruptions. "You said you were in a hurry, so I'll make this short. I'll admit that right after Andy died I had my doubts, because I'd always thought the vineyard would be for him. But Patrice persuaded me that we should go ahead, and that's just what we're going to do."

There wasn't time to get into J.L. Minkston and whether he had been pressuring her to sell out. That could wait. It was enough just to know she wasn't going anywhere.

As soon as Aunt Grace left I got on the radio to Larry and to the sheriff, told them that the Border Posse was in place, and the roundup and pawnshop raid should commence. Then I locked up the office and started my little stroll down toward the fairgrounds.

I could tell right away that something was wrong. Henshaw saw me coming, of course. I had expected we would go through some sort of confrontation about their permits for the assembly, and maybe about the sidearms most of them were carrying. Instead, Harlo started yelling things to other members of the group, and then pointing both up and down the road. The sheriff and his team had driven unmarked vehicles, but evidently Henshaw had spotted something. Either that or there had been a lookout down at the pawnshop. Whatever it was, things started changing rapidly.

The group began throwing things back into their van, and then they all jumped in and headed south with Harlo at the wheel. Before they had gotten more than 100 yards, a sheriff's department cruiser pulled out from behind a building and blocked both lanes of 83. Henshaw saw it right away and did a one-eighty that ended up sliding his vehicle broadside into a shallow roadside ditch. Then he gunned it, spraying gravel as he attempted to get back onto the pavement. By this time the sheriff had blocked things off to the north, and the Border Posse boys realized they were trapped.

Five of us ran toward the spot where Harlo had stopped his vehicle, which ironically happened to be right next to my office. We all had our weapons drawn, and the sheriff yelled for everybody in the van to get out and get on the ground.

Only two of the six complied. The other four scattered on foot, each in a different direction. We found out later these four were the ones directly involved in the marijuana project. They were lucky, because the sheriff had made an advance decision not to use deadly force unless provoked. Instead, following his orders, we all fired into the air over the heads of the fleeing Posse members. This brought all of them to a halt except one. Harlo Henshaw kept running. Probably by accident he found an unlocked door on the first building he came to, and ducked inside. It was the kitchen entrance to the Santa Rita Saloon, right where I suspected Frenchy and Aunt Grace might be practicing a new recipe.

I started running and yelled back to the sheriff at the same time. "Get the front door, Luis! I'll take the back. Frenchy Vullmers and Grace Slawson are in there, and Harlo's got a gun!"

It took me less than ten seconds to cover the distance between my office and the door through which Henshaw had disappeared. It was a risky situation. The other deputies were busy rounding up the remaining Posse members. I was alone, standing in front of a door with no windows, not having any idea what might be happening on the other side. I backed off a couple of paces but kept my sidearm at the ready.

"Henshaw, this is Cal Creede! You're surrounded! Throw your weapon out first, then come outside and get on the ground!"

There was nothing but silence.

"Listen Henshaw, nobody needs to get hurt here. You're in enough trouble already. Don't make things worse. Let your hostages go, and then come on out!"

It was the sheriff who broke the silence. "Cal, can you hear me? I'm at the front door, but it's locked and really heavy. I don't think I can break through."

"I hear you. Just cover the exit."

It might have been worthwhile giving Henshaw one more opportunity to surrender on his own, and to wait for backup, but I never got the chance. Instead, I heard the muffled but unmistakable sound of a gunshot.

"I'm going in, Luis!"

The sheriff likely warned me off, but I was too busy to hear him. For sure it would have been prudent to wait, and I might have done so if Frenchy had been the only one in there with Harlo. But because of Aunt Grace the decision was an easy one. I rushed the door, swung it open, and then pivoted inside with my pistol held high.

I needn't have worried. Harlo Henshaw lay on the floor, face down, and it was obvious he wasn't going anywhere. Frenchy Vullmers – all 200-plus pounds of him – was sitting on the man's back. Aunt Grace was there too, holding a large cast-iron frying pan in her right hand. Based on the glazed look in Henshaw's eye, she must have just used it.

Frenchy offered a simple explanation, but it was sufficient. "I believe he mistook me for a simple inn-keeper. Perhaps he did not know of my previous life."

"And the gun?"

He pointed back over his shoulder. "You will find it in that corner by the freezer. That is where it stopped sliding." Frenchy shook his head and sighed. "It is so easy, you know, disarming a man who knows nothing about weapons."

By the time I got Henshaw cuffed and back outside, everybody else was in custody. They all looked rueful except for Harlo, who appeared dazed and surly.

The sheriff reported that all had gone well in the raid on Henshaw's pawnshop. They'd made a big bust and nobody was home. "So, no surprises down there. Up here it wasn't quite so simple. But thanks to your quick action, it all worked out. So thanks."

"Turns out it was no big deal, thanks to Frenchy."

"Yeah, but you didn't know that going in, did you? So next time wait for backup, okay?"

I decided to change the subject. "Did Larry and Joe Ortega and the D.E.A. team find anything else interesting at Henshaw's place?"

The sheriff frowned. "Like what?"

"Like snakes."

"Why would he ... oh, I get it. You're thinking maybe the Border Posse was behind the Andy Slawson killing? That seems like a bit of a stretch. But anyway, nobody said anything about snakes, and it seems like they would have."

"Okay. I'll check with Larry when he gets back, just in case."

It felt great to think about the Border Posse riding off into the sunset. It was just wishful thinking that I might have gotten anything else off my to-do list at the same time.

~ ~ ~

The sheriff had called a paddy wagon to haul the Posse boys off to Nogales, which left him free to visit. He accepted my offer of a late cup of coffee, and we got down to business. I first raised the idea of a conference call with Game and Fish up in Tucson, once we had Larry and

Laura Floyd in the office.

Luis responded by pulling an envelope out of his shirt pocket. "Won't be necessary. Here's your search warrant for the Pendleton property. Oh, and we're going to subpoena his bank records too, but I've asked Ortega to handle that part."

"But don't you think we should talk to Game and Fish first?"

He grinned and shook his head. "Already taken care of. Jason Clark, he's head of their Tucson office, we go way back. They're fine with it as long as you take Laura along to represent the department."

I must say, the man did have connections.

He stopped to take a drink of his coffee, and made a face. "Old and cold, but never mind. What else? I need to get back to headquarters."

"Just two things then, I suppose." I handed the sheriff two plastic evidence bags, one with the soda can and one with the blood or whatever it was from the cave up in the Whetstones. "That's all we got except one snake and a bunch of skins. Maybe you can get some DNA or prints off these."

"DNA can take time, as you know. But I'll push Joe Ortega to make this top priority, and we'll see. What else?"

"Can you get me a photo of Ambrose Pendleton? Maybe off his driver's license?"

"Sure, but why? You know what the man looks like."

I explained about the woman at the feed store who may have identified Pendleton as someone who recently bought a large quantity of rat poison.

The sheriff said no problem about the photo, that he'd have somebody in the office send me one as an email attachment. "But what about Maria? How's she taking it?"

"Better, I think. It really got her down for a while."

Luis smiled. "She sure does love those goats, doesn't she? And you too I think."

Then he was gone.

Chapter 29

Executing a search warrant can be pretty routine, even boring, but not when you're half expecting a rattlesnake to jump out from every darkened corner. Since that might have been the case at Ambrose Pendleton's place, we were all on our toes.

Hazel Smith had a class that morning, and she was a critical part of the search team, so we didn't get out there until early afternoon. The team was Larry, Hazel, me, and Laura Floyd from Game and Fish.

Pendleton lived in a nondescript little stucco place with a detached garage, on a five acre lot about two miles southeast of Sonoita. The house needed paint and maybe a new roof. Apparently someone had done some serious landscaping in the past, because there was an assortment of native desert plants still in evidence, including stag horn cholla and ocotillo. But by now most of the plants were half-dead. It seemed odd, given the man's self-proclaimed interest in the environment.

He came to the door as soon as I knocked, like he must have been watching. I identified myself just for the sake of formality, even though we both knew each other. I showed him the warrant. He didn't look pleased, but neither did he look especially worried. It was not the best sign.

Then he spotted Laura's uniform and put on a surprised look. "What is she doing here?"

I wasn't buying it and apparently neither was Laura. "We are here, sir, to search for possible contraband wildlife. Now please step aside and let us do our work. The sooner we can get started, the sooner we'll be out of your way."

I liked her style, and I could see that Larry did too. He instructed Ambrose Pendleton to remain seated in his living room while we conducted the search.

It was a simple one-story home, with two bedrooms, a single bath, and no basement. Based on the fixtures and appliances I guessed the house had been built sometime in the seventies, making it one of the older homes in this particular development. The inside matched the outside in terms of deferred maintenance. The linoleum floor in the kitchen was stained and cracked. The rest of the house was carpeted in a dingy olive shag that had worn down to almost nothing in heavy traffic areas. I recalled what Joe Ortega had said about the apparent state of the man's finances, and it all seemed to fit.

But we weren't here for an appraisal, and it was time to get down to business. A quick walk-through suggested that most of the action was likely to be in the spare bedroom, where each of the four walls was lined floor-to-ceiling with shelving. It was the cheap kind with metal wall brackets you could get at any of the big box stores in Sierra Vista or Tucson. What made these shelves unusual were their contents, which consisted almost entirely of glass and wire screen terraria. The reptilian inhabitants were numerous and varied, including some that greeted us with an all-too-familiar assortment of hisses and rattles.

After passing out latex gloves and evidence bags, I suggested that Hazel and Laura start in the reptile room, while Larry took the rest of the house and I went out to the garage. I was especially anxious to get a look at the man's vehicle, and Luis had made sure that our search warrant specified not only the house but everything else on the property. We agreed to meet back up in about an hour to share our discoveries, and to do it outside at our vehicles in order to prevent the suspect from eavesdropping.

Pendleton's garage was full of the usual assortment of tools and yard implements, although as far as I could see he hadn't been using them very often. A dark green Toyota 4-Runner was parked inside. It was equally cluttered, and the hood was cold to the touch.

I started in the back of the vehicle, where much of the space was taken up with more cages. I took each of these out in turn and inspected it for any sort of contents, but they all were empty. Also in back was a collecting noose, much like the one used by Hazel Smith.

A cardboard box in the back seat was filled to overflowing with little canvas bags that could be closed by pulling a drawstring. It took me a while to sort through them all, but like the cages they all were empty. I didn't know exactly what they were, so I took one along to show Hazel, in case they had something to do with collecting snakes.

The front seats of Ambrose Pendleton's truck were clean and empty, but the floorboards were not. An assortment of everyday objects like empty soda cans, gum wrappers, and old newspapers cluttered up the passenger side. I picked through the whole mess, item by item, but was disappointed to find nothing with any obvious connection to our case.

The driver's side floorboard was another matter. There was the usual accumulation of dirt and gravel that inevitably finds its way into any well-used field vehicle. I bent down for a closer look, using my flashlight, and spotted something more green than brown, half-buried in the litter. It took about two minutes to tease the whole thing apart and transfer the object into an evidence bag. It looked familiar, some kind of a plant, and I was pretty sure Aunt Grace already had several just like it.

I was in such a hurry to share my find with the rest of the team that I almost missed something sitting on

Ambrose Pendleton's messy workbench. It was a red and yellow plastic tub, about six inches in diameter. There were warnings printed on the top and sides that said things like 'danger,' and 'poison,' and there was a black silhouette of a rodent with a red 'X' drawn through it. I put the tub in an evidence bag and walked outside, where everybody else was waiting by our vehicles.

Hazel and Laura had been in the reptile room, and it seemed logical to start with them. Laura deferred to the herpetologist lady.

Hazel didn't seem to be carrying anything as big as a snake, but she did have some evidence bags. "Well, there's good news and bad news. First, the man had eight rattlers of various species, but none of the rare kind. And his three Mojaves didn't look right. I got tissue samples and photographs, just in case. I'll have Willy check it out, but at this point I'd bet against any of them being from the Whetstones."

That sounded like all bad news, but I'd learned the hard way not to interrupt.

"So you're wondering about the good news?" She held up an evidence bag that had a bunch of snakeskins inside. "I found these in an empty terrarium. Based on their small size, I'd guess they're from either twin-spotted or ridge-nosed rattlesnakes. Of course they could be young of some other species, but it will be easy to figure that out once I'm back in the lab. All we have to do is compare the scale patterns on these skins with specimens in my collection."

It was Laura who answered my question before I had time to ask it. "And the twin-spotted and ridge-nosed are two of the three rare species he's got no business collecting. So it looks like we've got him for trafficking at least, if not for what happened to Dan."

Now it was my turn for show-and-tell. "I may be able to help out there." I held up the evidence bag with the green and brown plant tissue inside. "If Aunt Grace can match this with the specimens she collected off Dan's jeans and boots, we may have Pendleton for that as well."

Laura Floyd frowned. "But why? I mean it's just an ordinary plant, right? Couldn't Pendleton have picked it up anywhere?"

I shook my head. "Apparently not, if Grace has it right about just how rare this particular plant is in our part of the world. And I wouldn't want to bet against her."

Finally, it was Larry's turn. He handed me an ordinary three-ring binder. "I found it in the bedroom, in a drawer. You should open it up, but keep your gloves on."

I walked over to the hood of the Blazer, laid down the binder, and began flipping through the pages. It was a photograph album, and the contents were all-too familiar. First there were photos of Moss Winslow's vineyard, then a couple of overgrazed horse pastures, and then one of J.L. Minkston's trailer all bedecked out with flags and pennants. But it was the last three pages of the album that caught my eye. They were filled with photos of Maria's place, including the house, the dairy barn, and her corrals.

I handed the album back to Larry. "Bag this. I don't think it has anything to do with Dan or the rare snakes, but it may turn out to be a roadmap to his environmental targets." I looked around at the whole group. "All right people, anything else? What about weapons?"

I was thinking about Dan McCall's missing sidearm, but nobody said anything. "Okay then, let's pack it up. I'll go tell Mr. Pendleton he can have his house back."

Chapter 30

After Hazel Smith had left for Tucson, Larry and Laura and I did a postmortem back in the office. Laura wanted to do it over a late cup of coffee. Not such a great idea if you're inclined toward insomnia like I am. But it had been one of those days, so we all indulged.

Once we all had our coffee, I spread the evidence we had just collected out on the desk, and added one additional item. While we were gone the sheriff had e-mailed me a photocopy of Ambrose Pendleton's Arizona driver's license. I handed it to Larry, along with the rat poison I'd found in the man's garage.

"Take these over to the feed store, and find out if Myrtle Schwartz recognizes either of them."

"Right now?"

"Yep, 'cause we need to get all this evidence down to headquarters first thing tomorrow, at the latest."

"Got it."

With Larry gone, I now had a chance to speak with Laura alone, which had been part of the plan. "You did well out there today, so thanks for your help."

She demurred. "I didn't really do much except follow Hazel Smith around. But it was a good chance to get a look at Mr. Pendleton's collection." She shook her head in dismay. "Awful. Just awful."

"In what sense?"

"I've heard about people whose idea of getting close to nature is to own it. But this was my first chance to actually see such a thing. I think it's pretty sick, really. All those lizards and snakes, even a couple of box turtles, trapped inside their little cages."

"But unless it's illegal to possess any of them..."

"Oh sure, I understand Mr. Creede. But just because you *can* do something, that doesn't mean you *should.*"

I was beginning to like Laura Floyd. "Please call me Cal. We should be on a first-name basis now that Game and Fish has assigned you to this part of Arizona. You're going to find we think alike when it comes to the natural world. Oh, and that includes my friend Maria Obregon. And Larry too, of course, but you may already know that."

It was a bit ham-handed, but I couldn't think of any other way to get at the subject.

Laura either blushed or flared, but I couldn't tell which. "If you want to know about Larry and me, why don't you just ask? I think he told you that we go back a ways, but then it ended. Now maybe it's starting up again. I like him. I like him a lot. Is there anything else you need to know?"

Zingo.

"I like him too, Laura. I know that was pushy, but we're partners and partners watch out for each other."

Fortunately at that point Larry came back in the office, bringing the whole clumsy episode to a merciful end.

"Myrtle says yes. That's the kind of rat poison she sells, and Pendleton definitely bought some about ten days ago. So do you think he was the one that tried to hurt Maria's goats?"

"Hard to say, but it's possible. Now you kids get out of here. I gotta call the sheriff. I know he's expecting a report on the results of our search."

It was late afternoon and nearly quitting time, but Luis picked up after three rings. He was his usual gruff self, but I could tell he was interested so I filled him in.

"You need to get that stuff down here right away, Cal. But Joe Ortega said McCall's weapon was missing at the crime scene. No luck on that in your search?"

"Unfortunately, no. We looked everywhere. So I guess maybe if Pendleton took it, he must have ditched it somewhere."

"Yeah, maybe. Oh, and there have been developments on our end as well."

"What developments?"

"First, those blood stains you found in that cave over in the Whetstones? They were reptilian and not human, so that's not going to be any help. Second, we got some good prints off the soda can you collected from up there, but they don't match anything from our databases. Third, we've gotten into Pendleton's bank accounts, but it's nothing unusual or suspicious, I'm afraid. Just a few hundred dollars in checking, and one small savings account that doesn't pay diddly. So it looks like there's no current largess from Daddy."

Well, that certainly was a big bunch of bad news. "And if he's collecting rare snakes for a living, it must be a cash business. What else?"

"The forensics people have finished with Dan McCall's Game and Fish truck. It was clean, except for some prints on the hood that aren't his. We're trying to run those down, but so far no luck with them either."

"I might be able to help you on that." I told him about the photo album, which had a nice hard plastic cover, and which doubtless had been in Pendleton's hands.

"Okay, good. Can you come down in the morning, and bring all the evidence?"

"Will do."

It had turned cold outside by the time I locked up the office and got in the Blazer. The sun had dropped below the Santa Ritas, and a steady wind was blowing out of the northwest. There was a suspicious looking cloudbank up toward Tucson, maybe the portent of rain, though I'd heard no such report. I was anxious to see Maria, but there was one more stop to make first.

Aunt Grace was home and I'd told her why I was coming. We sat at her kitchen table under a good light. She took the evidence bag and examined it closely, using a small magnifying lens that hung on a silver chain around her neck.

"This looks right, Cal. I think we've got a match."

"And there's no chance the plant I found in Pendleton's truck could have come from someplace else?"

"I wouldn't say no chance, but it seems unlikely. As I already told you, according to the herbarium records at the University of Arizona this fern hasn't been seen anywhere in the state for the last hundred years. That's how far back their fern collections go. I'll check with Arizona State and UC Berkeley and Missouri Botanical Garden herbaria and a couple other places. But I doubt anything will turn up."

I'd brought along some extra evidence bags, labels, and chain-of-custody forms, just in case. We split the sample from Pendleton's truck in two, labeling everything and co-signing all the appropriate forms. She would keep half for a more detailed comparison with the fern fronds she'd already collected over in Gardner Canyon.

There was going to be big news for the sheriff tomorrow.

~ ~ ~

Maria had finished milking the goats and was fussing around about dinner when I walked in. I could tell she was fidgety about where I'd been, like she always was when things ran late. It was dark by now, and even colder, so there was no chance for our beer on the patio. Those days were getting scarce anyway now that fall had come. Instead, we sat together on a couch in the living room. She'd started a little fire in the wood stove, and it felt good.

I filled her in on my day and asked about hers.

"Oh, nothing unusual. The route is taking longer than it used to because I need to check on the goats at least twice during the day."

"Are some of your customers complaining about it?"

"Not yet. But it doesn't matter because I've cleared it with the postmaster, and she says it's okay as long as I get done by five."

"Are you still worried about them? The goats, I mean? How are they doing?"

"Of course I'm still worried. They're doing fine, but I don't think I'll be able to calm down until you catch whoever did this. Speaking of which, have you made any progress?"

I said "maybe," and then kicked myself.

"Maybe?"

"We're checking into who's been buying rat poison in Sonoita."

"And so you found somebody, but you're not going to tell me, right?"

"Probably shouldn't at this point. Just because we found a buyer doesn't mean he's the one that did it." Then I tried to put her on the spot instead of me. "You wouldn't want me to make a false accusation would you?"

It didn't work. I could tell right away because she got up and went out into the kitchen without saying anything. Apparently it was my day to get jammed-up with women, first Laura Floyd and now Maria.

I let things simmer a while and then went over to the refrigerator on the pretext of getting each of us another beer. She had her back to me, standing at the stove and stirring a pot of beans way too fast.

"Sorry, Maria. I know this goat business is getting you down, and I promise we're doing everything we can. Just because I can't talk about it doesn't mean I don't care."

She still didn't say anything, but I thought the stiffness in her shoulders relaxed a little and I took that as a hopeful sign. I decided to change the subject.

"You know Laura Floyd, she's Dan McCall's replacement with Game and Fish? She helped out today with the search on Pendleton's place. I really like her, and so does Larry by the way."

This seemed to get her attention because she turned back from the stove with a question. "You mean like, as in *like*?"

"Apparently. They seem to be spending most of their spare time together. Not that any of us has all that much of it these days."

Maria nodded. "Well, that's good. Larry's a nice guy, and he deserves to be happy."

I laughed. "Now you're sounding like somebody's aunt. They're not that much younger than we are."

"Somebody's aunt, huh? We'll see about that after dinner."

I could tell right away I was off the hook.

Chapter 31

There had been a light rain overnight, and the roads were still wet as I made my way across the valley to the office the next morning. Low clouds hung over the Santa Ritas and the Huachucas, like they often do after a storm has passed by. Otherwise the sky was clear and the air had a snap to it that I usually associate with the heart of fall. The grasses apparently had noticed this as well, because they were fully cured of any remaining summer green. The rolling hills and plains had taken on their winter mosaic of browns and yellows mixed with scattered patches of red ochre and gray. I knew it would stay that way until the next monsoon, which was at least eight months away.

I was just outside Sonoita when my cell rang.

"Hello, Cal? Say, this is Hazel Smith. Thought I'd bring you up to speed on things."

Sure enough, she was ready with one of her good news/bad news reports. But at least this time she started with the good news. "You know those little snake skins we collected from Pendleton's place? I've positively identified both of them as coming from ridge-nosed rattlesnakes. The scale patterns are a perfect fit. So we've definitely got the guy for illegal possession. Be sure to tell Laura and maybe the other folks at Game and Fish."

"Will do. And thanks, that's great."

I was almost scared to ask, but Hazel saved me the trouble. "Now as to those Mojaves that Mr. Pendleton had in his house. I can't be sure until Willy does his DNA thing, and that's going to take several more days. But I've compared them in terms of general appearance with the one that bit Andy Slawson? And I'm sorry to say they're not even close.

"Oh, and one final bit of news, but I'm not sure if it's good or bad. I had Willy do a rush job on the DNA from that sick snake we took from the Whetstones a couple of days ago."

"Yes?"

"It *is* a tight match to the one that you found in the mailbox. So this confirms the likely origin of your killer snake."

"And so now all I have to do is figure out who broke into that cave and took all her brothers and sisters?"

"Yep."

I thanked Hazel again for the help, and ended our call with a request that we stay in touch.

This was indeed bad news. It looked like we could bust Ambrose Pendleton for trafficking in illegal wildlife, but that was a far cry from nailing him for murder. It probably wouldn't even get him off the street, given the light sentences most judges handed down for that sort of thing.

If we were going tie Ambrose Pendleton to a killing, it would be for Dan McCall and not Andy Slawson, and we were going to have to do it with evidence other than snakes. The strongest evidence we could have gotten on Pendleton would have been finding Dan McCall's weapon somewhere on his property. Absent that, I could think of only two other possibilities. The first and most promising was the little fern that Aunt Grace had just identified. If it was as rare as she claimed, and I had no reason to doubt her, then finding it on the body and also inside Pendleton's truck would be powerful evidence. The other possibility had to do with fingerprints. The sheriff had said there were prints on the hood of McCall's truck that were not the victim's. Since Pendleton had a record, his prints should be on file somewhere. If we could match them with prints from the truck, that would be another way of tying the man to the crime scene.

I parked the Blazer in its usual spot and walked into the office. Larry was at the sink, filling his favorite mug with black coffee. It smelled good, and I helped myself to a cup before getting organized for the rest of the day.

"Hazel Smith just called with her usual mix of good news and bad news." I summarized her report for Larry.

Apparently he was not discouraged. "Just because the snake in Winslow's mailbox doesn't match the ones we found yesterday in Pendleton's house, that doesn't mean he didn't do it. He could have gotten that snake from someplace else."

"Sure, but it means we have no evidence."

"Then what about nailing the guy for the murder of Dan McCall?"

"We might be doing better there." I explained about the fern and the possible fingerprints connecting Pendleton to the McCall crime scene.

"Do you think that will be enough?"

"Better be, because at this point I don't know what else we've got."

"You think the guy's guilty, right?"

"Damn straight. All we've got to do now is present a convincing case, and that's gotta happen at least three times."

"What do you mean?"

I held up my right hand and started counting fingers. "First the sheriff , then the county attorney, and then a jury, assuming it gets that far."

Larry walked back to the sink, rinsed out his mug, and hung it back up before turning back to me. "Well hell, then, let's get started."

There were some things I wanted to do in the valley, so I asked Larry if he would be willing to deliver the evidence down to headquarters by himself. He readily agreed, but with an "oh, by the way" that involved taking Laura Floyd to lunch afterwards at a little shrimp place across the border we both knew about. They'd earned a break, so that was fine with me. I did suggest that he take Laura in to meet the sheriff. He thought that was a good idea, as did Luis when I called to set it up. They'd take all the evidence to the Property Department and sign it in. Then they'd walk upstairs to the sheriff's personal office and fill him in on results from the search of Pendleton's place. Joe Ortega would be there if he was available.

I helped Larry collect up all the evidence and shooed him out of the office. Then I called the sheriff back because I wanted to make sure we were on the same page about the logical next steps in the Pendleton investigation. My call went right through, but something in his voice told me he was not alone and that my call had been an interruption.

"Yes, Cal, what is it?"

"Just to clarify, Luis. Aunt Grace is positive the fern she collected at the McCall crime scene is the same one we found in Pendleton's truck. And Dr. Smith is sure the snakeskins we found in his house are from one of those endangered rattlesnakes. So as I see it there's nothing Joe or his forensics people need to do about either of these issues. I'll let you know if Dr. Smith comes up with anything more about the Mojaves, but like I said that doesn't look good. Where I need your help is with the fingerprints."

The sheriff suggested maybe I'd forgotten a couple of details. "So if I'm hearing you right on the snake evidence, we still don't have spit in the Andy Slawson case, correct?"

"No, but if we can make Pendleton for the McCall murder then maybe..."

"Then maybe what? He'll confess to both killings? I'm not holding my breath. And what about Maria and her poisoned goats? No leads there either, right?"

I guess it was a rhetorical question, because Luis didn't wait for an answer before he hung up. Something odd must have happened, because this wasn't like him. Or maybe it was, ever since my disastrous interview with Percy Butterfield. I could imagine Joe Ortega hovering in the background with a smug look on his face. He must have been thrilled to see the Boy Detective flame out.

~ ~ ~

Luis Mendoza had barely finished getting rid of me when the phone rang. It was Vicky McCall. She asked if we could meet, and I could tell from her tone that it was something important. I suggested her place, and she agreed. "Things are a bit of a mess around here, because we're packing. I hope you don't mind." I said I didn't mind at all, and that I'd be right out.

The McCall home was nestled in the eastern foothills of the Santa Rita Range, and the drive over took me through an exceptionally fine oak savannah. Maria and I had traveled the same road on the day Dan died, but I'd failed to appreciate the surrounding landscape because of the fading evening light. As much as I'm drawn to treeless plains, there is something magical about a grassland with scattered trees whose wide crowns do not touch, which is the formal definition of a savannah. Somebody once told me their appeal derives from our evolutionary ties to the savannas of East Africa.

There was only one vehicle in the McCall yard, a relatively new Subaru Outback. The back end was filled with boxes, but they appeared to be empty, which suggested that the moving process was still in its early stages. I got out of the Blazer, walked three steps up onto the front porch, and knocked. From somewhere inside a woman's voice said "just a second," but it was a full two minutes before Vicky opened the door. She looked better than the other night, but still pretty haggard. She also was flushed and a little sweaty. "Sorry about my appearance, Cal. I was moving things around in the kitchen, and those dishes are heavy. Please come in."

There were cardboard boxes scattered everywhere, most of them about half full. Vicky pointed to a couch that was the only uncluttered piece of furniture left in the living room. "The boys are away at school, so we're alone. Can I get you something to drink?"

I knew Mormons had restrictions about things with caffeine or alcohol, so I said anything would be fine. Vicky disappeared into the kitchen and came back in less than a minute with two cups of hot cider and a plate of cookies. She set them on a low table in front of the couch and sat down beside me.

Vicky hadn't said what it was she wanted to see me about, so I waited for her to take the lead.

"We're going back home to Kingman, Cal. And we're taking Dan's ashes with us. My parents are driving down tomorrow to help finish the packing. The mover comes the day after that."

"So there won't be a service here?"

"There was a small one at the church down in Nogales, but only for members of the local congregation. I just wasn't up to anything more. We'll do a big formal service at the church up north, and he'll be buried there in the family plot."

"I understand. But in the meantime, if there's anything we can do, please just ask."

There were tears in Vicky's blue eyes, but they held

steady on mine. "That's very kind of you, but I think everything is under control. Between our good neighbors and members of the congregation, I've nearly had more help than I can use."

I took a swallow of cider and set my cup back down on the table. It was hot, spiced with cinnamon, and just right for a cool fall day. "Maria and I are anxious to make a contribution in Dan's name, if that's possible. Like maybe a college fund for the boys?"

Vicky shook her head. "As you may know, our church has a very strong support system. Between it and Dan's pension, the boys and I will be all right financially. So instead I'm requesting that contributions be sent to the Game and Fish Department's general conservation fund."

"We'll be pleased to do that."

I followed her eyes as she turned toward the window and pointed outside. "You know this was much more than just a job for Dan. It was his passion. So we think that's the best way to honor his memory."

"We're going to miss you around here, Vicky."

"Thanks. But I didn't invite you out here just to say goodbye."

I had wondered when she was going to get around to it. "What is it then?"

"Well, first of all, I'd like to apologize for the other night."

I didn't think an apology was called for, and told her so.

"But it is, Cal. There was no excuse for my getting on your case about Ambrose Pendleton. I know you're doing all you can. I was under a lot of stress, and it just boiled over. Every time I think about that man, that he might get away with killing my husband, well you can imagine."

"If it is in my power, Vicky, we'll get him. It's just a

matter of finding enough evidence."

Then she surprised me. "I may be able to help you there because I have something to show you." She excused herself, went into another part of the house, and came back holding a small yellow notebook. It was cloth-bound and measured about five by three inches. "I found this yesterday when I was cleaning out Dan's desk. It's some sort of a diary. I didn't even know he kept such a thing."

She handed me the notebook and suggested I take a look at the most recent entries. I did as she instructed, thumbing my way from back to front. The writing was in neat black script, and most of the pages began with a date and location. Dan McCall had kept a logbook of his daily activities. The last entry was from the day before he died, and even with a cursory glance I noticed that the name Ambrose Pendleton appeared more than once.

"You can keep that, Cal, if you'd like. Though I'd like it back when you're finished."

I had a better idea, if she was amenable. "What if I made a copy?"

"Sure, I suppose that would be all right. But I do have one favor to ask."

"What?"

"I haven't read it all yet, and there may be some personal things in there besides just work. I'm hoping they could remain confidential."

"Of course. And we may need a favor from you in return. If and when we use this as evidence, you could be asked to testify about its authenticity."

"So you think it could help?"

"Can't say for sure until I give it a closer look."

One thing was certain. Dan's logbook would have been much more valuable if it had included an entry from the day he'd encountered Pendleton over near

Gardner Canyon. But evidently his custom had been to make entries after he'd gotten home from work, and that was the day he never made it. I had no intention of pointing that out to Vicky. Instead, I asked her for a mailing address in Kingman where I might send the diary.

I rose from the couch and thanked Vicky for the refreshments and especially for the notebook. She accompanied me to the door, where we parted with an awkward hug and the unspoken possibility that we might not be seeing each other again.

Chapter 32

The road east from the McCall place topped a low rise just before it dropped down to its junction with route 83. From that vantage point I had a sweeping view of the whole Sonoita Valley. It was clear, breezy, and a bit chilly. There was a trace of snow on the highest peaks of the Huachucas. I pulled off to the side of the road, slowed the Blazer to a stop, and looked out across the gray-brown, nearly treeless plain.

Luis Mendoza referred to everything from here all the way down to Nogales as "my county." I'd always thought it was overly possessive of him, like he owned the place or something instead of just being there to keep the peace. But lately I'd started thinking about the Sonoita Valley in the same way. Maybe it's just something that comes with a sense of responsibility. Those were my people out there. It was my job to keep them safe, and to bring justice to those who had it coming. Big ego trip? Maybe. But it also was a burden.

Lately, as in the last few days, I'd felt the burden lifting just a bit. Joe Ortega's grumbles notwithstanding, there had been some progress. We'd gotten the Border Posse off the street, or at least that seemed likely, and we'd taken care of their marijuana operation at the same time. Nobody was going to miss those bastards, and that was for sure.

So all that left were two murders and one case of attempted livestock poisoning. Oh, and a developer hell bent on obliterating another chunk of my favorite view, mostly by persuading landowners to do something with their land they didn't want to do in the first place. Suddenly I felt crummy all over again.

Such introspective musings probably are a bad thing. Fortunately or otherwise, something unusual interrupted this one before I had a chance to spin myself even deeper into a hole. There was an ugly plume of black smoke billowing up into the sky somewhere over near Elgin. It was in the vicinity of the Obregon homestead, but I couldn't be sure from this distance. I fired up the Blazer, along with lights and siren, and got on the radio to the local volunteer fire department. Then I drove east just as quickly as seemed prudent, or maybe just a little faster than that.

It turned out the smoke wasn't coming from Maria's place. Instead it was rising out of a field that once had been Moss Winslow's vineyard. The firefighters had gotten there before me, and they already were deploying their hoses as I arrived on the scene. It took us no time at all to figure out that the fire was no accident. Moss was there, and so were all of his field hands. They had built a bonfire out of the dead and dying remains of all his grape plants, and they were standing around watching as the brush pile went up in smoke. The plume bent east as it rose, driven by a west wind that also fanned the flames.

The whole thing was so far gone that the crew made the logical decision just to wet down the perimeter and let the fire burn itself out. I suspected that had been Moss Winslow's plan all along, given what he had told me about the disease that was killing his vines. Perhaps he had lit the fire in an effort to prevent the sickness from spreading to other vineyards in the valley. If so, it was an act of altruism coming from a man I wasn't sure had many such instincts.

It turned out that was only part of the story. My first clue was that Moss was wearing something odd around his head. I pulled the Blazer in behind the two engines from the volunteer fire department, and walked down Winslow's driveway to where he stood. We were about even with the fire, and I could still feel the heat even though the peak of the burn already had passed.

We exchanged hellos, and then I said how sorry I was that his vineyard had come to such a sad end. I pretended not to notice the thing on his head. It looked like a football helmet except it was metal and had these weird projections coming out of it, sort of like antennae on a giant aluminum grasshopper.

Winslow didn't say anything, and eventually I just couldn't help myself. "So, uh, what's that you're wearing, Moss?"

"When I send out a signal, I want to be ready for their reply. Just in case. It doesn't always happen."

"What signal?"

"The fire, of course." Then he pointed up into the sky. "In case they see it. I want them to know I'm ready."

I never had the chance to find out what Moss Winslow thought he was getting ready for, because just then J.L. Minkston drove down the lane in his big white Cadillac. He pulled up next to us, stopped, and rolled down his window. Moss didn't even give him a chance to say hello.

"Happy now, J.L.?"

"What happened here, Moss? And what's that thing on your head, for god's sake?"

"Not now, J.L., not now. Just get the hell out, okay? Can't you see it's all working out just like you planned?"

"I have no idea what you're talking about. But we gotta talk soon. I'll probably be back tomorrow, and you'd better not be wearing that stupid helmet or whatever it is."

Minkston caught my eye and made a twirling motion with an index finger just above his left ear.

Then he turned his Escalade around and sped back down the lane, spraying gravel as he drove.

By this time a fair number of rubberneckers had accumulated along the county blacktop, and I realized it was time to get back out there to handle the traffic. I said goodbye to Moss Winslow, but he was looking skyward again and I don't think he even heard me. One vehicle in particular did not stick around long enough for me ask the driver to please move along, which is what I did for everybody else. It was a dark green Toyota 4Runner, and the driver was Ambrose Pendleton. He did a U-turn in the middle of the road and headed back west before I even had a chance to make eye contact.

~ ~ ~

That night after dinner I settled down in the living room with Dan McCall and his diary, and started to read. Maria didn't say anything, but an hour later she wandered in wearing something that made me realize I'd settled in the wrong room with the wrong person. She sure didn't look like the mailman. I had one quick phone call to make, and then sheriff business for the day was going to be over.

As I had suspected, the McCall diary was not all that helpful, because it ended the day before he was killed. But it did reveal that Dan had become increasingly obsessed with Ambrose Pendleton during the last two weeks of his life. They had met in the field on at least two occasions, one in Sunnyside Canyon and another in the Patagonia Mountains. McCall had failed to find any of the rare rattlesnakes in Pendleton's possession either time, but his notes suggested that the encounters had not been pleasant. At least the diary could establish the fact that Pendleton knew he was being watched, and why.

Luis Mendoza answered his personal cell on the

third ring. He sounded tired and not a little grumpy, and I didn't blame him.

"Sorry to disturb you on a Friday night, Luis, but frankly I was a little concerned about our talk earlier today."

"Concerned how?"

"That maybe you've lost some confidence in me?"

His response surprised me. "Yeah, I was going to call you about that, but not until tomorrow morning. And then I was going to apologize. Just having a bad day, I suppose."

I wondered if his bad day had something to do with Joe Ortega hovering around, but I wasn't about to go there. "Actually, Luis, you were right about our lack of progress on the Slawson killing, or Maria's goats for that matter. But it does seem like we're getting someplace with Pendleton."

"You're right. And I have some news there, both good and bad."

"What's that?"

"Those fingerprints we got off the hood of the game warden's truck? They match prints we lifted off the photo album and the bucket of rat poison you took from Pendleton's place. And better yet, they match Pendleton's prints that were on file with the FBI."

"And the bad news?"

"The prints on the soda can you found up in the Whetstones? They're not his."

The conclusion was inescapable. "So it looks like we can link Pendleton to McCall, but not to Slawson."

"Right."

"Do you think we have enough to charge him with Dan McCall's death? You know he could have come into contact with the man's truck some time before the killing. McCall's diary even suggests such a possibility."

"At least it should be enough to bring him in for

questioning, especially in light of Aunt Grace's plant evidence. I think it's time for you and me to sit down with Joe Ortega and the county attorney. How early can you be here in my office?"

"You mean tomorrow? Can you get them in on a Saturday"

"Leave that to me. Can you be here by nine?"

"I'll be there."

Things certainly had gone better than the last time I talked with the sheriff. Maybe I was inching back out of the doghouse.

Chapter 33

Everybody in the sheriff's office that morning was crumpled and grumpy, including Luis himself. He'd had to make his own coffee because it was Saturday, and I suppose that was part of it. We all helped ourselves to a cup and then gathered around the sheriff's big mahogany desk. County Attorney Tom Bancroft was there, along with Joe Ortega and me. Luis sat in his oversized leather swivel chair behind the desk, while the rest of us lined up dutifully across the front. It was the same arrangement whenever he held court. Bancroft was a big heavyset man, usually given to pinstriped three-piece suits. Today he was wearing tan chinos and a bright green polo shirt. We probably had interrupted a day on the golf course.

We were there to talk about Ambrose Pendleton, and specifically what charges if any might justify an arrest warrant. The sheriff tossed me the ball right off. "Cal, would you summarize what we've got, just to make sure everybody is on the same page?"

I made the assumption that Tom Bancroft knew nothing. It probably wasn't true, but I couldn't be sure what Joe or Luis might or might not have told him, and so it seemed like a wise and safe tactic.

"We suspect Mr. Pendleton of possible involvement in three separate incidents. First, seventeen days ago someone put a rattlesnake in a mailbox up near Sonoita that ended up biting and killing a young man named Andy Slawson. It was a deliberate act, but we have no evidence suggesting that Pendleton was involved, other than the fact that he is known to collect snakes."

"Do you have any other suspects?" It was Bancroft.

"We have some possible leads, but nothing solid, no." I was worried that the County Attorney might take us off on a tangent, so I decided to get a little pushy about it. "We can come back to that later, but I'd like to stick with Mr. Pendleton for the moment, if that is okay."

The sheriff favored me with a barely perceptible nod.

"The second item is that the suspect appears to have been dealing in the trafficking of illegal wildlife, specifically some rare species of rattlesnakes. We have solid forensic evidence that he has kept these species in captivity in his home, which by itself is an illegal act. We also have circumstantial evidence that he has been selling snakes to a dealer up in Phoenix."

Bancroft interrupted again. "Are you sure this is a matter for Santa Cruz County? I understand these offenses are relatively minor, and that personnel from the Game and Fish department normally would handle any such arrests by themselves."

It sounded like somebody had already gotten to Bancroft, and I wondered how well he knew Joe Ortega. Maybe they played golf together?

"We have a Game and Fish agent working with us on the trafficking case, and if that was all there was to it, you might be right. But then last week Dan McCall, our local game warden, was found dead by his truck over in the Santa Ritas. We have reason to suspect Ambrose Pendleton in that case as well."

I proceeded to describe our evidence tying Pendleton to the murder scene, including the fern fronds, the fingerprints on Dan's truck, and the warden's diary. Then I stopped talking and waited for somebody to respond. It was Bancroft again, but he didn't go where I expected.

"I understand that the game warden's handgun was missing at the scene. I assume you haven't been able to tie that weapon to our suspect, or you would have told me so." Bancroft pivoted in his chair, away from me and toward Joe Ortega. "And the gun hasn't turned up anywhere, right?"

"Right. We've given out the make and serial number to all dealers in this part of the state, but so far nothing has come of it."

By now I had the distinct impression that Bancroft and Ortega has rehearsed things ahead of time. Luis apparently had come to the same conclusion, and he was in a much better position to do something about it than I.

"Let's leave the gun aside for the moment, gentlemen, and concentrate on what we've got." Luis started counting fingers. "First, we know from his log book that Dan McCall has had Mr. Pendleton in his sights for some little while. Second, we found Pendleton's fingerprints on the hood of McCall's pickup. And third, we found parts of the same fern in Pendleton's truck that was growing at the crime scene, some of which also was plastered to McCall's body."

Joe Ortega may have smirked just a bit, but at least he just sat there. It was Bancroft who kept interrupting. I suppose it was his job. "So this plant, this little fern or whatever the hell it is, how solid is that? I mean, couldn't Pendleton have picked it up somewhere else? After all, from what you're telling me, he's been spending lots of time lately up in those mountains."

I started to reply, but the sheriff held up his hand to stop me. "No, Tom, that's where we got lucky. We have this on good authority – and I mean *good* authority. That fern is so rare it hasn't been seen around here in at least the last 100 years. The odds that Pendleton got into it someplace other than the crime scene are remote at best."

It fell silent for a while in Luis Mendoza's office, except for the sound of Tom Bancroft's fingers tapping across the polished surface of the sheriff's big desk.

"Well, if you can find a judge who'll sign a warrant on what frankly looks like pretty scant evidence, I suppose we could bring the man in for questioning. But I'm not sure you're going to get that lucky."

At that the sheriff fumbled around in the top center drawer of his desk and pulled out a medium-sized envelope. "Actually, I already have a warrant for his arrest."

I may have said this before, but Luis Mendoza really knows how to make things happen. How he'd managed to find a judge even willing to talk to him that early on a Saturday morning, let alone to sign a warrant, I could not even begin to guess.

Chapter 34

We decided to act that same day. The arresting team would include Joe Ortega, Larry, and me from the department, accompanied by Laura Floyd from Game and Fish. I got Larry on his cell, evidently still at home, and told him to round up Laura and meet us in the office. There was a woman's voice in the background, so it may not have been hard for him to track her down. Joe was driving up separately, "In case this falls flat and I have to go back to Nogales by myself." My hope was that we would have to choose which one of us got to haul Ambrose Pendleton down to the county jail. But either way I was not about to miss out on his interrogation, assuming there was one.

Once gathered at the office, I issued bulletproof vests to everybody, following departmental protocol. We each carried a radio, along with sidearms and mace. It was hard to predict just how the man might react when we came knocking, but we were taking no chances.

We drove in three vehicles as far as the gate to Pendleton's property, where we left Laura's pickup to block his driveway and proceeded on back to the house and outbuildings in my Blazer and Joe's Explorer. It was quiet when we pulled into the man's front yard. The plan was to have Larry go around to the back door, while Laura checked the garage to determine if the Toyota was inside. Once Larry was in place and we got the indication from Laura as to whether the man was home, then Joe and I would proceed to the front of the house.

We did have a Plan B if Pendleton was gone. I

would remain on foot someplace on the property as a stakeout, while everybody else went back to the office to await my call on the radio. There was a risk involved – namely, that Pendleton might spot me upon his return and flee before we had a chance to give chase. But the risk was minimal as long as I stayed well hidden, and we judged that was a better alternative than having him see a bunch of law enforcement vehicles parked in the neighborhood as he was returning home.

We never had to find out if Plan B was any good. Laura wasn't in the garage more than ten seconds before she came back out and gave us the thumbs-up, at which point Joe and I walked up onto Pendleton's front porch.

I knocked, and then we both stood aside while Joe announced our presence. "Santa Cruz County Sheriff! Ambrose Pendleton, we have a warrant for your arrest. Open the door and come out with your hands up!"

Dead silence.

I got on the radio to Larry. "Anything back there? Over."

"Nope. All quiet here. But where's Laura? Over."

Neither Joe nor I had seen her since she'd come out of the garage and given us the signal to go in. But then my radio crackled to life and it was Laura, obviously in a whisper. "I'm around to the side, under a window. And I think I hear movement. Over."

Shortly after that I heard a loud thump, followed by the sound of someone running. Then Laura shouted, "Freeze! Get on the ground! Arizona Game and Fish Department! You're under arrest!"

We all broke for the side of the house, Larry rounding the back corner at the same time that Joe and I came around from the front. Ambrose Pendleton was face down in the sparse grass between his house and garage. Laura was in the shoot position about six feet behind him. Her legs were spread and she had both hands on her Glock, which she held steady and pointed right at the man's back. It looked like things were under control.

Larry ran up and cuffed the man and brought him to his feet. Only then did Laura holster her gun and start brushing an accumulation of grass and dirt off her uniform. She was pale and a bit shaky, but she had done just right and I think she knew it. Larry asked her what happened.

"I was hiding under the window, when he jumped out and landed right on top of me. Then he took off running. I think he was headed for the garage."

I asked if she was all right.

"Yeah, no problems."

At that point Ambrose Pendleton decided to start asking questions. "What's this all about? I haven't done anything. Why am I under arrest?"

Joe Ortega read Ambrose Pendleton his rights and then explained the charges, while I checked the man for weapons. Patting down a suspect is routine once he is in custody and secured. But there was nothing routine about what happened next, because under the man's shirt, tucked into his belt, I found a pistol. It was a Glock, and it looked like the one Laura had just inserted back into her holster. We would need to check the serial number, of course, but I was ready to bet we had just found the weapon Game and Fish had issued to the late Dan McCall. Somehow we must have missed the weapon during our prior search.

"Got him," I said aloud.

Pendleton went 'peaceable,' as they say in the old westerns. Not that he had much choice with his hands cuffed behind him, sitting alone in the back seat of my Blazer. The man made no attempt at conversation on our drive down to the Nogales jail, nor did he say anything to anybody else in booking as we escorted him to a holding cell.

It was late afternoon by the time all this was done, but both the sheriff and Joe Ortega wanted to begin the interrogation right then. Luis made doubly sure we'd read the man his rights, and then he suggested maybe we could get something out of Pendleton before he asked for an attorney. I sure didn't want to miss it, and so I called Maria to tell her what had happened and that I might be late. I think she understood, given the circumstances. She probably knew better than anyone how much pressure I had been under to bring this case to a close.

We didn't get much out of Pendleton that night. Even if we had, it likely wouldn't have been the best news of the day. That came when Game and Fish confirmed that the weapon he'd been carrying when he jumped out of his window was the same one they had issued to Dan McCall. Why he had decided to take it off the man's body up in Gardner Canyon was anybody's guess, because he wasn't talking about that or much of anything else.

We had him in a small interview room with no windows except for the one-way glass that connected to an adjacent observation room. The only furnishings were a small wooden table, thoroughly scarred with cigarette burns, and three purposefully uncomfortable straight-backed chairs.

Joe Ortega and I were in the room with Pendleton. Joe came at it from all angles, but he got essentially nowhere.

"What were you doing up in Gardner Canyon the day you ran into Dan McCall?"

"Where's Gardner Canyon? Who's Dan McCall?"

"How did you get that pistol if you didn't take it off McCall's body?"

"I found it."

"Where did you find it?"

"I can't remember."

"What if I said we have evidence that puts you at the crime scene where we found McCall's body?"

"What evidence? Anyway, it doesn't matter because I'm through talking. I want an attorney. I know my rights."

It looked like the interrogation had stalled, but I had an idea. I motioned to Joe that we meet outside, where I knew the sheriff and County Attorney Bancroft had been listening and watching through the one-way glass. Once we were all together, I made my proposition. "Before we lock him up for the night, and before he starts rounding up a lawyer, why don't we try him out on the rare snake business?"

Ortega asked why we should bother with small potatoes like that when we likely would be getting him for murder.

"Because I know he has a thing about rattlers, and it just might start him talking." I reminded Joe about a reptile dealer named Roscoe Danforth up in Phoenix who may have been trafficking in illegal wildlife. "Game and Fish have been trying to catch the man, but so far no luck."

Joe Ortega still didn't get it, but the sheriff did. "So if we charge Pendleton with illegal capture and sale of those little snakes, he might see a way out by agreeing to testify against Danforth?"

"Right. And if we lose him to a plea bargain on the snake business, it won't matter that much, will it? I mean, assuming we can get him for the McCall murder."

Everybody agreed to the plan, and they let me take the lead. Before going back into the interview room, I asked that a particular item be brought down from the evidence room. Back inside, I sat down opposite

Pendleton and laid a plastic bag on the little wooden table that separated us. In it was the collection of snakeskins Hazel Smith had taken from a terrarium in Pendleton's house the day we conducted the search.

We were alone in the interview room, because I thought he might get more talkative that way. Everybody else was listening and watching from next door.

"Do you recognize these?"

He barely glanced down. "They look like shed snake skins."

"They came from your house."

He rolled his eyes. "I keep snakes. They shed. So what?"

"We have an expert witness who is prepared to testify that these particular skins came from ridge-nosed rattlesnakes. You probably know they are a protected species."

"Maybe your expert isn't all that expert."

I mentioned the name Hazel Smith, and right away I could tell a light began to dawn. Pendleton's expression changed from smug to frown and he shifted uneasily in his chair. But he remained combative. "Yeah, well last I heard it's legal to keep their skins. Maybe I found them someplace and brought them home."

That was a stretch and he knew it, so I pressed the point. "A whole batch of them, that you just happened to drop into an otherwise empty terrarium? Does that sound reasonable to you?"

"You got a better idea?"

"Sure. You collected the snakes and then sold them to a dealer, but they happened to shed while you still had them at home."

"You've got no proof of that."

"No, but we – that is Game and Fish – are talking

to a dealer. His name is Roscoe Danforth, and we have a witness who saw the two of you together in Sonoita just last week."

"Who was that witness?"

"It was me. The two of you were having dinner at the Santa Rita Saloon."

Ambrose Pendleton got quiet, and I could almost hear the wheels spinning. My hopes rose that he could be heading just where I'd planned. "So here's what's going to happen, Ambrose. We're going to charge you with illegal possession of wildlife. And then we're going to charge you with sale of those same animals."

"You've got no proof of that, even if you could make the possession charge stick."

There was only one play left, and either Pendleton would take the bait or he wouldn't. "Well, it isn't my case, but suppose Game and Fish were to lighten this man Danforth's sentence if he gave them the name of his supplier. And that would be you."

He bit. "What if instead I testified that Danforth paid me for those snakes? Just hypothetically speaking, of course."

"Hypothetically speaking my ass." That's what I wanted to say but actually didn't because at that point Joe Ortega came into the room and took charge of the interrogation, along with Tom Bancroft.

Two hours later we had a signed confession from Ambrose Pendleton as to the collection and sale of illegal wildlife, along with a commitment from the County Attorney on a plea bargain. Pendleton would do no jail time, and pay only a small fine, if he agreed to testify against Roscoe Danforth up in Phoenix.

Pendleton either thought or pretended to think that he had just gotten off the hook. "So, can I go now? I admit I took those snakes and sold 'em, but this other stuff about a game warden? I'm completely innocent."

Then he stretched out his lanky frame and attempted cocky.

If any of us had thought that confessing to the snake caper would start the ball rolling on the McCall murder, those hopes were now gone. In fact they probably had been remote from the start. But Joe Ortega handled it just right. "No sir, you are not free to go. You remain under arrest for the murder of Warden McCall. We will resume that interrogation in the morning."

"What about my lawyer?"

"You are at liberty to begin making those arrangements, and we will not ask any more questions until an attorney is present, if that is your wish."

"You're damn straight it is. And I'll say it again. I did *not* kill that man, and there's no way you can prove that I did."

Chapter 35

I'd been back and forth to Nogales so many times in the last couple of days that my Blazer must have been wearing ruts in the highway. It had been another short night with Maria, and I was on the road by six-thirty. It had turned cool overnight, but there was no wind and only a hint of clouds to the northwest. It was Sunday, and the little town of Patagonia was barely awake as I drove through on my way south to Nogales. Wood smoke rose from a few chimneys, mostly from the older adobes down along Sonoita Creek. Despite the lack of traffic, or much human activity of any kind, I was careful to stay within the speed limit. Patagonia's town fathers and mothers were strict about that, which is one reason it stayed such a nice quiet place.

It turned out I needn't have hurried anyway. Ambrose Pendleton had retained the services of a very fancy lawyer from Phoenix. He was on his way down in a private jet, and expected to arrive sometime in late morning.

Luis invited Joe Ortega and me into his office for coffee while he explained what was happening. Apparently Pendleton had used his phone call the night before to get in touch with his father back in Connecticut. He must have been thrilled given the hour. Dad then used his attorney to make the contact in Phoenix, so that Pendleton could be represented by somebody licensed to practice law in Arizona. They never made clear why it had to be somebody from all the way up in Phoenix.

About ten o'clock we got word from downstairs that the lawyer had arrived. Straight off he had requested and was granted time alone with his client. By now Tom Bancroft had joined the three of us in the sheriff's office, and we took the opportunity to talk strategy for the coming interrogation. Once again Luis asked Joe to take the lead, with me in the room. He suggested that Joe begin much as he had the day before, but then move quickly on to the specific sorts of evidence we had against Pendleton.

Ambrose Pendleton's lawyer, Linus Spelling, was a compact man of medium height, with blue eyes, a full head of white hair, and a deep Arizona tan. He wore a charcoal gray suit with a matching gray tie and a burgundy shirt. The man looked to be in very good physical shape, and I guessed that his tan came from time on a tennis court rather than a golf course. Probably his country club had both. He oozed confidence mixed with arrogance, and I suspected we might have our hands full as we made our case.

We sat again at the little table in the department's interview room, and Spelling immediately took charge. Or at least he made an attempt. "Let me begin by stating for the record that I have now conferred with my client, and he once again declares his complete innocence of the charges you have brought against him. I will be making application for bail just as soon as this interview is completed, and I expect it will be granted expeditiously. Frankly gentlemen, from what Mr. Pendleton tells me you have no case. We expect full exoneration."

Either it was a bluff or Pendleton had just told Spelling some real whoppers. Either way, Joe Ortega was having none of it. In fact he pretty much ignored Spelling and addressed his opening questions to the suspect.

"Well, let's see about that. Mr. Pendleton, just for the record I'm going to start where we left off yesterday, to confirm your answers in the presence of your attorney. First of all, do you deny being present at the site in Gardner Canyon where we found the body of the deceased?"

Pendleton looked at Spelling, who gave a little nod. "Absolutely."

"And so you also deny removing Mr. McCall's weapon from the crime scene?"

"Yes. How could I have done that if I wasn't even there?"

"Then how is it that you came to have that weapon on your person when we arrested you yesterday at your home in Sonoita? The serial number is a match. We know it was McCall's weapon you were carrying."

"Like I already told you, I found that pistol someplace else."

"Where?"

Yesterday he'd forgotten, but apparently by today it had come to him. "Beside the road over along Harshaw Creek."

"How did you happen to see it there?"

"It glinted in the sun."

"The gun is black, Mr. Pendleton."

Ambrose squirmed a little, but maybe it was just his uncomfortable chair. "Nevertheless, that's how it happened."

Joe Ortega shuffled some papers in front of him, and then asked if either Mr. Spelling or his client would like something to drink. Pendleton asked for water. I volunteered to go get it, but Joe stopped me. "No, I'll go. Need to hit the head anyway."

We sat alone in silence for nearly five minutes before Joe came back in the room. I found out later he'd been conferring with Luis and Tom Bancroft about where to go next with the interrogation. Once Joe was seated and Pendleton had taken a couple of swallows of water, we got back down to business.

"So, Mr. Pendleton, if you deny any involvement in the death of Warden McCall, or even being at the scene, how can you explain the fact that your fingerprints were found on the hood of his pickup?" Pendleton started to speak, but Ortega put up a hand. "And how can you explain the plant material we found on the floor of your truck that matches similar, actually identical, material we took off the man's body and from the water nearby?"

Apparently Linus Spelling had read the evidence we had presented to the judge to obtain Pendleton's arrest warrant, because he was ready for this one. "My client is under no obligation to answer that, or any other of your other questions for that matter. But in the interests of clarity and justice, let me offer the following."

Clarity and justice? Spelling cleared his throat, took a sip of water from Pendleton's cup without asking, and proceeded. "First, as to the fingerprints. There are any number of ways they could have been left on that truck. My client has never denied knowing Mr. McCall."

Now it was my turn to interrupt. "Actually he did, just yesterday."

Spelling glared at me. "All right, so maybe he forgot. But I'd like to come back to this business about the plant evidence. Seems pretty flimsy to me. I mean, even if you can prove that the samples match, that doesn't mean they came from the same place. My client admits he spends a lot of time in the mountains around here, looking for snakes. He could have picked up those plant leaves anywhere."

Joe Ortega turned in my direction. "Perhaps Deputy Creede would like to explain a bit about that?"

So I did. "It wasn't a leaf, it was a fern frond. And that particular fern is so rare it's hardly ever been seen before in Arizona."

Linus Spelling loosened his tie. "What are you, some kind of a botanist or something?"

"No, but I'm real good friends with one. Her name is Grace Slawson, and she's a recognized expert in the field of forensic botany. I believe your client knows her too. Perhaps he would like to confirm her expertise."

I knew it was a smarty remark, but I just couldn't help it. "And here's what she'll testify, if it comes to that. That particular species of fern is so rare in these parts, the odds that your client got tangled up with it someplace other than at the crime scene are no better than a thousand to one."

Okay, so I made up the part about the odds.

Linus Spelling obviously was an experienced attorney, and he wasn't about to give up anything yet. But I could tell he was getting concerned. "So if that's all gentlemen, I believe we're done here. You can expect my client to be out on bail no later than this afternoon. We look forward to the opportunity to respond to this unfounded charge in court. In the meantime, I am formally advising my client not to say anything further on the matter. Good day."

Spelling rose to leave, and I thought it was over. But then Ambrose Pendleton said something unexpected. "I'd like to speak to my lawyer alone now. I have that right, don't I?"

We all agreed that he did. Spelling knew that 'alone' meant somewhere other than a room connected by speakers to the one next door, even if Pendleton didn't. So they left in the custody of a guard who took them someplace more private.

It seemed to take forever, as Luis, Joe, Tom Bancroft and I cooled our heels back in the sheriff's office. But eventually we got word that Ambrose Pendleton and his lawyer were ready to meet, and we found ourselves once again in the interrogation room.

Spelling started things off. "Against my advice, my client would like to make a statement."

Then it was Pendleton's turn. He looked nervous as hell, cramped and uncomfortable in his little chair. His face was beaded with sweat and there were large spreading stains under his armpits. He cleared his throat and started reading from a yellow tablet that Spelling had placed on the table in front of him.

I will spare you the details, but the heart of it was this. Pendleton admitted being at the crime scene. He'd been there collecting rare snakes when Dan McCall caught him in the act. They were tussling over the specimens when one of them bit McCall on the arm. At that point the warden fell backwards and hit his head on a rock. It was an accident, but Pendleton thought nobody would believe him, so he panicked and fled in his truck. Nobody was supposed to get hurt over a couple of little snakes. He was terribly sorry. End of story.

Linus Spelling then proposed a deal. Pendleton would plead guilty to causing an accidental death, with the understanding that there would be probation and community service, but no jail time.

Joe Ortega didn't even blink. "That's ridiculous. The charge here is second-degree murder, and we're more than happy to take that to a jury, given the evidence. You've got to do better than that, counselor."

Spelling spent some time thinking that over and then asked if he could have a moment with his client. "And please give me your word you'll turn off that damned sound system."

Joe said "sure" and we both sat there while the attorney and his client huddled together in a far corner of the room, with their backs to the one-way mirror. They were back in five minutes. Spelling indicated he would do the talking and we were not to address Pendleton directly.

"My client agrees to plead to one charge of

manslaughter. He does the minimum. Three years."

Now we were getting somewhere, but Joe and I needed to consult with the brass in the other room. We excused ourselves and went next door. I was surprised, but the County Attorney started with me. "Well, what do you think, Mr. Creede? It's been your case up until now."

Joe Ortega wasn't happy with that, and I didn't blame him. But neither was I going to defer, and besides it seemed like Bancroft and the sheriff had talked this over in advance. "Two things, I suppose. First, there were no witnesses, except for Pendleton and his victim, so we can't be sure what really . happened out there. But second, didn't Julie Benevides say the amount of damage to the back of McCall's skull was more severe than was likely to happen from a simple fall? And didn't the M.E. confirm that?"

Luis nodded. "So you're saying Pendleton really went after the man? That it was more than just a 'tussle,' to use his own word?"

"Exactly. So anyway, under the circumstances I think manslaughter is the best we can hope for. But three years is way too light. I'm no lawyer, but my guess is if we went after murder, even in the second degree, there could be trouble with a jury."

Tom Bancroft almost looked relieved. "I agree with you. But we'll counter with eight to ten years. This guy did a terrible thing, and he's gonna pay for it."

In the end, that's how it played out. But before we finished I insisted that Ambrose Pendleton answer two questions. Spelling said okay I could ask, but then he would advise his client whether or not to answer.

That was fair enough, but I made sure that Pendleton was looking directly at me and not at his lawyer when I asked my first question. "Why did you take Dan McCall's gun? It was one sure way we could link you to him, if we found it in your possession."

Apparently Spelling thought that was a harmless enough question, and indicated as much to his client.

"I've wanted a gun ever since I came out west, but I couldn't pass a background check because of my felony convictions back in Connecticut. So I just took it. Big mistake, huh?"

It sure as hell was.

"Okay, so here's my second and final question. Did you put one of your snakes in Moss Winslow's mailbox?" I knew that Hazel's evidence made that a remote possibility, but I just had to ask.

This time Linus Spelling got all excited and he started to object. But Pendleton brushed him off. "With God as my witness, no. Why would I do something like that?"

I was inclined to believe the man, and one thing was for certain. We had no evidence to suggest otherwise.

~ ~ ~

The snakes took comfort in the familiar feeling of their bodies entwined together in the small confining space. There was water to drink. Sometimes, miraculously, mice would come raining down from above, stunned and stupefied and easy to catch.

But still it was all wrong, and they were growing increasingly restless. They were trapped in a strange place, and they could find no way out. Worst of all, sometimes a person would come with a curved stick and take one of them away. All the others became agitated, just as they had when they were taken from their mountain cave in the first place. They tried to strike out at the person and kill it, but they failed every time.

Chapter 36
J.L. Minkston

He'd been dreading the call for a week, and today it finally had come. A banker from California, some big shot vice president named Smiley, was due to arrive in Sonoita that evening. He'd made it crystal clear what the visit was all about, not that Minkston really had any doubts. They were going to call in his loans unless he could demonstrate in hard numbers that both the shopping mall and the housing development were on their way to the black side of the ledger, which they weren't.

Somehow he'd convinced this Smiley person to meet him for a drink at the Santa Rita that evening. They were scheduled for a conference the next day in his office, and he'd been told to have all of his records available. Minkston knew if it ever got that far he was finished. There was just the slimmest of hopes that maybe they'd get to be buddies over the booze, and maybe the whole thing would go away, at least for a while. It was his last chance, and he knew it. The odds were small, but charm had always been one of his strong points and there was nothing left to lose.

Minkston locked up the house and got in the Escalade he'd left parked in the front yard of his home up against the south flank of the Whetstone Mountains. It was a clear and cool evening on the Sonoita Plain. There must have been a million bright stars twinkling overhead, not that he noticed.

He drove down his driveway out to its junction with 82 and turned west toward the lights of Sonoita. The powerful vehicle ran smoothly and quietly, almost driving itself. It was a good thing because his mind was elsewhere. He knew the little village of Elgin was out there somewhere in the dark, off to the south. He was thinking about his dreams for the place, and how they were just about to go poof.

J.L. Minkston was so lost in thought that at first he didn't notice the strange rubbery feeling down under his feet. The Escalade had just topped a low rise and begun a long gradual descent into Sonoita, when he heard a noise that was familiar but completely out of context. The noise was followed almost immediately by a stabbing, searing pain in his lower left leg. Still more puzzled than alarmed, he switched on the dome light and looked down, right into the triangular face of a rattlesnake. The animal was big and heavy and it was moving right for his crotch.

J.L. Minkston screamed. The car started to veer across the road all by itself, as if it had a mind of its own. He slammed on the brakes, but it was too late.

Chapter 37

Maria and I were in bed, just getting down to some important business, when the phone rang. The ID said it was the night dispatcher down in Nogales. I was surprised, because Larry had agreed to be on call that night.

I untangled myself and reached over to grab the receiver. "Hi, Ellie. What's going on?"

"Sorry about this, Mr. Creede, but I couldn't reach Deputy Hernandez. We've had a report of a wreck on Highway 82 just east of Sonoita. Apparently a car has rolled off the road, with somebody inside. I've already notified fire and rescue."

"Okay, thanks. I'm on my way."

As soon as I got out of bed Maria started rearranging the pillows and blankets as if that had been her plan all along. "I thought you were off duty tonight. Don't you ever get a break? Don't I?"

I explained the circumstances, and hoped she understood. Her frown may have diminished a little, but only just, by the time I was dressed and heading for the door. "Don't wait up. There's no telling how long this might take."

I ran out and jumped in the Blazer, turned on the flashers and the siren, and headed north on the Elgin road, then west on 82. About three miles outside Sonoita my headlights illuminated heavy skid marks angling across the highway toward an embankment on the south side. At the same time I spotted the flashing red lights of emergency vehicles rapidly approaching from the west.

I pulled off to the side of the road, grabbed a big

flashlight out of the console between the front seats, and ran across to where I could look down the embankment. A white Cadillac Escalade lay on its side about fifty feet below, with the driver's side down. I slid down the slope and peered in the passenger side door. There was a man inside that I recognized as J.L. Minkston. He may have moved, and then I thought I heard a moan. I tried both doors, but they were jammed. Fortunately by this time both an ambulance and a fire truck had arrived on the scene, and the rescue personnel already were getting organized. It was a great local crew.

I called back up to the highway. "Get the jaws of life! There's somebody trapped in here. He looks alive but pretty badly hurt. There's blood all over."

I needed to get back up on the highway and start handling traffic. Some spectators already had begun to accumulate on the side of the road, and there could easily have been another accident. I clambered up the slope and began to direct traffic, at the same time keeping an eye on the rescue activities unfolding below.

In about ten minutes they had Minkston out of the vehicle and onto a stretcher. In response to my query, a voice came up from out of the dark. "He's alive, but just barely. We're calling for a helicopter to fly him to the trauma center down in Nogales. This one looks real bad, and he needs help fast."

"Did he say anything?"

"Not a word. I'm not sure he's really conscious, but there is some eye movement."

~ ~ ~

In less than an hour the helicopter had landed, loaded up J.L. Minkston on board, and taken off. About this time a wrecker from Sierra Vista showed up. They were unbidden, at least by me, and I supposed they had been following radio traffic on a scanner. In any event they were here, and it seemed like a good time to get the vehicle back on its feet.

Two men got out of the wrecker, ran a cable down the slope, and hooked it to the car. Then they tightened the cable and easily righted the vehicle. They were in the process of deciding the best way to pull it back up onto the highway when I told them to stop. "Hold it you guys. Let me get a look inside before you move it anymore."

I walked back down the steep slope to the crumpled Cadillac and scanned the interior with my flashlight, starting with the front seat. Evidently the man had been wearing his seat belt, because the medics had needed cut it away when they pulled him out. Next I shined my light into the back seat, and instinctively jumped back. Wedged up against the rear console was one of the biggest rattlesnakes I'd ever seen. It appeared to be dead, and nearly beheaded by the impact of the crash. I couldn't be sure in the dim light, but it looked like a Mojave.

The wrecker crew had already started tightening the cable again, but I waved them off. "Don't move the car! This looks like it might be a crime scene. I'm going to unhook your cable, and you can go for now. It's likely to be daylight before we're gonna want to move this thing."

The two men mumbled something about 'maybe we'll see you tomorrow' and drove off, clearly in a funk. Not my problem.

I scrambled back up the slope and got on my cell. There were lots of calls to make, some of which I didn't want going out over the radio. First I contacted the trauma center in Nogales, reminded them about the helicopter that was now on its way, and said to check the victim for a snakebite. Then I called dispatch and asked Ellie to mobilize a crime scene crew for first light.

There seemed little point in having anybody fumbling around in the dark. The Cadillac and its contents weren't going anywhere.

I tried Larry and he picked up, sounding groggy. I explained the circumstance and he apologized without explanation for the fact that he'd missed the earlier call from dispatch. I didn't push it. "That's okay. Just get your butt over here pronto. And bring coffee and some snacks. We're about to have a long night."

Finally I punched in the number for the sheriff's personal cell. I figured if he didn't want to be disturbed he'd have the thing turned off. He answered on the third ring and I told him what was happening.

Luis sounded incredulous. "Another snake event? Did it bite him?"

"I don't know, the medics didn't mention it. They probably didn't even see it because they were so busy prying J.L. out of his car. I called the trauma center just now to tell them to look for any fang marks or swelling."

There was a lengthy pause. "Cal, what in the world is going on up there? I thought we had this snake business all sorted out, what with Pendleton's arrest and all."

"Maybe, but don't forget we weren't able to tie his collection to the snake that killed Andy, and the only thing he's actually copped to is the supposedly accidental death of Warden McCall.

"Anyway, Sheriff, I gotta go. The rubber-neckers are starting to pile up again."

"Want me to send up some more help?"

"Thanks, but I don't think that's necessary. Larry's on his way, and we should be able to handle traffic. I just hope the crime scene crew gets here first thing in the morning."

"Let me see what I can do about that."

Once Larry arrived I couldn't resist going back down to the remains of J.L. Minkston's Escalade for one more look-see. I knew better than to mess with anything before the forensics people had a chance to do their job, but a simple look around couldn't hurt.

The snake, or what was left of it, looked to be about five feet long and as big around as the widest part of my forearm. I counted nine rattles on the tail, a pretty good indicator of the snake's age.

I tried to recreate the accident in my mind's eye. The most likely scenario was that Minkston had driven off the highway in a panic once he'd discovered his fellow passenger. Maybe it actually bit him. We wouldn't know that until the trauma folks down in Nogales had done their job. But how did the snake get in his car in the first place?

It began to feel like Andy Slawson all over again.

To quote the sheriff: "Just what in the world is going on up there?" Sure, maybe someone planted the snake in the car in hopes it would bite J.L. and kill him. But just like with Andy, what made the perp think it would work? A snake that size would pack a very big wallop, but death was far from assured even if a bite did occur.

And then there was the biggest question of all, the one that really made my head hurt. With Ambrose Pendleton and even the Border Posse out of the picture, who had been responsible and what was their motive?

I told myself to get a grip. The snake in front of me was dead, just like the one I'd shot in front of Moss Winslow's mailbox a scant two weeks ago. Somebody had put this animal in J.L. Minkston's car, and it probably was someone I knew. Finding him or her was just a process of elimination, and there weren't that many suspects left.

Then it occurred to me. Wasn't Minkston himself

one of those suspects? We still couldn't make him for poisoning Moss Winslow's grapes or Maria's goats, let alone for the snake that killed Andy. Grounds for a search warrant were scant at best. But the man had motive in all three cases. Suppose he'd put that snake in his own car planning to deliver it someplace? Suppose it had gotten loose and caused the accident? There was no sign of a cage or anything else inside the Escalade that might have held a snake. But still, I had to wonder.

I climbed back up the slope to join Larry Hernandez in a much-needed cup of coffee, hoping for three things. The first was that Hazel Smith could shed some light on the origins of another dead snake. The second was that J.L. Minkston would manage to stay alive, and that he might have some things to tell us. And the third, of course, was that Maria would remain her patient dear sweet self, in spite of everything.

Chapter 38

I suggested that Larry and I take turns guarding the remains of J.L. Minkston's Escalade that night, but he let me off the hook. He made a remark having something to do with the Lone Ranger and Tonto. I really couldn't figure it out, but then he told me to get the hell out and that was clear enough. Maybe he felt guilty about missing the call from dispatch on account of his being distracted. I had a pretty good idea about the nature of his main distraction these days, but we didn't need to get into that.

By the time I got back home it was close to midnight, and Maria was dead to the world. I took a chance and called the trauma center at the hospital down in Nogales. Whatever category comes next after dead tired, that was me. But if Minkston was awake it might have been worth the trip while his memory of the night's events remained fresh. And who knew, he might even let something slip.

Fortunately or otherwise, the surgeon was still at the hospital and he let me off the hook. Minkston was alive but heavily sedated and in no position to speak to anyone. It would be tomorrow at the earliest. I asked for details, and got plenty.

There had indeed been a snakebite to his lower leg, but it was responding well to anti-venom. The bigger problems were elsewhere. He had suffered a blow to the left side of his skull that had caused a severe concussion at the very least. There were numerous facial abrasions, and his left ear was nearly severed. There were compound fractures to both his upper and lower left arm, plus a broken collarbone and pelvis. His condition was listed as critical.

~ ~ ~

I must have been asleep for several hours when the alarm went off the next morning, but it seemed like no more than a half hour. Maria already was out in the barn milking her goats by the time I struggled out of bed and headed first to the coffee pot and then to the shower.

When she came in I was on the phone to Larry. Julie Benevides and another deputy already were gathering evidence at the wreck site. I reminded Larry to get the snake for Hazel Smith when forensics had finished with it, and then to call a wrecker. If there ever was a vehicle that was totaled, it was Minkston's Cadillac.

He wanted to know my plans for the day.

"I'll be in Nogales trying to get something out of Minkston, assuming he wakes up."

Two hours later I was in the waiting room of the intensive care unit at the Nogales hospital. The receptionist said that Minkston was still unconscious. It wasn't clear when or even if it was going to be possible to talk to him. She promised that somebody would come out and talk to me whenever there was something to report.

I was surprised when the sheriff came walking in and took the seat next to mine. He read my look and was quick to offer an explanation.

"No, Cal, I want to be in on this myself. J.L. Minkston is prominent in your end of the county, or at least he's likely to be once his projects are a bit more mature. It will look good if I show a personal interest. Believe me on this one. I've learned the hard way."

"Aren't you making a big assumption there?"

The sheriff shrugged his broad shoulders. "Perhaps, but we'll have to wait and see. Perhaps he learned a lesson in those other places where his developments were, shall we say, less than successful?"

"So you're taking no chances?"

"Something like that. And after all, what is there to lose? At the very least I can help you interview the victim of a possible crime."

"Aren't you forgetting something?"

"What's that?"

"That he may be a suspect as well as a victim?" I reminded the sheriff that Minkston had motive in at least two of my ongoing cases.

"Well sure, Cal, but I thought that after tonight..."

The sheriff paused, and then a light came on. "So you think maybe Minkston was delivering that snake someplace? That he'd loaded it into his own car?"

"It's possible. Not likely, but possible. That's why I'm anxious to talk to the man."

"Well sure, then, I see your point." The sheriff snapped his fingers. "And say, what about his wife? Does she know about the accident?"

"I didn't even know he had a wife."

"Yeah, he mentioned it briefly at the Rotary breakfast last month. I think there's some kids too, maybe college age. Two girls as I recall. It was Sally Benton who told me that. Apparently she and Mrs. Minkston went to the same eastern prep school way back when."

"Sally's in Rotary?"

"Yep. She doesn't come all that often, but she's a generous contributor to our various causes."

I was surprised to learn that J.L.'s wife and Sally Benton ran in the same circles, or at least had done so in their younger days.

The sheriff had an incredible memory for detail, especially about the people in his county. It was an essential adaptation for somebody in politics, and it was one more reason I almost certainly would never achieve the rank of sheriff. There were other reasons, too. For one, whoever heard of a sheriff living at the wrong end of his county, out in the middle of nowhere on a goat dairy?

Luis made a couple of calls, setting in motion the search for J.L. Minkston's wife and daughters. It took a while, but Sally Benton turned out to be the key. She happened to know that Joyce Minkston had been at their time-share in Maui for nearly a month. Mrs. Minkston contacted her daughters who were away at college as soon as she learned about J.L.'s accident. Everybody was headed home to Arizona.

The sheriff and I needed to talk strategies before any possible interview with J.L. Minkston. Fortunately, there seemed to be plenty of time.

There was one aspect to this thing that was particularly troubling, and about which I was anxious to gain the sheriff's opinion. "So, Luis, I expect even if we do get to talk to Minkston that he's likely to be pretty bad off."

"Sounds like it. What's your point?"

"Well, just suppose he incriminates himself, like maybe admitting he tried to poison Maria's goats. With no lawyer present, and even if we did manage to Mirandize him..."

The sheriff nodded. "He's in such bad shape, still under the influence of god knows what kinds of drugs, so none of it would be admissible."

"Right. We probably couldn't even get a search warrant under those circumstances. So how should we proceed?"

He thought about that for maybe thirty seconds, and apparently made a decision. "Carefully, that's for damn sure. I think we start by showing our concern, maybe ask him what he remembers about the accident, and then just let the man talk. Maybe he'll spill something we can use, if not in court at least to guide our investigation – uh, make that *your* investigation."

I appreciated his endorsement, and it sounded like a plan, but two more hours went by before we finally had the chance to put it into action. A nurse told us he was in Unit 7, that we could stay no more than fifteen minutes, and that she would be right outside in case anything happened. At least we would be alone.

J.L. Minkston was in bed of course, hooked up to tubes and wires leading off in various directions to a bewildering array of bottles and monitors. His head was heavily bandaged, and his left arm was suspended in a cradle. His lower left leg was twice the size of his right, and propped up on a pillow.

Luis and I took seats on opposite sides of his bed, and I cleared my throat. J.L. stirred, blinked open his eyes, and then feebly turned his head in my direction.

"Hello, Mr. Minkston. It's Cal Creede. I'm here with Sheriff Mendoza, and we're sure sorry about your accident. How are you feeling?"

I waited for a response, but got nothing other than a brief nod.

"We'd like to ask you a couple questions if you're up to it."

J.L.'s voice was hoarse but clear. "I thought you'd be here sooner. I don't remember much about the crash they say I had."

"Do you remember the snake?"

He frowned. "What snake?"

I knew that head trauma sometimes caused a loss of short-term memory, so I decided to take a different approach.

"Do you leave the doors of your car open when it's parked?"

"No, shut and locked at the office. Just shut, don't lock it at home. Why?"

"When did you last drive the car? Before the accident that is."

"Can't remember. Probably yesterday. What day is it anyway?"

I decided not to answer that. "Have you seen any strangers around your place in the past few days? Have you had any visitors at all? Can you think of anybody who might want to hurt or trick you?"

Minkston closed his eyes, and I thought maybe he'd fallen back asleep. But then he opened them again and uttered a single word. "Smiley."

"Beg pardon?"

"Smiley."

I had no idea what he was talking about. "Who is Smiley?"

"He's ... a sonofabitch." For the first time that night J.L. Minkston showed signs of real agitation, turning his head from side to side and waving his functional arm in the air. I almost called the nurse, but the sheriff put his hand up.

"Not just yet, Cal. Let the man talk if he wants to."

It turned out he wanted to.

"Should've gone after Smiley, not these local losers. Now it's..."

Minkston faded away for maybe ten seconds, but then he came back. "Now it's too late."

I wanted to ask him what was too late, but apparently the sheriff had a different idea. "What losers, Mr. Minkston?"

That was when we hit the jackpot. "Why Moss of course, and that Slawson woman. They're both losers." Up until now he'd been looking at the sheriff, but now he turned his head in my direction. I could tell he was fading fast. "And Maria Obregon. She's your girlfriend, right? Well she's a loser too."

I wanted to ask more, but that was when the nurse came in and told us it was time to leave.

Luis and I were walking back to our vehicles in the hospital parking lot, when he asked if I knew anything about this Smiley person that Minkston had just mentioned.

"No idea, but we need to find out. Maybe his wife knows."

Luis shook his head. "I've got a better idea."

"What's that?"

"Maybe you need a search warrant to get at the bottom of this Smiley business. Maybe there's a paper trail, either in his office or at home. And you just never know what else might turn up during the search."

"Like what?"

"Like rat poison, or some bedraggled grape stems, or maybe even a basement full of snakes?"

I had to hand it to him. Sometimes Sheriff Mendoza was just damned brilliant.

Chapter 39

It had been a long day in Nogales, and I'd been running pretty much bat-crazy nonstop for the last three days. Once again I was in a hurry to get home to Maria. But it was Monday night and Larry had agreed to handle the two-fers event at the Santa Rita. I knew he'd be there when I got back to Sonoita, and I wanted to talk to him about how things had gone at the Minkston wreck site. I was especially anxious to learn whether he'd had any luck getting the snake we'd found in Minkston's car delivered to Hazel Smith.

So instead of heading directly on back to the Obregon homestead, I pulled off into the gravel lot in front the Santa Rita and walked inside. Frenchy was behind the bar and he motioned me over as soon as he recognized who it was. "That's terrible news about J.L. Minkston. How's he doing?"

"Hard to tell. He was busted up pretty badly. They'll know more in a couple of days."

Frenchy snapped his fingers. "Say, that reminds me. There was some guy in here last night looking for Minkston. He hung around until nearly ten, then said he was going back to Tucson. He asked me to tell Minkston to get in touch if I saw him. He seemed upset."

"Do you remember the man's name?"

"Yeah, I wrote it down here someplace." Frenchy fumbled around beneath the cash register and eventually pulled out an order pad with something written on the back. "It was Smiley. Didn't give a first name."

Larry was down the bar chatting with Al Treutline.

I waved him over to an empty table.

"How did it go today with Minkston's wreck?"

"Not bad. Julie Benevides and her crew finished up about mid-morning, and then I had a wrecker take the man's Caddy to impound down in Nogales. They dusted everything and got a bunch of good prints. But here's the really interesting part. The Escalade's brake lines had been cut."

"So this was more than just a snake event?"

"Sure looks that way."

"And speaking of snakes, did you get it to Dr. Smith?"

"I did. She actually drove herself all the way down here to pick it up."

"Did she say anything? I mean about the snake?"

"Yep. She said it's a Mojave for sure, and that it looked a lot like the ones from the Whetstones, along with the one that came from Moss Winslow's mailbox. She said somebody named Willy something-or-other would do the DNA and she'd get back to us."

Larry stopped to take a swallow from the bottle of *Dos Equis* he'd carried over from the bar. "So how did it go with you today?"

I brought Larry up to speed on the interview with Minkston, such as it was, and about his physical condition. "His family should be getting back sometime today, if they're not already here. Turns out there's a wife named Joyce, and two daughters. We probably should call over to the man's house tomorrow, just to check. But not now, because something may develop."

Larry drained the last two inches from his bottle and set the empty down on the table in front of him. "Develop?"

"Yeah, I think Luis may be about to work another of his judicial miracles and get us a search warrant for Minkston's house and office."

"Based on what?"

"Minkston kept mumbling today about somebody named Smiley. From what Frenchy just told me, it looks like maybe they were supposed to meet here last night. Anyway, Minkston said Smiley was the one he should have gone after, instead of the people he called local losers."

"And who were these losers he was talking about?"

"Maria for one. He also mentioned Moss Winslow and Aunt Grace."

"Good God almighty. So who do you suppose this Smiley person might be?"

"No idea. But if I had to guess, I'd say it's somebody connected to Minkston's finances. We need to find out."

"Got it. So anyway, Cal, where do you think we stand on all this? I mean with Pendleton in jail, somebody else must have put that snake in Minkston's car, right?"

"Seems likely. The man didn't get bit until Sunday night, and we arrested Pendleton mid-day on Saturday. It's possible, I suppose, but damned unlikely that the snake could have been in his car since Saturday morning without it being noticed. And besides, if Hazel Smith has it right the snake that got Minkston isn't like the ones Pendleton kept at his house."

"And Pendleton denied having anything to do with the Andy Slawson deal, right?"

"Right."

"So we've got another killer out there, right?"

"Right."

"Well, shit."

"Right again. That makes three in a row."

I rose to leave, telling Larry I'd see him in the office next morning. I gave Frenchy a wave and headed for the door. Just before I got there, in walked somebody

I'd never seen before in the Santa Rita. It was Moss Winslow. And right behind him was my old pal from the *Tucson Gazette*, Percy Butterfield. What the hell were they doing together?"

Moss didn't look happy to see me, but Butterfield's ruddy round face lit up in recognition. "Well good evening there, Deputy! Great to see you again! I was just about to buy Mr. Winslow here a drink. We've had a long and most interesting day."

"Doing what?" I couldn't help but ask.

"I'm working on a local interest feature about UFOs, and I must say Mr. Winslow here is quite the expert. Ever hear about sky serpents? Well I sure hadn't. Like big snakes in the sky, right Mr. Winslow?" Butterfield rolled his piggy little eyes, but only after he had turned aside so I was the only one who could see it. "Well anyway, Deputy, won't you join us for dinner and a drink? It's on me."

"No, sorry, I can't. It's been a very long day, and I need to get home."

Percy Butterfield was not to be deterred. He moved his short but substantial girth in front of the door and blocked my way out. "Yes, you have been busy lately, haven't you? I've been reading the press releases from your headquarters down in Nogales about recent events. But those are such sterile things, and so I have a couple of questions before I let you go."

"Sorry. Sheriff Mendoza has made it clear that I am forbidden to engage with you in any more wide-ranging conversations. And last I checked, my decision to stay or leave here is not in your hands."

"Well then, can you just confirm a couple of facts for me? I'm guessing you'd rather do that than have me report about your lack of cooperation."

I could feel the jaws of a trap starting to close, and made a snap decision about the best way to minimize the impending damage. "As long as we stay within the bounds of the department's official communications, I suppose that would be all right."

"Good, Deputy. Very good." Butterfield pulled a notebook out of his hip pocket and flipped through some pages that I could see were cluttered with a tiny scrawl. "Well first of all, is it true that Mr. J.L. Minkston was bitten by a rattlesnake when he wrecked his car last night?"

"Yes, that is true."

"And what can you tell me about his condition?"

"You'd have to check with the hospital in Nogales about that."

Butterfield flipped more pages. "And is it true that you have arrested one Ambrose Pendleton for killing a local game warden, and that he has agreed to a plea deal?"

"That is my understanding, yes."

"And is it true that this Mr. Pendleton is a collector of rattlesnakes, some of which are illegal to possess?"

"Yes."

"So if I'm following all of this, Deputy Creede, you have a local man who collects snakes, whom we know is capable of murder. And you also have two unsolved crimes involving snakes." Butterfield paused to consult his notes again. "One of these involved the Slawson boy who was killed by a snake in a mailbox. We've already discussed that. But now we have this more recent event involving Mr. Minkston, right?"

"Right."

"So, would I be correct to assume that Mr. Pendleton is a suspect in these two incidents as well?"

Moss Winslow had just been standing there looking bored. But Butterfield's last question brought his head up. "Seems like it to me, Cal. Pendleton obviously is some kind of a snake nut, and now we know he's a killer to boot."

I wasn't about to get into Hazel Smith's evidence suggesting that Pendleton's snakes probably weren't the culprits in either the Slawson or Minkston cases. Maybe I did it just to bug Butterfield, but I couldn't see the harm in releasing one obvious fact about the whole business. "Well, we can't be sure about any of this, gentlemen, but it's highly unlikely Pendleton put that snake in J.L. Minkston's car."

This got Butterfield's attention. "And why is that, Deputy?"

"Because we already had him in jail when it happened."

Chapter 40

Some days don't turn out like they're supposed to. That's fine if you like surprises, but not so much if you like predictable. Maria once told me she thought predictable was boring and that surprises were a lot more fun. In hindsight, this was a day when she would have been lots happier if things had stayed predictably boring.

The morning started out like many others. Maria and I left for work at about the same time, with tentatively plans to meet for lunch in the office if I was still in town. We agreed to stay in touch. I pulled off the highway into my usual parking spot, while Maria drove on to the post office, where she would pick up the mail awaiting her delivery.

The door to my office was ajar. This was strange because I thought Larry was the last one who'd been there, and he was good about things like that. I went inside and looked around, expecting some signs of disturbance, but found none. Still, an odd feeling came over me as I went to the sink and fired up the coffee pot. Something seemed out of place. I just couldn't put my finger on what it was.

Larry showed up about a half-hour later, and I asked him about the door. He assured me he'd locked up the night before when he left for his duty at the Santa Rita Saloon.

"Does anything seem different in here?"

Larry shrugged and wrinkled his nose. "Nothing, except maybe that smell."

"What smell?"

"I don't know really. It seems sort of musty in here,

which is odd if the door was open all night. Maybe it's the smell of burned coffee." He pointed to the pot. "How long has that thing been on?"

"Not that long. Maybe this old place is just rotting away. The sheriff could be right. Maybe we ought to move into something newer."

He laughed at that. "Yeah, maybe we'll show up for work one day and the whole thing will have collapsed overnight. Any news from Nogales?"

"Nothing yet."

We were waiting for word from the sheriff about a possible warrant to search J.L. Minkston's home and office, which was our top priority for the day. We'd both finished two cups of coffee before the phone finally rang. It was Mary Gonzales from the sheriff's office, calling to report that there was some sort of delay, but that we should stand by. Apparently Luis was having trouble working his usual magic with a favorite judge.

Larry decided to go out on patrol, and I agreed. When and if the warrant came in, I would let him know and we would meet at the man's house.

The call didn't come in for another two hours, which gave me plenty of time to sit around stewing in my own juice. And believe me, that's what it felt like. Sure, we had Ambrose Pendleton locked up for the killing of Dan McCall, but now there was this incident with J.L. Minkston. Obviously there was another killer loose in my jurisdiction, and it probably was some real nut case who could do it again.

I had a feeling, not for the first time, there was some sort of clue right in front of me, if only I could bring it into focus. Something was familiar, but it hung out there just beyond my reach.

I was lost in these thoughts when Mary called to say they finally had the warrant, and that it was coming as an attachment to an email. I had my usual moment of panic that always came when I was faced with downloading something off the computer. It was too bad Larry wasn't around, because he was the tech guru of our little operation. But he had managed to teach me which key actually turned the damned thing on, and even how to boot up the e-mail program. After about ten minutes of fumbling around with a variety of unproductive options, I finally had something on the screen that looked like a search warrant. The only remaining challenge was getting it to print. I thought I had that problem solved when the printer made a rude noise indicating that it was out of paper. Odd, I thought, because we had reloaded the thing just two days ago.

The computer paper lived in a large drawer in the lower right side of my desk, so I pulled it open and reached in for a new ream. What I got wasn't paper. I don't know if the hiss or the rattle or the pain came first, because it all seemed to happen at once. I grabbed my right wrist and toppled backward out of the chair. Then a Mojave rattlesnake surged up out of the open drawer, and spilled onto the floor.

Things got a little blurry after that, but the next thing I remember was the sight of Maria coming in the door. She didn't have to ask what had happened because the snake made it all too obvious. I watched from the floor, fully conscious but too stunned to move. Maria did not hesitate. She grabbed a fire extinguisher off the wall and threw it down toward the recoiling snake. But it was only a glancing blow, and the snake immediately rose up and struck in Maria's direction. Fortunately the strike fell short and the extinguisher rolled away far enough for a safe retrieval. She picked it up and threw it down a second time, and then another time after that. Both were direct hits. I could tell the snake was still alive because its head kept moving, but the rattle and heavy body lay still. She must have broken its back.

By now I was trying to get up off the floor. My right hand and wrist were starting to hurt, and I felt both dazed and confused. Maria came over and helped me back up into my chair.

"Cal, we've got to get you to the hospital. *Now!* Can we take your Blazer? The mail van is slow and it doesn't have a siren." She shook her head. "No, that's not right. I need to call Rescue. They're right across the street."

"Sure, whatever you want to do. It hurts, and my head is starting to spin. I think the poison is starting to affect more than just my arm."

As Maria and I sat waiting for the ambulance, the same odd feeling swept over me that had been there all morning. Something was illusive but familiar, and now it seemed closer than ever. I almost had it in my grasp, but then things began to fade away.

Chapter 41

It was a cold night in the desert, but I was sweating and shivering at the same time. The tent was small and cramped, and I was not alone. There were snakes all around, of many different kinds. At first they were lethargic, but then I heard a flute somewhere in the distance and the snakes began to move. Some swayed in time with the music. This was not Arizona, I was sure of that. Probably it was Afghanistan, but there was nobody around to ask. A pistol lay in the dirt next to me, but my fingers were numb and swollen, and I could not pick it up to defend myself. I was convinced the snakes were coming after me, but there was nothing I could do. A strong odor filled the inside of the tent, sort of musty and acrid and damp all at the same time. The odor was strange, yet somehow strangely familiar.

"That's it! It's the smell! The smell of the snakes!"

I bolted upright but then fell back because of the terrible pain in my arm. I looked around and realized I was in a new place. I was in a bed, and there was a man in a white coat standing at the end of it. He had gray hair and there was a stethoscope hanging around his neck. Sitting in a chair next to the bed was my beloved Maria. I realized it had all been a dream, the part about the tent and the desert and the flute music. But something else stuck that was very real.

Some parts of it were coming back to me now. I remembered the incident in the office, the ride in an ambulance with Maria at my side, and something vague about a hospital. But mostly it was the smell. The smell just before the snake had struck.

"How long have I been here? What day is this?"

Maria put her hand gently against the side of my face. "It's Wednesday, Cal. You've been here nearly a whole day. Lots of people came to see you last night, but I don't think you were aware."

"Who? Who came to see me?"

"Aunt Grace and Frenchy and Larry. And my parents, of course. They drove over from Patagonia. And I called your parents, so they know about it too. But are you all right, Cal? You shouted something about snakes just before you woke up, and now you're soaked in sweat." She turned to the man in the room with us. "Is he all right, doctor?"

I didn't give him a chance to answer. "I'm fine, Maria. I'm fine. But I've got to get out of here! I know who did it, and there's no time to waste."

"Who did what?"

"Who killed Andy Slawson! And it's probably the same person who tried to kill Minkston. Where are my clothes? You've got to help me get dressed!"

This time the doctor was not going to be put off. He came around to the side of the bed, put his hand on my shoulder, and looked straight down into my eyes. "Now hold on there young man. You shouldn't be going anywhere just yet. You suffered a serious snake bite."

"I know that doctor, but I feel fine except for this arm. I'm a deputy sheriff and there's something critical that I have to do. I want to be discharged, and I'll take personal responsibility."

The doctor shook his head. "It's just too soon, son. You responded well to the anti-venom, so we don't think there's been any permanent damage to your heart or your central nervous system. But it's too soon to tell about your arm. We need to keep you under observation for at least two more days, or maybe three."

Maria became a co-conspirator. "He's right, Cal.

You know as well as I do that a bite from a Mojave rattlesnake can do real neurological damage. We mustn't take any chances. And besides, can't Larry or the sheriff take care of things?"

Larry or Luis probably could have made the search and possible arrest I had in mind, except for one thing. It might all be a bust, and a really embarrassing one at that. I decided to stall for time, since there was a call I needed to make in any event. There was a phone on the little table next to my bed. "Maria, can you get me the number for Hazel Smith?"

"Sure, Cal, I've got it stored in my cell. But why her and why now?"

"You'll see. Just help me punch in the numbers, okay?"

Fortunately, Hazel was in.

"Tumamoc Hill. Smith speaking."

"Good morning Dr. Smith, this is Cal Creede."

"Oh, good morning Cal. And it's Hazel, remember? Good to hear from you. And we're still working on the Mojave that came from that man's Cadillac. As I told your partner, Deputy Hernandez, it looks very much like the one that killed Andy Slawson, and also the other one we got from the Whetstones. But these DNA profiles take time. So what can I do for you?"

"I have a question, and I know it's going to sound silly."

"Sure, Cal. What is it?"

"You remember the other day up in the Mustangs we talked about whether people can smell rattlesnakes?"

"Of course I remember."

"And you said maybe some people could but you couldn't, or at least you never had? And so you're skeptical?"

"Yes?"

"So now I'd like your best guess. Could this be real, this thing about smelling rattlesnakes? I mean is it something I could stake a criminal case on? Or at least a search warrant?"

"Well now, that is an interesting question. There have been rumors about rattlesnake odors for years. Some people say yes, others no. As far as I am aware, there have been no definitive scientific studies showing that rattlesnakes have any particular odor that humans can detect, at least under normal circumstances. A sick snake maybe, or certainly a dead snake. But like I told you up on that mountain, I personally have never smelled a live snake."

"So there's nothing to it?" I felt things slipping away again.

"Well, no, I didn't say that. In fact, those rumors about rattlesnake odors are so persistent and widespread, I have often wondered if some people actually can smell them."

"These people who claim to smell the snakes. What do they say it smells like?"

"I thought we'd already covered this."

"Maybe, but please refresh my memory. I wouldn't be asking you about this if it wasn't important."

"Well, all right. Again, there are different stories. Some say it is a sharp musty smell, like a wet dog. Others claim it smells like, if you can believe this, a cucumber or an overly ripe watermelon when you first cut into it."

I felt a stirring of hope. I wasn't sure about watermelons, but to me those caves in the Mustangs and the Whetstones had a wet, musty, slightly putrid odor. So did a particular old house in the Sonoita Valley, and so did my office, at least as of yesterday.

I thanked Dr. Smith for her time, hung up, and made a decision. Arm or no arm, it was time to act. I could have this all wrong, and it could cost me a demotion or even the whole job. But the risks associated with inaction were much greater. I asked both Maria and the doctor for some privacy. She shot me a look, but eventually complied. Then I picked up the phone and called Nogales.

The sheriff was in.

"Good morning, Luis. This is Cal and I need your help."

"Sure, anything. We all heard about your bite and we're really concerned. I assume you're still in the hospital and that's where I want you to stay. Don't worry about the office. Larry has things under control. Just concentrate on getting yourself well."

"Thanks, but there's something else." I told the sheriff what I suspected, and what I wanted him to do.

He was dubious, to put it mildly. "Well I guess I could do that for you, but I gotta say it sounds crazy. You're basing this on what rattlesnakes smell like? Really?"

I did my best to convince the man, and eventually it must have worked.

"All right then, but let me handle this. Assuming I can persuade Judge Corona to sign a warrant, I'll bring Joe Ortega and do the search myself. You have my word on that. Even if you get discharged, you should just go back to Maria's and rest. My God, Cal, you're less than one day removed from a Mojave bite!"

"No, please Luis, I need to be in on this. This is my case, and my ideas may be completely off the mark. If anybody's made to look the fool here, maybe even get sued for false arrest or something, it has to be me. Like you said, this might be crazy. And besides, I really am feeling okay. My hand is swollen and a little numb, but otherwise I'm okay. Really."

"If you tell me one more time that you're 'okay,

really' I'm likely to stop believing it."

"No, really ... I mean, uh, it's just that I have to do this Luis, can't you see that?"

"What I see is that you are a proud man, Señor Creede. But you are also my friend, and a good officer. One of my best. So we will do this together. I only hope that we both do not live to regret it. What sort of help should I bring?"

"Bring the crime scene crew and Joe Ortega I suppose. And I'll make sure Larry knows about it."

"Assuming I can get the warrant, when are we going to do this?"

"Well, there may be a little snag there."

"Snag?"

"The doctor won't let me out of the hospital."

"*What?*"

"Yeah, I know. But really Luis, I'm..."

"No, you're not, Cal. You're not okay, so just cut the crap."

"But you'll talk to him, right? The doctor? Like give him an order or something?"

The sheriff laughed. "My powers may be great, Deputy, but normally they do not extend to telling doctors what they may or may not do with their patients."

"But you'll try, right?"

There was a long silence followed by a sigh. "All right, then. Put him on. I only hope that I do not live to regret this."

Chapter 42

In the end, they let me out. There were conditions, all of which I reluctantly accepted. First, they secured my arm in a sling and told me to keep it there no matter what. Second, I was not to use my right hand at all, even bound up as it was. Third, if the search and possible arrest involved any sort of physical confrontation with the suspect, it would be handled entirely by others at the scene. Finally, Maria would do all the driving, and if in her judgment my condition changed, she was under orders to get me back to the hospital at once.

"Changed how?" she asked the doctor.

"Like if he becomes light-headed, or if there is a sudden change in his heart rate."

"Up or down?"

"Either one." Apparently the doctor saw the worry in Maria's face. "However, his vital signs are stable now, as they have been for the past six hours. As long as he avoids any strenuous physical activity, he should be okay." Then the doctor actually grinned. "You have a tough guy on your hands, Ms. Obregon."

I could have kissed the man.

Four hours later, six people in three vehicles headed east out of the Sonoita office of the Santa Cruz County Sheriff's Department. Maria was the only civilian, and she drove my Blazer. Larry Hernandez took his Jeep, while Luis, Joe Ortega, and Julie Benevides followed in a departmental van. My hand and arm were swollen and painful, but my head was clear.

The drive took only about fifteen minutes. The day

was cool, clear, and breezy. The gravel track leading back to the white wood-frame house was by now familiar. A scattering of gray ashes over blackened soil was all that remained of the vineyard. We pulled to a stop and everybody got out. It was quiet, except for the repetitive creak of the old windmill out in back as it turned slowly in the wind. I led the way up onto the porch and knocked, using my left hand. There was no response. I knocked again, normally at first, then much harder. Still nothing.

"Moss, it's Calvin Creede. Are you in there? I'm here with the sheriff. Please let us in. We have a warrant to search your place."

A muffled voice came from somewhere inside.

"You go to hell, Creede, and take the sheriff and your warrant with you! Just go away and leave me alone. I haven't done anything to anybody. So you go away now. Just leave an old man in peace."

"No can do Moss, we need to come in. Please open the door."

A cow bellowed somewhere off to the north, out beyond the windmill, but no further sounds came from inside the house.

Luis took charge. "Mr. Winslow, this is Sheriff Mendoza. I have a warrant to search your house and premises, issued by Judge Corona down in Nogales. Now you open this door. If you've got nothing to hide, this can all be over in a few minutes, and we'll be out of your hair pronto."

"You mean Manny Corona? Hell, I've known those Corona boys all my life. None of them's worth anything. I'm not about to pay any attention to a so-called warrant one of them claims to have signed."

The sheriff signaled Joe and Julie to go around to the back of the house. Then he drew his sidearm and instructed Larry to do the same.

"Cal, stand aside and let Larry and me go in first. Watch out for your hand. Larry, let's move."

Larry nodded, took a step back, and kicked in the door. Luis and I followed him inside, but we didn't get far. Moss Winslow was standing across the living room with a shotgun pointed right at us. But he didn't pull the trigger. Instead, he turned and disappeared through a darkened doorway. We heard descending footsteps and then the sound of a door being slammed shut.

Larry ran across the room, hesitated at the top of the stairs, and looked down. "Cal, is there any other way out of this basement?"

"I don't think so, Luis, but Moss never gave me a complete tour of his house. And anyway, let me go first. He's more likely to listen to me. He's a crazy old man, but we know each other."

"Well, get over there then." The sheriff must have realized he'd just asked me to disobey the doctor's orders. But in the heat of the moment all of that seemed a world away.

I took a few tentative steps down the stairs leading to the basement and called down into the darkness. "Moss, it's me, Cal Creede. Now why don't you just put down the gun before somebody here gets hurt, and come on up. Whatever the problem is, I'm sure we can work things out."

In truth, I was far from sure that things could still be worked out with Moss Winslow. For openers, the old man had just threatened the sheriff and two of his deputies with a gun. For another thing, there was a distinctive smell coming up from the basement. It didn't smell exactly like watermelon or cucumber, but it sure as hell did smell familiar.

I made my way farther down the stairs, both cautiously and slowly, until I got to the point where the steps turned on a landing and then led directly to the basement door. It was closed. For all I knew the old man was standing on the opposite side of that door with his shotgun at the ready. In fact it seemed likely. I have never thought of myself as any sort of coward, but I'm not completely stupid either.

I called back up over my shoulder. "Luis, the door down here is closed. What should I do?"

"Don't go in there, Cal. It's too dangerous. Larry just checked, and there's no other exit. That old man is trapped. All we have to do is wait him out."

I had just started my retreat back up the stairs, when I heard a sound. Actually, it was two sounds. One was that of an old man, and he was sort of whimpering. The other was the sound made by a room full of Mojave rattlesnakes, all buzzing and agitated.

Okay, so the Mojave part was just a guess.

On an impulse, I turned back and hurtled down the stairs, putting the full weight of my good side against the basement door. The sheriff would later describe it as the most foolish thing he'd ever seen in nearly thirty years in law enforcement. But the door burst open, and there before me stood Moss Winslow. He was trying to reach the trigger on the shotgun, but he was having trouble because he had the barrel of it in his mouth. I got to him first, grabbed the gun and threw it across the dimly lit room. He pulled back in horror and then turned toward a makeshift pen filled with the writhing tangled bodies of at least a dozen snakes.

Moss Winslow's last act as a free man was attempted suicide by snakebite. But it didn't happen, because I grabbed him around the neck with my left arm before he had a chance to throw himself into the pen. I hurled him to the floor, just before Larry came up behind me.

The arrest of Moss Winslow on suspicion of

murder and attempted murder was not without some further excitement. The old man screamed and thrashed about as Larry dragged him up the stairs and out into the yard. Joe Ortega then pinned him to the ground, while Luis cuffed his hands behind his back and read him his rights. He remained sullen and uncommunicative as we loaded him into Larry's Jeep.

Joe and Julie Benevides stayed behind to work the crime scene. They were not amused by the snakes, but they had come prepared to collect several because they might prove critical should the case come to trial. I made a mental note to contact Hazel Smith about taking the remainder for DNA analysis, after which I assumed and hoped she would release them close to a particular cave back up in the Whetstones. Winter was coming, and those snakes had to find shelter if they were going to make it until spring.

Larry drove Moss Winslow directly on to the Nogales County Jail, while Luis, Maria, and I went back to the office in my Blazer. I was tired and my arm hurt, but I could see that they both wanted to talk. The sheriff's radar must have been working, because he excused himself and went outside, giving Maria the first shot. She definitely took it.

"Well, that looked pretty rough and tumble back there. You do recall the doctor made me the responsible party." Her dark eyes flashed in real anger.

"Yeah, sorry, Maria. It was just that I thought..."

She put her hand up to stop me. "I'm not sure you were thinking at all, deputy. Now let me see your arm."

She gently untied the sling from around my neck, cradled my right hand in both of hers, and bent in for a closer look. "Well, I guess it's okay. How are you feeling?"

"I'm fine, Maria. I never used my arm back there at all. Larry did all the heavy stuff. There was no danger."

"You mean other than the fact that you and a crazy man with a shotgun were on opposite sides of the same door?"

I guess she knew more about the events just passed than I realized.

Maria announced that she was going home to take care of the goats, and that she would be driving the Blazer since it was the only thing available.

"Then I'll be stuck here."

She shook her head. "No you won't. The sheriff doesn't know it yet, but he'll be bringing you home as soon as he's finished with you. And trust me, it won't be that long." Then she stomped out.

I heard loud voices outside, followed by the sound of a vehicle door slamming shut. Shortly after that the sheriff came inside.

"I think my godchild may be a little upset with us."

"No kidding."

"I guess maybe she has the right. But you seem to be okay. I suppose you were lucky."

"Maybe, Luis. Except for the swelling and some pain, I think it's coming along just fine. And thanks for letting me go along today. It looks like we got the right guy."

The sheriff settled in Larry's chair. "Yeah, I suppose we did. Assuming a basement full of snakes means what you think."

I reminded the sheriff we also had one piece of evidence that could prove critical. "And don't forget that soda can we collected from the cave up in the Whetstones. Didn't you say they got some prints off of it?"

Luis snapped his fingers. "Say, that's right. We'll compare them with Winslow's as soon as he's gone through booking. But in the meantime, I gotta ask. What led you to suspect Moss Winslow in the first place?"

"I guess it started when Professor Smith recognized

the similarities between the snake that killed Andy and her collection from the cave in the Whetstones, and then we found all that evidence of disturbance inside. At that point I was pretty sure somebody had deliberately collected up a bunch of snakes, that it probably was somebody local who knew they were there, and that Andy Slawson's death was no accident."

"Sure, but how did you know it was Moss?"

"I didn't. But then somebody put a snake in J.L. Minkston's car. Since Ambrose Pendleton was already in jail, there weren't that many other possibilities. And then there was the smell. That was the clue that finally penetrated my brain. It took a while for me to remember where I had encountered that odor, in addition to the caves, and then just yesterday in my office. It had been on my first visit to Winslow's house, the day Andy Slawson was bitten. His whole place had that smell."

"So Moss put that snake in his own mailbox? But why?"

"Damned if I know, Luis. Maybe he's just crazy. Maybe there is no logical reason. And I'm still not sure about the identity of the intended victim. If Moss told me the truth that first day – that he asked Andy Slawson to put some letters in his box – then he must have planned for Andy to be the victim. But I'm not prepared to rule out Maria, either. She was due to deliver the mail that day, and she almost certainly would have put her hand in the box."

Luis Mendoza stood up to leave. "We should learn more about all this when we interrogate Winslow. There's plenty of time for that tomorrow. But right now it's time to get you home before Maria chews my skinny old *trasero* any closer to the bone."

All the way back to the Nanny Boss's Goat Dairy, I just couldn't get that image out of my head. I was really sorry he said it.

Chapter 43

The next morning I insisted on driving myself in to work. The arm was lots better, and I think even Maria recognized I was on the mend. It had been a chilly night, so to speak, but she seemed so friendly over breakfast that I figured both Luis and I were back out of the doghouse.

Larry was in the office making coffee. As soon as we both had our cups filled I asked him if there had been any word from the sheriff about Moss Winslow.

He shook his head. "Haven't heard a thing. But I do need to bring you up to speed on something before I head out. It has to do with J.L. Minkston. While you were busy over in Sierra Vista dealing with your snakebite, the sheriff came through with a search warrant. We got a look into the man's house as well as his office."

We walked over and sat down on the usual sides of our shared desk. In the midst of everything else I had forgotten all about the developer. "And?"

"And, three things turned up. First, apparently Minkston talked about somebody named Smiley when you and the sheriff visited him at the hospital in Nogales?"

"Yes?"

"We found out from records in his office that Willard Smiley is vice president of a bank in California that has invested heavily in the man's developments around here. And it looks like they're calling in his loans."

"So Mustang Estates is headed for the toilet?"

Larry took a swallow of coffee and set his cup back

down on the desk. "Looks that way. I expect the sheriff can give you more details."

"I'm surprised he didn't mention it to me yesterday."

"Maybe he decided you already had enough on your plate for one day."

"Yeah, I suppose so. But anyway, you said there were three things about the Minkston search. What else?"

"We found two interesting things at the man's house. First, there was a big canister of rat poison in a shed out in the back yard. We took a sample to compare with the pellets you found in Maria's barn. Not that it would prove conclusively he was the one who poisoned her goats, but it's a place to start."

"Damn straight it is." I shook my head in disbelief. "I can't believe he would do something like that. What a greedy sonofabitch."

"Yeah, and maybe desperate too."

Larry had that right. "But listen, I need to let you go and then call the sheriff about Moss. So tell me what else you found at Minkston's place."

"Maybe the weirdest thing of all. Turns out he has a little vegetable garden. In amongst the remains of last summer's tomatoes and beans were a half dozen of the sorriest looking grape vines I've ever seen."

"Huh. What did you do with them?"

"Left three and took the others to Aunt Grace. Hope that was the right thing to do. I told her what the deal was, and asked if she could identify whatever was wrong with them. Didn't you say that Winslow's vineyard got some sort of fatal disease before he burned it down? So I'm thinking maybe there's a connection."

It looked like the final pieces of this whole crazy puzzle might be falling into place. "I think you're on to something Larry."

"How so?"

"I think it's possible that Minkston deliberately poisoned Moss Winslow's grapes. And he may have had some help."

Larry looked puzzled. "Help from who?"

"It's from whom."

"What?"

"Never mind. I think he may have had help from Andy Slawson."

Larry left on patrol, literally scratching his head. There would be time later to bring him up to speed. Right now, I needed to talk to Moss Winslow. I called the sheriff. He was in and didn't even let me get started.

"He confessed."

"Who, Winslow?"

"Yep. At first he just sulked and asked for a lawyer. So we got him one, a Public Defender from Tubac. Pablo Torres. He's one of the best in the county, so they can't go after us on that."

"And then he confessed?"

Luis chuckled over the phone. "Well, not right away. It was only after we told him his prints matched those on the pop can you took from that cave up in the Whetstones."

So that was it. "Well I'll be damned. And he copped for both the Slawson kid and Minkston's car accident?

"Got it in writing, and with no strings attached. One count of attempted murder for Minkston, one count of murder second degree for Slawson. Torres kept telling him not to, but it didn't seem to make any difference."

"What about the snake that got me?"

"He wouldn't say anything about you. We tried, but no luck."

"What were his motives for Andy and Minkston?"

"No idea. He signed the confession and then just shut

up. He said there's only one person he was willing to talk to, and you're it."

"That's good, because there's some things I want to ask him as well."

"Then you'd better get your butt down here. Are you okay to drive?"

I told the sheriff I was. Then I got Larry on the radio, caught him up on what was happening, and locked up the office.

~ ~ ~

Forty minutes later I was in the Nogales jail, waiting in an interview room for a guard to bring in Moss Winslow. Pablo Torres already was there. In about five minutes Moss came in, dressed in prison clothes. They had him cuffed at his wrists and ankles, which seemed excessive. I asked the guard to take off the restraints, which he did. Then I asked the guard to leave, and he did that too. We sat on opposite sides of the rectangular wooden table. Pablo Torres was next to Minkston.

"Hello, Moss. I hear you want to talk."

"Where the hell have you been, Cal?"

I asked permission to use a tape recorder. Torres started to object, but Moss put his hand up. "Sure, go ahead and turn the damned thing on. Makes no difference to me."

I asked Moss to state his name, after which I added mine, Pablo's, the date and time, and the circumstances of our interview. I knew right where I wanted to start. "Moss, did you set out to kill Andy Slawson on purpose? Why? He never did anything to you."

Pablo Torres immediately interrupted. "You don't have to answer any of these questions, Mr. Winslow, and my advice is for you to remain silent."

Moss shook his head. "Silent, hell. Look boy, my

goose is cooked and I know it. That's why I confessed. You're just wasting your valuable time here. And as for Andy Slawson, that kid was worthless and lazy. Only his Auntie Grace really cared a damn about him. But there is one thing I want you to know. He wasn't supposed to die."

This was news to me. "So you didn't mean to kill him? Then why did you set him up like that? It doesn't make sense. And for the record, I think he was an okay boy. Aunt Grace set great store by him. You broke her heart when you killed him."

"Well, I guess that just couldn't be helped. How was I to know he'd be stupid enough to stick his nose into my mailbox? I just had in mind he'd get bit on the hand, or maybe not even that. I just wanted to teach him a lesson and get some revenge."

"What does that mean?"

"It means he had a hand in killing my grapes, that's what it means!"

I remembered Larry's story about seeing Moss and Andy Slawson going at it one day out in the old man's vineyard. "So Andy introduced that disease to your place?"

Moss shook his head. "Not by himself he didn't. It was J.L. Minkston. He was the one that got hold of the sick plants. Then he paid Andy to plant some in my vineyard. Turns out the kid did yard work for Minkston, and they hatched a deal. I guess he paid Andy a bundle. And then Andy was supposed to have a story ready in case I caught him at it. He told me all about it that day when we had our little confrontation."

"What was the story?"

"Andy was supposed to say that J.L. had found some new interesting varieties of grapes and just wanted to try 'em out at my place."

"But you didn't buy it?"

"Not when all my plants started to look bad. That's when I got a man down from the university, some sort of grape expert, and he told me what was going on."

"And so for that you tried to kill two people?"

"I already told you the boy didn't have to die. I just wanted to teach him a lesson."

"Suppose Andy had managed to get the mail into your box without arousing the snake. Then it could have been Maria who ended up being bitten. Did you think about that, Moss?"

The old man shook his head, and for the first time he looked genuinely remorseful. "Guess I didn't. Sorry about that, Cal. I've got nothing against your Maria. Seems like a nice gal to me. You know, the real sonofabitch in this whole thing is J.L. Minkston. He's the one I was after. The snake in my mailbox? That was partly just a diversion, so you wouldn't suspect me when Minkston got what was coming."

"What about me, Moss? Did you put that snake in my desk?"

For a while I thought he was going to deny it because he didn't answer right away. But finally he just shrugged and said it was something that "couldn't be helped."

"How's that?"

"Because I knew you were getting close. The other night at the Santa Rita, when you told me that fella' Pendleton already was in jail the day Minkston had his car crash? I knew right then you were gonna figure things out. So you left me no choice."

I shook my head. "We always have choices, Moss."

I knew the time had come to talk about the really big thing staring both of us in the face. And it wasn't the proverbial elephant in the room, it was a basement full of rattlesnakes. Even before I asked him I knew things were going to get weird. But I had to do it, because I knew there could be no closure without it. "Why the snakes, Moss?"

He got a dreamy faraway look in his eyes and said nothing for nearly a full minute. When he did finally speak it was not to me but to Pablo Torres. "You need to leave now. Cal and me are gonna talk private." Then he shifted his gaze back to me. "And you need to turn off that damned tape recorder, okay? This is just between us."

I guess he didn't know about the one-way glass, or the likelihood that the sheriff was listening to our conversation.

As soon as Torres left Moss began to talk. "When I was a boy I used to tend cattle up in the Whetstones for my dad. I think I already told you about that, about how beautiful it was up there, with the views and the night sky and everything. And maybe I told you that was where I first saw the aliens, and also where I ran into a bunch of snakes?"

"I remember we talked about those things, Moss."

"But I may not have told you about the connection."

I sensed we were coming to the heart of the matter. "What connection?"

"A cosmic connection. The aliens told me to do it."

"They told you to try killing people with snakes?"

"That's right. Once I figured out what Minkston was doing, I went back up into those mountains for advice. They're good at advice once you're hooked up. Remember I told you about the sky serpents? To them, snakes are like a religious icon. They use them a lot themselves. So that's what they told me to do."

"So you took those snakes out of the cave and brought them home?"

"Yep. And they were real happy about it too. Like I was doing their bidding."

"You were doing the snakes' bidding?"

"Not the snakes' bidding, you ignorant fool." He pointed skyward. It was as if he had a clear view of the heavens, even though we were buried deep inside the County Jail in a room with no windows. "No, I did *their* bidding."

If Moss Winslow ever had to face a jury I was pretty sure "the space aliens made me do it" would not have been a good defense. Unless his plea had been utter insanity, in which case he might have had a chance.

I had one more question. "But why so many, Moss? You had a whole room full of those Mojave rattlers."

He took off his rimless glasses and rubbed his eyes. Then he pulled a red bandana out of his pocket and wiped the lenses before putting them back on. "Don't know for sure. I guess they might have come in handy when another situation developed."

There didn't seem to be much else to say, except goodbye. I dropped by the sheriff's office on my way out. He'd heard the whole thing, just as I had suspected. We both agreed it would have been easy to charge him with attempting to kill me in addition to Andy Slawson and J.L. Minkston, but we also agreed it probably was best just to leave things as they were.

The case was closed.

Chapter 44

Outside, the skies over Nogales had turned cloudy and a gentle west wind carried the sweet smell of distant rain. My spirits rose as I climbed in the Blazer and started the familiar drive back to the Sonoita Valley. Then I drove past Harlo Henshaw's pawnshop and they fell a bit. There were no vehicles out in front, nor any signs of life inside. The barred and empty windows reminded me of the ignorance and intolerance infecting the man who once had run the place. He would not be missed in my county.

I did not feel the same way about Moss Winslow. It was true that he had committed one murder and attempted others, and I was among his intended victims. He surely would pay the price, and I doubted we ever would cross paths again. But there was something about the man, a texture and a depth that the likes of Harlo Henshaw, or even J.L. Minkston and Ambrose Pendleton, would never approach. God knows it wasn't his thing with extraterrestrials. That was as foreign to me as the space aliens themselves.

Moss Winslow cared about his grapes so much it had driven him to violence, but it also reflected a passion that I judged possible only in someone who loved this land. I had seen it in his eyes and heard it in his voice, most especially when he looked out across his vineyard before it got sick, and when he reminisced about his early days high up in the Whetstones. So I was prepared to forgive Moss, up to a point. Someday I would ask Aunt Grace how she felt about that, but it would not be soon. She loved the land just as I did, maybe even more, but her loss had been too close and too dear.

By the time I got to back to Sonoita the clouds had dropped down low and heavy, enveloping the whole valley in a steady rain that obscured all the surrounding hills. The roads were wet, and my tires hissed on the pavement as I slowed to a stop in front of the office. Larry's Jeep was gone, and I assumed he was still out on patrol. I almost got him on the radio, but decided against it. If there were trouble and he needed help, he would call.

It was late afternoon when I pulled up in front of the old Obregon adobe, but Maria had not yet returned from delivering the mail. I knew that wet weather sometimes slowed her down, so I was not surprised that she was running late. I could have called her cell, but I told myself it was too soon to worry.

Maria's first order of business when she got home would be to feed and milk the goats. I knew she would be tired by the time she got off work, and that my taking care of the animals would be a welcomed favor. I had no trouble putting out their hay and grain, but my hand was still too swollen and painful for me to do the milking. It probably was just as well because my relationship with the goats remained a work in progress. They never were as generous with their milk for me as they were for Maria.

I was just finishing up with the feeding when I heard the sound of her Honda pulling up in the yard. We met outside the barn, and she did not look happy.

"What happened?"

"Oh, nothing really. But I had to step through a puddle to get at one bank of mailboxes. My feet got wet, and so I've been cold most of the afternoon."

"Why don't you go inside and change clothes? I've already fed the goats." I held up my right hand. "Sorry I can't milk them, because of this. But I'm sure they can wait."

She shook her head. "No, it's better for them and for me if I get this over with. We have things to talk about later, and I don't want to be interrupted."

We went back inside the barn together, and I watched and learned as usual. It was easy to see why the animals gave more milk for her than they did for me, even with two good arms. She talked to each of the does individually as she milked, and she had such a calm and patient way of doing things it seemed almost mystical. If the herd ever grew large enough to require milking machines, that would be another matter. But for now, when it was all by hand, I knew I could never be her equal.

It was going to be a wet and cold night, so while Maria finished in the barn I collected some split mesquite from a box we kept next to the kitchen door. I carried it inside and laid a fire in the wood stove that sat against the far wall of our living room. By the time she came in the wood was crackling and our little house was beginning to heat up. Boomer, her Labrador Retriever, already had begun to warm his backside in front of the stove.

Maria excused herself and went into the bedroom to change out of her wet clothes. "I'll be right back. And I'm really anxious to find out how it went today."

We had gotten into the habit of talking about my work, especially if a case involved her personally, which in the present instance it most certainly did. She was a good listener and her advice invariably was succinct and to the point. She was understandably curious about Moss Winslow and his snakes.

I was pretty excited about the apparent resolution of all my current cases, and anxious to talk, but there was some other business to take care of first. "I'm feeling the need of a little celebration, and besides it's too cold for beer. What say I bring out the expensive stuff?" The expensive stuff was a bottle of Maker's Mark bourbon that we kept for special occasions.

I had two glasses of the amber liquid ready, each with a pair of ice cubes, when Maria came out of the bedroom. She was drying her hair with a towel and wearing a blue terry cloth robe. As near as I could tell that robe was all she had on, which definitely portended well for the evening ahead.

We sat together on an old leather couch in front of the fire, and I told her everything I knew about the Winslow case. The conversation then widened to include all of my recent adventures, including my dealings with Ambrose Pendleton, Harlo Henshaw, and J.L. Minkston. By the time I had finished it was dark outside.

Maria wanted to know if we were going to arrest Minkston for poisoning her goats. This was a touchy subject, because it was the only case on my current list where we had no solid evidence. The rain had slackened for the moment, so I used this as an excuse to go outside for another load of firewood. Once that chore was accomplished, and I had taken a sip of Maker's Mark, I had run out of excuses.

"Like I said, Larry found rat poison in the man's house, and it matched the kind we found mixed into your grain. But it's a common brand, so that's probably not enough."

Maria nodded her understanding, but I could tell she wasn't happy about it. "And you said Minkston is in financial trouble?"

"Big time, apparently. So at the very least it looks like his whole Elgin operation is going down the tubes. And of course maybe he'll confess, not only to poisoning your goats, but also to introducing that disease into Moss Winslow's vineyard. We've got some evidence there."

Maria drank some bourbon and put her glass back down on the table. "What's that?"

"It's hearsay, but if Moss Winslow is telling the truth about his conversation with Andy Slawson, then it was Minkston who got hold of the sick plants and paid Andy to plant them in the vineyard. We know for sure that Minkston still had some of the sick plants in his yard. So assuming Andy was telling the truth, and assuming Moss is willing to testify to that effect, then we might have a case."

"That's a lot of assumptions."

"You bet, but it's all we're likely to get."

Maria thought about that. "So it was Minkston, and not Winslow or Pendleton, who turned out to be the real snake in the grass."

"Snake in the grass?"

"That's an old expression. It means somebody who's sneaky and treacherous. Apparently the saying goes all the way back to Virgil."

"Virgil who?"

Maria laughed, and shook out her beautiful black hair that by now was nearly dry. "No, just plain Virgil, silly. The Roman poet? You're the one who majored in literature. You're supposed to know these things."

"And Virgil wrote something about snakes in the grass?"

"Yes he did. Of course he wrote in Latin, and it was one damned long time ago, so you might have missed it."

"And how is it that a mere biology major happens to know this particular fact?"

"We learned it from Dr. Smith in herpetology. She gave lots of examples of the ways in which snakes have been portrayed in literature as evil and sneaky."

I sighed and shrugged. "All right, fine. But now I'd

like a favor. Just for tonight, isn't there some subject we can talk about that doesn't involve snakes?"

Maria smiled. Then she leaned against my shoulder and brought her face up close to mine. "I have one. Let's talk about us."

"Us, meaning what exactly?"

"Well, we've got the house nearly back to where it was before the flood, and it looks like your work load finally may be returning to something like normal. So I'm thinking maybe it's time to take make some long term arrangements."

I had been badgering Maria about getting married for nearly a year, but so far she had always found a way to put me off. She had never said no, but she hadn't said yes either. So I wasn't about to let this possible opportunity slip away. "Good. I accept your proposal of marriage. When are we doing this?"

"But I didn't..."

"Yes, you did."

She giggled. "Okay, I guess I did."

"So now let's get to the when part."

It was then I learned that this whole thing had been a setup, because Maria had some news. "I ran into Aunt Grace at her mailbox today, and we talked. Turns out she and Frenchy Vullmers are getting engaged, and they plan to make the announcement next Monday night at the Santa Rita. We're invited. So I'm thinking, as long as they have all those people rounded up in one place, perhaps we could make an announcement of our own?"

I liked her thinking. "Is Aunt Grace okay with this?"

"She was thrilled."

"Good, then. In the mean time I'll put Larry on call, so we'll have the whole weekend to ourselves."

"You've earned it, Cal. We both have. It's been a crazy what, nearly three weeks since this whole thing started?"

"The most chaotic time of my life, outside of Afghanistan. And I'm sorry you got dragged into it."

"That's all right, except now you have to make up for it."

"How?"

"I'm sure we'll think of something. But first I'm hungry, so let's eat."

Later that night the storm opened up in earnest. It spooked Boomer, who was frightened by thunder. As a result he kept trying to get into bed with us. On some nights that would have been all right, but this was not one of them. I finally had to throw him out. The sounds of rain on the roof mostly drowned out his whimpering just outside our bedroom door, but I'm not sure we'd have heard it anyway.

Chapter 45

Two-fers night at the Santa Rita Saloon usually did a brisk business, but this particular Monday was off the chart. It was obvious as soon as Maria and I walked in that somebody had spread the word. Most likely it was Aunt Grace, although I suspected Maria may have been a collaborator. Most of the Regulars were there, of course, including Al Treutline and Sally Benton, along with both sets of our parents. So were Luis and Serena Mendoza. Larry Hernandez was there with Laura Floyd glued to his side. They seemed to have eyes mostly for each other.

I'm not real good at mingling, but obviously this was an occasion that required it. Maria must have decided it was a good idea that we mingle separately because she disappeared into the crowded room shortly after we arrived.

There were some real all-stars among the invitees. First, Hazel Smith came up out of the blue and introduced me to her husband. I learned that his name was George and that he was president of a bank in Tucson. Then Frenchy Vullmers came over with a full bird colonel in tow, a distinguished looking gray-haired man in dress uniform. Frenchy was a little vague about their relationship, but I gathered they had been colleagues back when he had been posted to Fort Huachuca, where the colonel now was commandant.

After about fifteen minutes of mingling I found myself cornered by Hazel, Sally Benton, and Al Treutline. It soon became obvious that they were well informed, and they had lots of questions.

First, everybody had heard about the snakebite,

and they all wanted to see my hand. By now the swelling had gone down considerably, and I no longer felt much pain. But my fingers still looked like little cigars, and they probably noticed I had been trying to avoid shaking hands. Hazel warned about side effects. "Those neurotoxic bites are not to be fooled-with, Cal. I've seen cases where symptoms like heart arrhythmia developed months after the bite. So you be careful and watch yourself."

I promised I would.

Then there were questions about Moss Winslow and J.L. Minkston.

Sally Benton took the lead on this one. "That's just amazing about Moss. Has he confessed? Why did he put the snake in his own mailbox?"

I caught Luis Mendoza staring hard at me from across the room. He shook his head. It was barely perceptible, but it was there. The man didn't miss much.

"I'm sorry Sally, but the case isn't fully resolved yet, and I really can't discuss it. All I can tell you is that Moss has been charged with a murder – that's Andy – and with the attempted murder of J.L. Minkston and possibly of a peace officer – that's me. We're not sure about that one yet."

"That old bird always did seem kind of goofy to me," said Al Treutline. "But what about Minkston?"

"J.L. is still down in the hospital in Nogales."

Sally made a noise like she knew something. "I talked to his wife Joyce today, and she said he's doing better, that they might be able to bring him home in about a week. You know there's one thing worrying me about all this, Cal. If J.L. deliberately poisoned Moss Winslow's grapes, isn't he guilty of a crime too?"

"That's going to be for the County Attorney to decide, Sally. It might be a hard case to prove."

"I hope this doesn't mean an end to Mustang Estates and all of J.L.'s other plans," said Al Treutline. "Those developments are just what this valley needs to get our economy really pumping."

Of course I felt otherwise, and I was pretty sure Sally Benton did too. But neither of us said anything.

At this point Frenchy Vullmer's distinctive baritone boomed out across the room, and we all turned in the direction of the bar. He stood behind it, with a row of six unopened champagne bottles lined up in front of him.

"Good evening ladies and gentleman, and thank you all so much for coming. My establishment and I are honored by your presence."

Frenchy cleared his throat and waited for the crowd to quiet.

"So now, I wish to make a little speech. As many of you know by now, I have proposed marriage to Grace. She is your Aunt Grace, but I do not think of her in that way. She is to me the total good of women. I think she is about to agree to my offer." Frenchy interrupted his own speech with a chuckle. "Can you imagine, she thought I was courting her only because of her possible vineyard? But no, grapes were just a way I could think of to approach her. I knew she wanted to have something for the future of Andy, so I thought of the vineyard. But I do not care so much about grapes. I would be happy just to be with her and watch the grass grow when the monsoon comes. That is how I feel."

"Bravo, Frenchy, bravo!" It was Maria who interrupted, and then we all applauded. But Frenchy put his hand up, because he had not finished.

"I just want to be with such goodness and kindness. Grace brings a memory of my beloved older sister, Ariel, whom you do not know. Ariel carried notes for the *Resistance*, and she was killed after the war in reprisal. This was a long time ago, in France, but all joy left my family then. Now I know that I can make Grace happy, and perhaps she would like to travel. I can take her to France and Switzerland and Belgium, should she wish. She could see where I was born. And you know she is a very good cook. We could cook together, invent good things, Escoffier, not this food here." He stopped to wave his hands around the room. "And I would eat better and not be so fat, eh?"

We applauded one more time, and then Aunt Grace walked up and joined Frenchy behind the bar. She stood there in silence, waiting until she had our undivided attention. At least half the crowd had been her students at one time or another, so that did not take long. Once it was quiet she began to speak, just like we all remembered from grade school. Just like then, we all paid attention. And just like then, she got straight to the point.

"My dear Patrice, I am honored to accept your proposal. But lest you misunderstand, we shall do much more together than simply watch the grass grow. When we first met, you persuaded me that you knew all about grapes. I believed it then, and I still do. But now you say that was just a means to win your way into my heart? I'm afraid that was a miscalculation. Because, *mon ami*, we are going to plant that vineyard, you and I together, and it will be the best in the valley. And we shall do it in honor of my Andy."

Aunt Grace stopped to wipe away a tear. It was dead quiet in the Santa Rita Saloon, except for a handful of people who suddenly felt the need to blow their noses.

She went on. "As I look out on all of you tonight, I see many people who once were my pupils. That gives me both joy and strength. And so I thank you, one and all. But especially I would like to thank Cal Creede. It was your hard work, along with that of your colleagues, that has brought peace back to the Sonoita Valley. For that we should all be grateful."

The crowd applauded again, and I caught Maria's eye from across the room. Her smile was simple and direct, and I thought she looked beautiful. Then somebody yelled 'speech!' and I was momentarily panicked. Fortunately Grace came to my rescue, because it turned out she wasn't finished with her own. She pointed to the bottles lined up in front of her. "Before we open the champagne, it is important for you to know that we are here to toast more than just Patrice and myself. Cal and Maria Obregon have chosen this occasion to announce their engagement as well."

With that she invited the two of us, along with our parents, Hal and Doris Creede, and Ernie and Cecelia Contreras, to come up to the bar.

I don't remember many other details about that evening, except that there was plenty of backslapping and toasting.

~ ~ ~

It is customary to end certain tales by saying that we all lived happily ever after. In fact we pretty much did, probably more than any of us had a right to expect. Nobody would confuse the life of a deputy sheriff with that of a fairy tale. But as long as Luis Mendoza stayed in office, and Larry Hernandez remained my loyal partner, I knew they would have my back. And as long as Maria stayed true to herself, I knew the old Obregon homestead would be my refuge. There would be challenges ahead, but on that happy night at the Santa Rita Saloon these blessings were more than enough.

Acknowledgments

Our thanks to the following individuals for their advice, encouragement, and assistance:

- To fellow members of the Red Herrings writers' group, Beth Eikenbary, Milt Mays, and Jean McBride, for critical comments on earlier drafts of *Death Rattle*, and for helping us get better at the writing craft;

- To Cynie Murray, our loyal book rep in Santa Cruz County;

- To our family, Laura, Larry, Anthony, and Dominic Hernandez;

- To Shirrel Rhoades and Chuck Newman of Absolutely Amazing eBooks;

- To the readers of our first Arizona Borderland Mystery, *Coronado's Trail*, for their constructive suggestions and for encouraging us to write more in the series;

- To Rusty Travis, who suggested we add a map to this and all subsequent Arizona Borderlands Mysteries, in order to better orient the reader;

- To Dr. Tom Ranker for his help with the identification of rare ferns in Arizona;

- And most especially to the late Dr. Hobart Smith, herpetologist extraordinaire, who taught us all we know about rattlesnakes, but who is in no way responsible for our pushing the lore of these remarkable animals perhaps a bit past their normal limits.

About the Authors

Carl and Jane Bock are retired Professors of Biology from the University of Colorado at Boulder. Carl received his PhD in Zoology from the University of California at Berkeley, while Jane holds three degrees in Botany, a B.A. from Duke, an M.A. from the University of Indiana, and a PhD from Berkeley. Carl is an ornithologist and conservation biologist. Jane is a plant ecologist and an internationally recognized expert in the use of plant evidence in criminal investigations. She is co-author with David Norris of *Forensic Plant Science* (Elsevier-Academic Press, 2016).

The Bocks spent nearly forty years studying the natural history of the region in southeastern Arizona that is the setting for their Borderlands Mystery series. They have co- authored numerous articles and two nonfiction books based on their fieldwork in the Southwest: *The View from Bald Hill* (University of California Press, 2000), and *Sonoita Plain: Views from a Southwestern Grassland* (with photographs by Stephen Strom; University of Arizona Press, 2005). The first volume of their mystery series, *Coronado's Trail*, was published in 2016 by Absolutely Amazing eBooks.

Now largely retired from academic life, the Bocks presently divide their time between Colorado, Arizona, and the Florida Keys, mostly fly fishing (Carl), fighting crime (Jane), and writing fiction.

ABSOLUTELY AMAZING eBOOKS

AbsolutelyAmazingEbooks.com

or AA-eBooks.com